BEYOND HATE

by

Jim Williams

DORRANCE
PUBLISHING CO
EST. 1920
PITTSBURGH, PENNSYLVANIA 15238

The contents of this work, including, but not limited to, the accuracy of events, people, and places depicted; opinions expressed; permission to use previously published materials included; and any advice given or actions advocated are solely the responsibility of the author, who assumes all liability for said work and indemnifies the publisher against any claims stemming from publication of the work.

All Rights Reserved
Copyright © 2021 by Jim Williams

No part of this book may be reproduced or transmitted, downloaded, distributed, reverse engineered, or stored in or introduced into any information storage and retrieval system, in any form or by any means, including photocopying and recording, whether electronic or mechanical, now known or hereinafter invented without permission in writing from the publisher.

Dorrance Publishing Co
585 Alpha Drive
Pittsburgh, PA 15238
Visit our website at *www.dorrancebookstore.com*

ISBN: 978-1-6366-1137-2
eISBN: 978-1-6366-1730-5

DEDICATION

This book is dedicated to the victims of terrorism in the past, at this moment, and in the future.

In every man's heart there is a devil, but we do not know the man as bad until the devil is roused.

James Oliver Curwod

BEYOND HATE
BOOK 1

CHAPTER 1

Tim… I Never Imagined

I'm an old guy. Older than I ever thought I'd get. Too much drinking, smoking, and life's stresses will catch up to you and I did them all. I owned bars, so too much drinking, smoking, and stress makes me a prime candidate for an early checkout. But somehow, I'm still here and I experienced an episode I shouldn't have survived. What I tell you now is true. I lived through it and I still don't how.

Before I begin you need to have a little background. About ten years ago my wife died… cancer. She survived, if you want to call it that, for almost four years after she was diagnosed. The last year was the worst. We'd spoken many times about my life after she was gone. I promised that I'd never marry again and she said, "You have to marry. I don't want you to be alone. Promise me that you'll marry." I agreed just to give her peace, but knew that would never happen. My life was over once she was gone. I just accepted that.

I suppose you might think I'm weak when I tell you that less than two years after she died, I began to actively date. I was lonely and looking for a new life partner. To be honest though, the first year it was all about sex. I had been married a very long time and didn't have a clue about relationships. The women I met were naturally older, but not as old as me, usually twenty plus years younger. I was, still am, an attractive guy, have a little money and a good personality so I usually didn't have a problem hooking up. My relationships might have lasted as long six months but I always had a problem after a while. These ladies had baggage. It might have been their drinking, their family interference, lack of personality, intelligence, or whatever. I could never find anyone I wanted to spend the rest of my life with.

I decided to go "off-shore" to find someone. I figured that foreign ladies didn't carry around the heaps of endless bullshit my American women seemed to have. Anyway, I quickly avoided Russian and other European dating websites. I joined a few, but it was immediately apparent that these ladies only wanted a way out of their poverty and marrying a "rich old American" was their meal ticket to freedom. Honestly, I'm still amazed that so many American guys traveled 3,000 miles to Europe to just get laid and spend thousands to meet these gold-diggers.

I came to the conclusion that Asian women would be my best bet. I did a lot of Googling and discovered, if you can believe all you read on Google, that an Asian lady's culture and their personalities were a kind of throwback to the women of my earlier times. They respected their men, were good homemakers, and, to me at least, were kinda sexy. These are the traits I remembered in my wife and the girls that I knew so long ago growing up in NYC. I know, I know, what I just said has probably pissed off a few of you. But it's true to me anyway.

I thought about where I would begin my search. Forget about Japan and China. These countries are doing well and I figured that any woman that wanted to leave was maybe a little too desperate. Thailand, Cambodia, and Vietnam were off the list too. I focused on the Philippines. English was pretty much spoken all over the country, the Philippines had a both a great history and an excellent current relationship with the USA, and from what I learned the women there were great. Our money was good too. The big problem I anticipated was that as a Catholic country, divorce was not an option for married but separated Filipinas. I figured if a met the woman I was looking for, there would be a problem if her marriage had not already been annulled. And now begins the crazy episode that almost killed me.

I joined a few Filipino dating websites. There's a twelve-hour time difference there so our day time is their night time. I'd go online after I closed my bar and got home, usually about 3 or 4 pm in the Philippines. There were always plenty of women online, all eager to chat. Almost all spoke English or could write it so I had no problem communicating. I'm old but not stupid and could usually spot a phony. I must admit I fell for the "my kids are starving" scam a few times and wired a little money through Western Union. I was beginning to think this was a mistake until I met Jenny.

She was the right age and beautiful too. She was a mix of Spanish, Chinese, and Filipino… long black hair and a drop-dead figure. Jenny spoke perfect English and was intelligent and engaging in our conversations. She had been married years before, had two grown kids, not living with her, and her marriage had been legally annulled. She never asked for money or help of any sort. From what she told me, she had owned businesses and property so I figured she had a few bucks. I was interested.

"Hi Jenny. How are you doing today. You're looking great as usual."

"Hello my dear. How was your day? You look very tired. Do you work hard today?"

"Honey, I always look tired about this time of day. Yes, I did work hard. I know you don't drink, but thank God Americans do. It was a good night at my bar. Nice crowd. Not too many drunks. Oh, did I tell you I like drunks?" I laughed.

Jenny was a Muslim, didn't drink, but she wasn't a practicing Muslim. About five percent of the Philippines is Muslim and her province of Mindanao is where most of them lived. She had already told me a little about her upbringing and it sounded difficult. Her people were poor farmers. Her uncle and his family had been slaughtered by the Japs and her father was captured and forced to work for them for three years. I had grown up poor but from what she told me, no way near as destitute as her family.

"Have you ever visited Asia, Jack?" she asked.

I used Jack as my name on all the websites I visited. I was pretty sure her name wasn't Jenny either.

"No… only Europe. Mostly when I was in the army," I lied. I had served in Vietnam, never wanted to talk about it. "I think I'd like to go though. Maybe you'll invite me sometime. Show me around."

"I would enjoy showing you around my city. Perhaps you'll plan a visit."

Our relationship was still at the "getting to know you" stage, no commitments or promises at this point. We then talked about places we had been, hers being much more interesting than mine. She had traveled to Dubai, been to Hong Kong, the Arab Emirates, Thailand, Singapore, and spent a great deal of time in Saudi Arabia.

I was curious. "Why so much travel Jenny? Business, work?"

"It was mostly work related. I was a partner in an auto parts dealership and I needed to travel a lot."

That much travel for "auto parts" seemed strange to me, but I didn't want to be nosey.

"Wow... impressive... Any memorable experiences along the way?"

"Oh, sure Jack. What do think a single woman traveling alone, doing business, especially in a Muslim country? There were many experiences."

I waited for her to elaborate but after a long pause, I could tell she wasn't going to and I didn't ask.

We chatted on... her kids, her house, the weather. Talking about all the usual crap two people think the other was interested in. Ordinary life stuff. But I enjoyed talking and listening to her. She was in the middle of telling me what she was planning to cook for dinner when a strange look, maybe fear, showed on her face. I heard a noise and suddenly two guys, one tall Italian or Arab looking and a shorter Filipino teenager, appeared behind her on my computer screen. She had stood and turned to face them when they came into the room. She said something to them I couldn't make out. They were on her quickly and the shorter of the two punched her in the face, knocking her to the floor and out of my sight. The bigger one then reached and pulled her up by her long black hair and began hitting her, hard; I could see her blood now. They were cursing in her language which I didn't understand.

"Stop! Stop hitting her!" I screamed.

Jenny had been using a headset and they couldn't hear me and my telling them to stop wouldn't have made any difference. The tall guy had his knife at her throat and with a quick, powerful motion, cut it straight across. Her blood spurted, some of it hitting the computer screen. Jenny was dead. There was no doubt in my mind. He had killed her and I saw it happen. As he wiped the bloody knife on her blouse, he noticed my screen image for the first time. He came close... looking directly at me... black dead eyes. We stared at each other for what seemed to me forever but probably not really more than a few seconds. He retrieved the headset and screamed into the microphone, "FUCK YOU!" before the screen went black.

4

CHAPTER 2
Jenny... Beginnings

I am female, Asian, a peasant, and was married at fourteen.

It was the custom in the mountain village where I was born for parents to arrange marriage for daughters at a young age. Especially where very poor families received "gifts" from the groom's family. My older sisters told me to run away before it happened to me but I was foolish and ignored them. I was brought to my husband's family home a few days before our marriage ceremony and the night before I was raped by him while his parents slept in the next room. This was not our custom but I was fourteen, frightened, and a virgin. I told no one.

I spent the first two years acting as a servant to him and his cruel family with whom we lived. He quickly tired of me and began pursuing many other girls, some he stayed with for a time, away from our home. I had my two children before I was 17 and was glad that he had found sex somewhere else.

I never undressed or allowed him to see me naked and after a time he became possessed to have me naked before him. No matter that he beat me or tried to tear away my clothes, I always resisted and he gave up since he never wanted his parents to hear me screaming in the next room. He had been visiting one of his women for a few days and returned late as I was sleeping next to our new baby. I woke and saw a light shining in the room and realized he was standing at the foot of our bed. His need to see me naked was strong and he lifted the thin sheet that covered me and shone his light on my body. At first, I struggled to wake and when I understood what he was doing, I kicked out and my foot hit him squarely in his face with great power. He screamed in pain and hurried from the room.

The next morning, his face was swollen and he looked away from me. At that moment, something happened inside of me. I realized that I was stronger than him and by his look, he understood that as well. This was the moment "I grew up". I began then to plan for a better life away from him and his family.

In time, I ran away. It was difficult, but I was young and unafraid. My older sister helped me and took my children into her home. She and her husband hated my husband and his evil family. They would not approach my sister because they feared her husband and his family who were well known as fierce members of the peasant armed force then fighting the corrupt government of our country.

We had some relatives working in the city and I hoped that they would aid me in finding work and give me a place to live. Early one morning I tearfully kissed my two babies farewell and walked many miles to the highway and the bus that would take me to my new life.

The city was crowded and dirty. I had lived in the mountains where the air was fresh and clean. I smelled forest and listened to the music of bird songs every day and now they were no more. Nothing good could live in this place. I did not speak the dialect of this city well and had difficulty finding my cousins. I was in great despair when I came to the place in which they lived. I was greeted warmly as was our custom and fed. I knew they had little, but we always shared. They showed me where I would sleep and in the next few days, after I became acquainted with my place in this city, my cousin took me to the fast-food restaurant where she worked. I was hired as one who cleans and prepares food for sale. It was not a difficult work but required long hours with very little pay. We were not allowed to eat any of the food prepared there but sometimes, when the manager wasn't aware, we gathered the leftover discarded food and brought it home. My money was shared with my cousins and the rest sent to my sister caring for my children.

In time, I became accustomed to my new life. I realized that there needed to be better opportunities for me in the future, but from where and when they would come, I did not know. For now, I worked, I lived, and my children survived.

One night after work, walking to my home, an older man approached me. This was not the first time he did so. I am told that I have beauty and men enjoy a beautiful girl. I would not talk to him but he persisted, "Pretty one please let me speak with you. I mean you no harm. Listen to me for just a moment. I have something important to say to you."

I gave him an opportunity. Perhaps he would then leave me in peace. "What do you want? Why do you follow me and ask me to speak with you?"

"Perhaps you wish to earn more money. I can help you earn a lot of money." The man showed me his dirty hand which was filled with money.

"I am not a street whore. Let me go and do not bother me with your evil offers of money."

"No, no, I know you are a pure woman. I am here to offer you work that will pay you more money than you can imagine. Just take a little of your time and follow me. You'll be forever grateful that you did."

I did follow him because I love my children and wanted more for them.

My name is Aadab Koo, I am a Muslim woman, a Filipina, and a fool.

CHAPTER 3

Tim... Brain Chaos

It's hard to explain how I felt. It kinda reminded me of how I felt after a bar fight. My face was burning, my stomach in a knot, and my heart was jumping out of my chest. I had just witnessed a murder. How was I going to report it? Jenny lived in the Philippines but I didn't even know where. She never told me anything other than she grew up on the province of Mindanao. I picked up the phone and called 911.

"911. What is the nature of your emergency?"

"I just saw someone murdered."

The operator asked a lot of questions that I couldn't answer. I began to think that she didn't believe me. I sounded like some kind of nut job. I couldn't blame her if she just hung up.

"Sir, I don't think I can be of any assistance. Would you visit your local police station and file a report? I'm sure they'll know what to do."

I agreed and immediately took off for my local police station. I walked. I needed to clear my head. It was 5 am and I was beat.

"Mr. Ryan, what you're telling me is very unusual. I believe you, but what do you expect me to do? You don't have much information about the woman who was murdered. She lives in a foreign country and I have no way of investigating."

The young detective seemed baffled after listening to my recounting what I witnessed. I was still in shock and not completely coherent.

"Oh... ok, ok, I understand detective. Maybe you could write a report and send it to the Philippines Embassy or something? Make it official."

He agreed, but I think he just wanted to get rid of me. He told me to go home, get some sleep, and then write up everything I saw and include information about Jenny, the website, and the two guys who killed her. I should bring my report back and he would get it into the proper hands at the Embassy.

Hell, I couldn't sleep. I wrote up my report and made two copies. One for the cop and one I sent to the Philippines Consulate in NYC. It was six weeks before I heard anything and it wasn't NYC police or the Philippines police that contacted me. It was Homeland Security.

I got a telephone call at the bar. The guy said he was an investigative agent for Homeland Security and he wanted to sit down with me and review what I had seen when Jenny was killed. He said he had read my report but had some questions. I told him absolutely, anything I could do to help. I asked if he had any information on what had happened. He was friendly but told me to wait until we spoke more about it in person. He and I agreed it would be more convenient for him to come to my house and we met the next afternoon before work.

"Thanks again for seeing me Mr. Ryan," Agent Tully said after we got settled at my kitchen table with coffee and Danish.

"Call me Tim. My real name is Thomas but everybody calls me Tim. What can I do to help you sir?"

Tully laughed. "Sir? Call me Dan. Tim, I read your report and by the way so did the Philippines Criminal Investigation Group, kinda like our FBI. Let me give you an update on what they've uncovered so far." Dan read from a report in front of him. "They tracked down your dating website and went through the membership records. They had three ladies with the nickname 'Jenny' listed and found two of them right away…. alive. The membership records didn't include any address information so they used the computer IP address to secure a physical location. Your friends real name was Aadab Koo, age 43, single, and living alone. She lived in a big city called Davao on the island of Mindanao. Their report included a little about her life. She owned her home, was a good neighbor, kept to herself, and her two kids were known to stop over and see her on a regular basis. Here's where it gets a little sketchy. They didn't find her body. It had already been removed and buried. Her murder had already been reported by her daughter. They searched her house and they found a lot of blood and the room where her computer was located looked like a battlefield. That pretty much ended their investigation, Her body, already buried, murdered, but for now it was just an unsolved murder as far as they're concerned." Dan took a sip of the coffee I made for him.

"Holy shit!" I said.

Dan looked me in the eye. I liked this guy. "To be honest Tim, originally, nobody here even looked at your report in any great detail. Your local cops sent it directly to the Philippines Embassy and copied us since the word 'Muslim' was included and the country is on our list of possible terrorist activity. When we received the Filipino cops report, some bells went off. First and foremost, Ms. Koo's name is on one of our watch lists. The manner in which she was killed was on our radar and your description of her killer was spot on with a guy we've been looking for a long time."

"You said Jenny is on a watch list. Was she a terrorist? I can't believe it. I didn't know her all that well, but she seemed normal whenever we talked. How can that be, Dan?"

"Terrorist? Maybe, maybe not. She had known terrorist contacts. She might have been involved with money, recruitment, spying, or was just an innocent bystander; it's possible she didn't know who she was friends with. We don't really know. Whatever her involvement, it got her killed. That's why we hope you can help us. Tell me in as much detail what you saw when she was murdered."

You know, you really can't trust your memory. I know this is true by conversations I've had with lots of people over the years. They forget details, make themselves more important or tell you about some event that you know they never witnessed. This was not the case of my memory of Jenny's murder. Every minute detail would be etched in my mind forever.

I drank a mouthful of cold coffee and began describing what I had seen. Dan didn't interrupt but he was making notes as I spoke. When I finished, I was drained. Describing it was like re-living it and I almost felt the same as I did when I saw it happen.

"Want to take five, Tim? Wash your face or something before we continue?"

"It's early, but I need a drink." I fixed myself a Jameson, neat, extra crispy and downed it in a quick, practiced motion. "You want a taste Dan?"

"Thanks, but not right now. If you're up to it, I have some questions."

"Shoot."

"Give me your best description of the white asshole who murdered Jenny."

I did and Dan had more to ask.

"Left-handed or right?"

"Left."

"Any tattoos or scars, anything distinguishing that you could see?"

" Hmm… I think he had a long scar over his left eye up toward his scalp and I think a remember a hint of a tattoo or maybe a scar on his right arm where it wasn't covered by his shirt."

"Height?"

"I'm only guessing… maybe 5"10', less than 6 foot."

"His hair color… full head, bald, what did it look like?"

"It was pitch black, full, he needed a haircut. I told you before his beard was black, long… but now I remember, it had a little grey in it."

"Tell me about his eyes again."

"Black as hell. Evil looking. He'd scare people just by lookin' at 'em."

Dan had been writing all this down. "I know he only said a few words Tim, but could you tell me about his voice."

I thought about his voice. I could hear it clearly now. "Well, it was deep, no accent."

"English sounding? American maybe? I know this is a reach, but what do you think if you had to recognize it again?"

"I'd recognize it."

"Ok, that's good. I'm gonna show you some photos. See if any of these guys look like him. Ok?"

Dan placed a stack of twenty or more photos of Arab looking men on the table before me. "Take your time Tim… give a good look."

It was hard to id my guy if he was even there. They all were bearded, dressed mostly in robes and some were profiled pictures. I held aside the three that kinda looked like him but I was not 100% sure.

"Dan these guys are the best match, but I'd need to see better pictures to be able to tell you if he's the guy."

"I have a video I want you watch. The guy may be in it." Dan set up his laptop and brought up a video I had seen once before on the news. It showed about ten guys in orange jumpsuits, each held by an

ISIS guard who was their executioner. These prisoners were captured Kurd or Syrian soldiers or something. They knew they were about to die and I remember thinking when I first saw the video, *Why the hell don't they try to escape or at least go down fighting?* Dan stopped the video at one guy holding a prisoner by the hair. He had an ugly knife at the guys throat, ready to behead the poor bastard. Something clicked, maybe it the way he held his knife, his eyes, there was Jenny's killer. No doubt in my mind at all.

"That's the guy Dan. That's him."

CHAPTER 4

Jenny... "Money Down... Then Panties Down"

He led me to a street filled with bars. He held my arm tightly so I would not run away. I was frightened when I entered. It was dark, dirty, and crowded with noisy men, all drinking and stinking of alcohol. I had never seen such a sinful place. I was young but had lived long enough with a man to understand men's lust. The loud music and seeing the young naked girls dancing and walking among the tables filled with drunken men made me sick. "Is this what I was to become?" I felt shame and regret. How had I come to this moment in my life? I knew poverty and I knew despair, but seeing this place of dishonor and knowing that I was to become a part of it, now doomed me for an Eternity of Shame. I felt my soul lift from my body and float away from me. I was truly alone. I must remain strong for my children.

I was brought before two men and an older woman waiting in a room above the bar.

"She's a pretty one. Where did you find her?" the woman asked.

She spoke Tagalog and I understood most of her words. My dialect was Visayan and I had some understanding of English and Tagalog from working in the fast-food shop.

"Take off your clothes child," she commanded.

I didn't understand. Become naked in front of these men? I just stood there until the three men held and stripped me of my clothes. I tried to cover myself and began to cry.

"She's a pretty one. What is your name?"

My voice was weak. "Aadab"

"We will have to change that... no Muslim names here," they were now laughing.

"We will call you Jenny. Say your name... Jenny."

I was taken away to another room, still naked.

"This is where you will sleep Jenny. One of the girls will teach you. You will stay naked for a time while you are being trained. You will not leave here until you know what you need to do when you work. You will give all the money you earn to Madame; she will pay you. You will have more money than ever before if you work hard and don't create any problems. Do you understand me Jenny? Can you work hard?"

I forget much of what happened the next month. I had a teacher. She taught me how to dance and make the drunken men give me their money. Soon I learned that I must give them my body as well. I planned for the time when I would leave this terrible place and be with my children. My sister knew where I was. This is how I remained for two years. But I learned, I learned well. I first learned Tagalog, then improved my English. I forgot Allah and prayed only when I could. I was Muslim in name only. Soon I forgot that as well. I became cunning, first in seducing lustful men to want my body. I made it a game. Give them just a hint of what I could provide and then make them pay and pay. In time, I managed to save some of my earnings even after taking care of my children's needs. I was a good worker and began to command the other girls and Madame depended on me.

"Jenny, I want you to help us find new girls. You will be paid much more than you earn here for each one you bring us. Would you like to do that?" Madame was a woman lover and I had seduced her.

"How much will I earn?" I asked. I laughed when she gave me a number. "No, I will find new girls and this is what I want to be paid."

I then began my new life away from the life of shame. My heart was hardened and I didn't care about the misery I would be bringing to young innocent lives. I wanted money. One of the workers taught me how to drive and I was given an automobile which I needed to take me into the provinces and then transport my new girls back to the bar. I found the work easy. I was old enough to be a sister of the innocent children I would meet. I carried gifts for their parents and lies for their young hearts. Ignorance and poverty were my allies. I even recruited within Muslim communities. This was more of a challenge but I spoke their language, pretended to practice their beliefs, and understood the particular lies that would make them believe a better life awaited them.

In time, my success became known and owners of other bars using girls asked me to help them as well. I made more money than I could ever imagine. I bought a house and my sister and my children lived a better life. I could spend some time with them and I was happy.

In time, the foul evil deeds I had done became known. The young Muslim girls lost in the unholy places of the city sometimes were able to escape before the drugs and despair took their young lives. My name became hated in my Muslim Provence and I learned that a fatwa had been issued against my life.

I needed to leave the Philippines before I was found and killed. Because of my well-known success in recruitment, I then became a source for enlisting women to work in Arab countries as domestics and nannies. In the beginning, I traveled to many countries and met with rich families taking orders for the women they were seeking. I encouraged my own younger sister to leave and work in Saudi Arabia for a minor royal family as a maid. I earned almost the same amount of money as before. I was happy until my sister became missing and could not be found. I had heard that women in foreign service were sometimes treated as slaves and sold to others and this was my sister's fate. I never saw my beloved sister again.

CHAPTER 5
Fatwa

Mohamed Wahid was normally a loud, overbearing man, but not today. He was summoned to appear before Mufti Ibrahim Abu and argue the "futya" he initiated against the apostate, Aadab Koo.

"Learned One," he began. "This evil woman has corrupted the children of Allah's faithful servants. She has led them into lives of sin and unholiness. She has deceived the parents of these children telling them only lies and making false promises on the nature of the work she was recruiting their children for. Many of these children turned to drugs and alcohol and led unclean lives working in foul places of sin and unholiness."

Wahid went on and described how the Koo woman, who was at one time Muslim, committed these terrible and unforgivable acts of evil. He finished by asking that an "ifta" be issued and she should die for her great sins.

The Mufti was familiar with the woman Koo and her great sins and issued the ifta.

Aadab Koo.... Jenny.... would surely be executed for her sins.

CHAPTER 6

Paul Asoph... aka The Snake

I think I was about ten or eleven when I lost my love for my Catholic religion. Strange how one bad experience can haunt you all your life.

It was a cold Saturday and my Grandfather asked me to help him with something. He lived across the street from us and I guess I loved him more than anyone else in my family. I can't remember what he wanted me to do but it kept me busy all day and I missed going to confession that afternoon. When I got home, I told my mother I wanted to go to confession that evening and after dinner, she had my father, who never went to church, take me.

Us kids were told by the nuns to only go to early confession on Saturday, never at night. It didn't seem like a hard and fast rule to me and I had gone late once or twice before.

My dad sat at the back of the church while I waited my turn to confess to the parish assistant pastor. He was old and I don't remember too much about him. I know he never visited our school like all the other parish priests. I picked him because he had the shortest line waiting to confess.

I knelt inside the confessional box waiting for him to finish with the old lady on the other side. I recall her being loud and I could hear her confessing some of her sins. I thought over the standard sins I usually confessed and readied myself for my turn.

The small window on my side opened and before I could even say "Bless Me Father". The priest shouted, "You don't belong here, get out of my confessional!" and slammed the window shut. I didn't know what to do and in my shocked state remained there for a minute or so. When I finally left, I was crying. My father came toward me and asked what had happened.

I was too upset to tell him and only when we left the church could I speak without sobbing. I told him as best I could what had the priest yelled at me. My dad is not Catholic. He's from Lebanon and belonged to some other Christian faith. When I finished, we stopped walking and he turned and headed back to the church.

"No dad," I shouted. It didn't matter what I said, he was on a mission.

He banged on the confessional door, "Come out of there you son of a bitch!"

The priest wisely remained inside and didn't answer. Dad banged the door a few more times and finally left with me trailing behind. I never felt the same about being a Catholic after that.

My name is Paul Asoph. I am a mixed-race kid from Bay Ridge, Brooklyn. My mother is Irish-Italian and my dad is native born Lebanese.

I grew up in a middle-class neighborhood with my two sisters and we all attended both Catholic grammar and high school. My early life was pretty normal. My father and his parents had left Lebanon during the civil war there and assimilated into American culture without any problems. I was smart and a good student. Early on I discovered that I had a thing for languages. My grandparents only spoke Arabic and I learned the basic elements of their language at an early age. I studied Latin, French and Spanish in high school and then later in college and became fluent.

CHAPTER 7
The Snake's First Strike

Father Sullivan was a pedophile. He had hidden his sin in darkness for all his evil life as a Catholic priest. There had been murmurings among his congregation about his overly affectionate manners with some of the kids in the grammar school he ministered. But good Catholic parents could never convince themselves that there was ever anything wrong, "He's a priest, for God's Sake. No way he would ever do anything bad to a kid." Sullivan was cunning. He covered his tracks and only molested young girls he believed he could control. One was a twelve-year-old, Mary Lepore. She trusted him and believed that his touching her and then her touching him was ok. He told her it was ok. She was an innocent maturing young woman and liked his attention anyway. It all ended when Sister Marie-Mountford discovered them lying naked together one afternoon.

Sullivan was immediately transferred to another parish and Mary began psychiatric counselling, paid for by the Bishop. Her parents were outraged.

"You must understand that Father Sullivan is a sick man Mr. Lepore and the church is getting him the help he needs," Bishop McKeever said in his most authoritative voice. Lepore could cause trouble and he needed to close this down as quickly and quietly as possible. "Mary is undergoing counselling and will be fine, she's young. What else can we do?" McKeever would offer money, a large sum if he had too. But he could tell Lepore was not going to cooperate. He was pacing and shaking his head.

"Perhaps, well... maybe the church might be able to help your family with some financial support. It's not full compensation for what happened of course Mr. Lepore, but it might help ease your concerns about the future." McKeever knew he didn't say that right, but the offer now floated in the air. He waited for Lepore's response which came quickly.

"Fuck you McKeever and fuck your fucking church. You're as big a bastard as Sullivan and I'd like to wring both your necks. Get the fuck out of my house! NOW!"

The Lepore family were next door neighbors to the Asoph's. When Mrs. Lepore tearfully told Mrs. Asoph all that had happened to little Mary both women cried. The same day all the Asoph family knew the tragedy of Mary Lepore and her oldest son, Paul, quietly vowed revenge.

Six months later, Father Sullivan had almost forgotten his problem at Help of the Angels parish. He was settled in his new parish, he liked his assignment and planned for his next victim. Of course, he didn't think of these children as victims. It wasn't about them anyway... it was his needs, his lust that needed to be satisfied. He had already chosen the thirteen-year-old that he was cultivating. He'd take is slow. No need to rush.

Paul Asoph was also patient. He didn't have a lot of free time... college, part time work... but what time he had, he used to observe Sullivan. It hadn't been difficult to uncover Sullivan's new parish. It was just a short drive and he found a good location to watch his comings and goings. In the beginning it was very difficult for him not to just leave his car and attack Sullivan, but eventually, he was able to contain his passion and act as an observer.

Paul knew from the start that he would kill Sullivan and he knew he had to plan carefully. He had no gun or access to one. Probably too noisy anyway. He dismissed using a rope to choke him, Sullivan was bigger than he was and probably stronger too. He settled on a knife. He went to the internet to learn how to kill with a knife. He bought a good long bladed hunting knife and practiced. It felt natural in his hand, almost a part of him. In time, Paul began to feel excitement at the thought of killing. In the beginning he wanted to kill Sullivan to avenge Mary Lepore and rid the world of a monster. Now he wasn't so sure about his motives. Part of him felt a strange excitement and he wanted the experience. He wasn't sure why, he just wanted to kill.

Paul's killing plan began to take shape. Sullivan was alone in the church sacristy for five minutes after he said daily 7 am mass. The altar boy always left immediately and the few parishioners headed out and never waited to talk with Sullivan. The street was usually empty and the church grounds were thick with trees and hedges. There was little chance of anyone seeing him after he killed Sullivan. He knew there would be blood, lots of blood and some would get on him. He knew that police forensics were good and he had to be sure he left no traces that could connect him to the murder. An alibi was out. He couldn't come up with one that would hold up. The priest always left the church through the front door and Paul decided to hide in one of the pews at the back and attack him as he passed by. It would be quick and deadly.

"Go in peace. The mass has ended," Father Sullivan blessed the half dozen parishioners and with the altar boy following, walked to the sacristy. He suddenly realized his mind had been on auto pilot during the entire mass. His thoughts had been fixated on his new little girl, Anne. He would see her today and planned to begin the touching. She was a simple girl and respected him. It wouldn't be difficult.

He finished dressing into his street clothes and left the sacristy. Sullivan never saw or heard Paul come up behind him. There was a quick sharp pain deep in his throat and he felt his knees give way as he fell to the marble floor. Father Sullivan was dying. He had sinned. He had never understood why he sinned or why he never sought God's forgiveness. His dying brain filled with a mist of imagines... his life... his choices... his sins. And now, he would remain alone in his Eternity, forever existing in the images of his sinful and unforgiven life. God's will be done.

Paul stood over the body. He was surprised it had ended so quickly. He hadn't felt any fear before his attack and he felt nothing now. He quickly left the church and walked at a normal pace to his father's car. His drive home was short and he entered through the back door. He removed his bloody clothes, put them and his shoes in a plastic bag which he would burn later. He had first cleaned and then threw the knife down a sewer. He felt good. He began to sing as he showered away the crusted blood from his body. Paul felt strong and alive.

A week later the police came to question the Franco Lepore. A few days later Paul was approached as he opened the front gate to the street. "Excuse me young man. Excuse me... do you have a minute? I'd like to ask you a few questions." Paul stood still. His eyes widened, his mouth went dry and he felt a tremble course though his body. Paul knew this guy was a cop. Should he run? No... stand and wait.

"Can I help you sir?"

"Hello young man. I'm Detective Molloy. I'm investigating the murder of Father Sullivan. I spoke with your neighbor Mr. Lepore. We're just speaking with people in the neighborhood who might have some information. Did you know Father Sullivan?"

"Ah, yes from our church but he's not here anymore. I think he left for another parish. I heard he was killed. Too bad. I didn't really know him. Just from church that's all." Paul began to calm down.

"Ok, did Mr. Lepore or any of his family ever talk to you about Father Sullivan?" the cop was making notes and watching Paul for a reaction.

Paul's mind was racing. Should he say yes or no to the question? The Lepore's told everyone they knew about the trouble Marie had with Sullivan. The cop probably already knew that.

"Well maybe, I mean, they mentioned that they heard he had been killed... stuff like that."

"Stuff like what? You seem nervous son... what's your name?"

"Paul Asoph. I'm not nervous, just worried about being late for school, that's all."

The cop stood close, too close, and Paul began to sweat. *What if he asks me for an alibi?* Paul thought.

The cop closed his note book and backed away a few steps.

"Ok Paul. Thanks for your help. I don't want you to be late for school. Have a nice day now," and with that, he turned and left for his car.

Paul felt sick. He was going to throw up if he didn't get moving. He thought, *Why didn't I expect this to happen? I have to be ready.*

CHAPTER 8
Some Answers for Tim

"Who the hell is this bastard? And why did he kill Jenny?" I asked.

"I think I'll have that shot of your Irish now," Dan answered.

I poured us each a healthy one and waited for Dan to drink.

"Slainte Mhath," he said, raising his shot glass.

"Slainte."

We downed our whiskeys backed up with a sip of coffee.

Dan sighed. "Nice. This guy is an American. Grew up right here in New York, Brooklyn to be exact. His name is Paul Asoph but he goes by the Arab name Usnan, which translates to "Snake". Appropriate don't you think? From what we know, he comes from a good family, went to Catholic grammar and high school and then on to NYU. He speaks at least four languages and did well in school. His folks came over here in '81 during the civil war in Lebanon. Grandparents and their kids, their son married a local Brooklyn girl, Paul's mom. There were three children in the family. Paul got a little squirrelly in his college senior year, his folks told us he gave up his Catholic faith and became a Muslim. Oh, and NYPD had an eye on him in their murder investigation of a local parish priest. The detective in charge was doing a normal neighborhood check and he got a bad vibe when he spoke to the kid. Nothing he could put a finger on though. The dead priest had his throat cut. Sounds familiar doesn't it?"

I needed a smoke and stepped outside with my pipe for some air. Dan needed to pee so we took a short break.

We sat back down. I had made some more coffee and I noticed that Dan liked his sugar. Me, straight up and black.

"Ok Dan, tell me what happened with this prick? How did you get on to him?"

"He left the US after college. He wasn't living with his family back then and they told us he went to Lebanon. He had dual citizenship there and it was easy for him to go. The country was in a mess, still is for that matter. Did you know that a quarter of million displaced Palestinians' had settled there? It was totally controlled by Hizballah and they had taken over. Our guy apparently fit right in. He taught languages at a university in Beirut. Probably where he finished his Muslim education. Anyway, he went off our radar for a few years and we picked him up again in Syria. He had left a trail and from our informants we could see that he had attracted some attention. Most likely his language skills and being an American citizen helped. Al-Qaeda tasked him to travel. maybe raise money, recruitment or just be a spy. He was in Europe for over a year, travelling around in different countries. There's some evidence he might have killed a few people in his new line of work; me... I think he might have become a serial killer. At some point he goes back to Lebanon and when the Caliphate is formed, he's right in the middle of it. That's where the video of him beheading the Syrian soldier came from by the way."

Dan stopped and looked at me. "Is this upsetting?"

I was fidgeting and he could tell something wasn't right.

"No... not at all, but something is bothering me Dan. Why are you really here and why the hell are you telling me all this shit? I'm just a civilian and I feel like you're giving me too much information. Why do I need to know all this stuff?"

Dan laughed a little at that. "Simply put buddy, you may be in danger. You have a right to know why."

This came from left field. "I'm in fuckin danger? What the fuck. Why am I in danger?"

"Tim, listen... you witnessed a murder. You identified the murderer who's happens to be a world class terrorist. And what's worst, he may know who you are. Your report went to the Philippines, it had all your information in it. Who knows where that report wound up? That's why I'm here and that's why you're getting this briefing. Just let me finish and we'll figure out what comes next, ok?"

I really didn't know what to say. "You got any good news for me Dan?"

"Yeah, I like your coffee."

We both chuckled at that.

"Ok... where were we? He and Al-Qaeda got their asses kicked by the Iraqi army with our help and with a lot of help from the Kurds. They had the last big battles at Ramadi. But they weren't done though. Still aren't for that matter. Asoph joined ISIS in Raqqa, but ISIS got the shit beat out of them there. Lost their caliphate. Their new plan was to switch the caliphate to Asia, specifically the Philippines. The head asshole ISIS guys managed to get a lot of the foreign fighters out. Our guy included. Paul, or Snake as they called him, wound up in the middle of it all.

CHAPTER 9
Paul's Itch

I am sick. I don't mean physically sick, mentally sick. I struggle with my sickness every day. I need to kill. It's the only way I can keep my sanity if that makes sense. I left the States and came to Lebanon because I was on the verge of being caught. Back in New York I had murdered a priest, an old man and my sister's boyfriend. I enjoyed killing them. The priest was my first. He deserved to die and I have no regrets. The old man was an opportunity. It just happened. My sister's boyfriend was someone I knew. I had no strong feelings of dislike for him, I just killed him because I could. I almost got caught killing him and maybe in my sick mind it was a way to get even with my sister whom I hated. I don't know.

Brian Hastings had seen a lot in his life. He was in his seventies and if anyone took the time to notice, well he had accomplished a lot considering he began life with nothing. Grew up poor, managed to put himself through college on the GI Bill, married, three kids, owned a little business and had a good life. That was until he was diagnosed with cancer. He just found that out. His doctor's appointment finished... just got news his life was almost finished as well. He wasn't shocked by the news, just a little angry. Now he was on his way home.

Hastings lived in Bay Ridge, Brooklyn all his life. His doctor's office was in a short subway ride away and for years he had been thinking about changing doctors. *Too late now*, he thought. Doc Whalen was as old as he and with the cancer he wouldn't consider changing anyway. The subway had been part of his life since he was a kid. The good old

4th Ave. local, now called the "R", had taken him to all parts of his world. He and his wife, his kids, friends... travelling... all the subway trips to Coney Island, Manhattan, school, on and on... Brian actually liked riding on the subway, but tonight with the final news of his pending demise he was hardly aware of anything, especially the young man standing behind him on the train platform.

If you asked me why I killed, I would tell you, "I don't really know." But I can tell you how I feel though. Think of anytime your mind floated above your body. Remember that feeling of total calmness and how time itself seemed to stop. You're just a spectator, watching yourself... there's no control over what your body is doing. You don't feel any horror or remorse. You're just compelled to watch.

I felt it take hold of me. I never anticipated it. It just came and before I had always controlled it, except now, it was strong; I just gave in. I saw him just standing there on the subway platform. He was an old guy and I knew I wanted to hurl him in front of an oncoming train. All these thoughts just flashed through me in an instant and there was no planning involved. This was just my overwhelming need to kill... end another life. No passion... just kill.

I came up behind old man and pushed him hard in front of the slowing "R" train. Hastings barely felt the push. He hardly felt his body slam against the leading train car. In his last instant of life, all he felt was blackness... then nothing.

It was done. I heard a woman screaming as I quickly, but not too quickly exited the subway platform. I was certain that no one saw what I had done. I had been hidden by a pillar when I pushed the old man and the platform wasn't all that crowded anyway. Maybe the train's motorman caught a glimpse of me... I don't know. It all happened too fast and most likely he was startled by seeing the body flying off the platform into his train.

A few days later I read that they had ruled the old man's death as a suicide; why, I don't know.

Did I mention that I have two younger sisters? Ellen is thirteen months younger and Susan is two years younger. I don't love them. Especially Ellen. She and I were always competitors in everything. It began early. I resented her being born. Why did my parents have more kids anyway? They had me, didn't they? Ellen was my dad's favorite. I wasn't anybody's favorite except for grandpa. She was the smart one. I'd get a "B" and she'd come home with all "A's". She had friends, I didn't. Ellen was kind. I wasn't. Ellen was pretty and had boyfriends. Me, I liked girls but they didn't like me. Ellen's current boyfriend was a guy I knew; his name was Tom Doolin. He was about my age but a big strong guy. I didn't dislike him but I never thought of him as a friend either. Tom had a car and he and Ellen were always driving around Bay Ridge. I killed Tom Doolin and I almost got caught.

One rainy Saturday afternoon I was walking to the library and getting soaked. I heard Doolin's car horn beep at me as he passed by. *What a prick*, I thought. *He could have given me a ride.* About an hour later and heading back home I walked past his house and there he was, in his garage, his car jacked up. He loved that piece of junk and was always working on it.

He saw me. "Hey Paul... come here buddy. Want a beer?"

I waved and walked into his garage and took the cold bottle he offered. I don't really drink but it was hot and muggy.

"Thanks Tom. What are you doing?"

"Ha. What does it look like? Stick around and I'll teach you how to fix a brake pad and a noisy muffler."

The cold beer tasted good. I leaned against the garage wall and watched Tom as he slid under his car. He began banging away at something and I could hear him signing... I guess he was happy.

"Is Ellen home?" he shouted.

"I don't know... probably."

There Tom was, under his car, helpless. All I had to do was kick out the car jack and he'd be crushed. I didn't want to do it. My mind was in chaos. D*on't do it!* it screamed. I dropped the beer bottle and it broke into pieces. I watched my foot kicking the jack. The car began to shake.

"What the fuck? Paul what the fuck are you doing?" Tom screamed. He was scrambling to get from under the two-ton car just as it crashed down on his head. His blood streamed from underneath. His feet quivered a few seconds and stopped.

I stood frozen in place and then I ran all the way home. Three hours later the police were there. They had questions for me.

" Paul. What can you tell us about Tom Doolin's accident? You were there, right?"

I couldn't deny it. I had left my goddamn library books in the garage and I figured my fingerprints were on the pieces of the broken bottle of beer I had dropped. And who knows, there may have been a witness or two seeing me running away.

I began to cry. "I'm scared sir. I saw it happen and I couldn't do anything. Is Tom dead?"

"Tell us what you saw. Calm down."

"We were talking. Tom was working on his car, the muffler or something. He kicked it and the car fell on him. I ran. I know I should have tried to help him. I just ran. I was scared. Is he ok?"

"What did Tom kick Paul?"

"I don't know... the thing you use when you have a flat. The thing that holds the car up. The jack. He didn't mean to kick it. We had a couple of beers and I guess he kicked it by accident. Is he ok?"

"You shouldn't have run away son. Why did you leave him there?"

"I know, I know... but I was scared, blood. There was blood everywhere. I just freaked. I had to get out of there."

"Then why didn't you call for help when you got home?"

"What? I don't know. I got sick," my fake crying grew louder. "Is he ok?"

"No, I'm sorry to tell you this but Tom died."

I let out a scream. "I should have helped him... I should have helped him. Oh God... I'm so sorry."

CHAPTER 10
Paul's Epiphany

I believe in God, Father Almighty. I don't believe in religion. I had been born Christian, made Catholic by my mother and had been incessantly taught first by nuns, then brothers, and in college, priests. All good people if one can define good. I'm sure they sinned as much as anyone else, probably not the "big" sins but by their own beliefs... sins none the less. I often wondered what their confessions were like? "Bless me Father for I have sinned. It has been just a few days since my last confession. I felt lust in my heart and committed two sins of self-abuse. I laughed when I saw another person injured." And on and on, could God really care? I'm sure they would envy my sins.... Real, horrible, unforgivable sins. I came to the conclusion that I believed in God. How could you not? God is an intellectual and moral necessity, but I didn't love God. I don't love anything or anyone.

After college I decided to find work in Lebanon. I had dual citizenship and had begun to hate America anyway. I applied to a university in Beirut as a language instructor and was quickly hired. My father and grandparents were delighted with my decision. Pop and Grandpop always told me how beautiful Lebanon was and that if it wasn't for the Palestinian refugees they would have never left. They contacted my relatives and asked them to help me find a place to stay. In reality, I wanted nothing to do with my Lebanese relations but agreed to see them when I arrived. The university had already arranged on campus housing and since I spoke decent Arabic, I knew I'd have little if no problems making my own way.

As I flew into Beirut, I had an epiphany. Lebanon was fucked up. There were no real police forensics. Probably no real police either. Killing had become a way of life there. I could kill and kill and I would never be caught.

CHAPTER 11
Snake Identified, located... Philippines

They called him Bong Bong at work. His real name was Hannan Roces and he was a captain in the Davao City Police Department, in charge of intelligence gathering. He was a lazy man but an intelligent one. His promotions came because he was smart and his superiors recognized his skill at solving problems. Bong Bong knew he had reached the top rung of his career and he was worried. He would retire in a few years and he was broke. He had five kids by three women and they were all looking for his pesos each week. The police pay was very very low and most cops survived on graft. In Tagalog graft was said as "nakawan sa gubyerno, pangunguwalta sa gubyerno, katiwalian". Of course, Filipinos didn't take the time to use the Tagalog words, so graft was graft and always said in English. Everyone knew what it meant.

When Bong Bong was a street cop, he'd shake down everyone on the street for almost anything. Sometimes he'd bring home a chicken or bananas, sometimes a pocket full of pesos. In his senior position he now made a lot of pesos. Small time drug dealers and thugs paid him for information and he had plenty to sell. But he never provided information that would get cops hurt or killed, just ordinary stuff about planned police drug raids and street sweeps for prostitutes and bar checks. Davao was a big city and his intelligence information reached every corner. The city now had a new mayor who was a genuine tough guy. He had gotten elected on the promise of cleaning up this city and it was working. Drug dealers and users were being killed every day by police hit squads. Bong Bong's income was slowly drying up.

"Captain Roces, captain, do you have a minute? I've got a report you I think you should see."

The young cop was afraid of Bong Bong. He was the new cop in this office. He was here because he wanted to get away from street assignments, they were getting too dangerous and he paid his sergeant to have him transferred. They all told him not bother Bong Bong and stay on his good side. Don't upset him or he'll kick you out.

"What's so important?"

"It's a report from Manila sir, about that incident concerning the woman who had been murdered, Aadab Koo. I thought you would want to review it."

"Put it on my desk and I'll look at it later. What's your name?"

"Ah, James Garcia sir."

"Thanks Garcia. I'll be at lunch if anyone wants me. "

It was almost two hours after he returned from lunch that Roces picked up the folder Garcia had left for him. He vaguely remembered the investigation into the murder Koo woman. What interested everyone was the manner in which it had come to the attention of the Filipino Police. Some American in New York claimed he witnessed her murder on an internet dating site.

This file contained old information but it was the new documents that most interested Bong Bong. There was a new section compiled by US Homeland Security that described in great detail what the American eye witness had seen during the attack on the Koo woman. Apparently, Homeland Security had now established a positive identity for the American attacker and was alerting the Filipino CID that they were interested and available to support their efforts in capturing this guy. His name was Paul Asoph, aka "Snake" by his ISIS comrades. The "Snake" file was extensive. This guy had been an ISIS VIP and had both hands-on combat experience and according to Homeland Security, and had been part of the ISIS recruitment management unit as well.

This information is worth money, Bong Bong thought. He knew that the American CIA might become involved at some point and that made it all the more valuable.

Bong Bong picked up his throw away cell phone, left his office, walked a block, and made a call to his contact in Butig Town. The man he was calling was a policeman related through marriage to one of the Maute brothers, leaders in the Moro Islamic Liberation Front (MILF) which had just publicly announced its allegiance to ISIS. Butig Town was the epi center for MILF activity in Mindanao.

Making a call like this was dangerous. Bong Bong was not a Muslim, had no particular dislike of Muslims like many of his countrymen but like most Filipinos, was concerned with the militancy of the MILF which threatened military action against the State. They had orchestrated the bombing in Davao's market and now were active on Police radar.

"Hello."

"Hello sir. How are you today?"

They were having this conversation in Visayan, a local dialect.

"My brother, I have very important information for our friends. I think it is valuable and for the right price, I would share it."

"Could you tell me something about this information sir?"

"It concerns some foreigners who recently arrived there and what the US Government is seeking. That should be enough for your friends to understand. Oh, and be sure to tell them to watch out for a 'snake'. It might bite them," Bong Bong laughed his little joke.

"What favor are you hoping for my brother? Could you tell me an amount?"

Bong Bong told his contact what he needed and reminded him to add something extra for himself. They arranged for a return call time and ended the conversation. He smiled at his expected good fortune and returned to his office.

Two days later he got his return call. It was dangerous to speak openly on a phone, but he recounted all the important information in the Koo investigation file. His caller was most interested in his Snake information. The caller acknowledged that the Snake was in fact close by and he would relay the information. They arranged payment to be made in the usual way and ended the call. Bong Bong was concerned. Their conversation was a long one and if the phones were monitored, he would be in danger. He didn't know it but he was already in trouble. A US airborne listening source had recorded all that was said together with the locations of the callers.

Bong Bong was late for work as usual. There were two CID agents waiting patiently in his office when he arrived.

"Good morning Captain Roces."

They both noticed his sloppy appearance. He was overweight and his uniform didn't fit. While waiting, they had made a cursory examination of his office and could glean nothing through the mountain of unfiled reports, notices and other documents that cluttered everywhere.

"Why are you here? What are you doing in my office? Who are you guys?" Bong Bong always found being aggressive was a good defense most of the time, but inside he was frightened.

"Don't bother to sit down captain. You're leaving with us... right now." They had flashed their id's and Bong Bong didn't dare resist. His Chief watched them leave. "He's fucked," he whispered to no one in particular.

A day later Bong Bong was stripped naked, tied hand and foot, and lay on a prison cell floor. He had been questioned the previous day, confronted with the evidence of his telephone call to Butig Town, and labeled a traitor by his interrogator. He denied everything even in face of the overwhelming evidence. He knew that he was at best, going to spend the rest of his life in jail, at worst, killed. He considered his options. He would hold out as long as he could. Tell them nothing, perhaps save his life with information bargaining.

They brought him from his cell and handcuffed him to a wooden chair in an interrogation room. The interrogator was a different one from the day before. He was shirtless and big. He shut the door and now stood within inches of Bong Bong's face. He smelled bad.

"I want you to confess and I will make it easy for you. There's no need for me to hurt you if you confess. You must answer truthfully and I will not hurt you. Do you understand what I am telling you?"

Bong Bong decided not to say anything to this monkey.

His fist caught Bong Bong's chin, knocking over the chair and putting him on the floor.

The big man opened the door and a police officer entered, carrying a roulette wheel. From his place on the floor Bong Bong already knew what was coming. This was known as the "Wheel of Torture" and he had heard from other cops that it was sometimes used in interrogation.

The monkey man up-righted his chair and had him face the wheel. "Do you want me to take a spin? Never mind. Don't talk, say nothing captain. I don't get to use the wheel very often. But you are a traitor to my country and you deserve punishment."

The wheel spun... where it stopped would be the particular torture inflicted. He spun it and when it stopped, it showed "Pacquiao".

"Ahhh... good. Now I will beat you hard for twenty seconds like Manny and then we spin again."

Bong Bong told all he knew after three spins. He was executed the same day.

CHAPTER 12
Tim's Bad News

Dan Tully had just entered his office when his chief called him to the conference room.

"What's up Boss?"

"You remember that guy you interviewed in the Paul Asoph aka Snake case? He saw the girl killed on his computer? Ehh... name Tom Ryan, right?"

"Sure. Good guy. What's the problem?"

"I just received a report from the Philippines... Ryan's name was definitely passed onto the ISIS branch in Mindanao. There's a rumor that some mullah there issued a fatwa against Ryan. They don't want the Snake to be identified as a killer living in the Philippines."

"Can't the Filipino cops catch this guy? They could extradite him and we could probably hold him and we could charge him here."

"Not much chance of the Filipino cops catching him Dan. This guy is holed up deep in Indian country and it would take an army to go in after him."

"Could we put Ryan in protective custody then. Keep him under wraps until the Snake is captured?"

"We could, technically, but he'd have to agree. Give him a call and tell him what's up and see if he wants our help. That's about all we can do for now."

Dan Tully decided to deliver the warning message in person. He knew where Tim's bar was located on 10th Avenue and 45th Street and was a quick subway ride over. The bar was right in the middle of the newly renamed Clinton neighborhood, they use to call Hell's Kitchen. Originally a very seedy, tough dangerous place to live, it was now becoming the next Yuppie enclave. Rents were still moderate by city standards and it was a real neighborhood. It was clustered with many small mom and pop shops, restaurants, and parks.

Dan liked Ryan's bar the first minute he entered. Old dark wood furnishings, long bar with a lot of brass and mirrors, no bar stools, just a foot rest and a slight tangy smell of beer and cigarette smoke. In earlier days it would have been called a "Man's Bar". There was mostly likely a back room and separate entrance for the ladies as well.

Tim was bar tendering with an attractive older woman who was handling food orders. It wasn't too crowded but considering it was going on 3 pm, not a bad sized crowd for this time of day.

"Welcome to Buddy's Shamrock Tavern Mr. Tully. It's good seeing you again. What can I get you?"

Tim reached over the bar and shook Dan's outstretched hand. Both were smiling and anyone noticing could tell they were friends who liked each other.

"Good to see you again Tim… maybe a soda, no ice and a menu. I skipped lunch. What's good?"

"Fish and Chips, corned beef and cabbage, and the Sheppard's pie are all good today. Think about it while I pour your soda. Sure you don't want something a little stronger?"

"Naw, thanks I'm good… working… I'll have the fish and chips."

The waitress had heard what was ordered and headed toward the kitchen in the back. The jukebox started playing some sad sounding Irish song and Tim had an annoyed look on his face.

"Billy. For fucks sake…. Can't you pick something else lad. I've listened to that same damn song twenty times today."

Tim place the soda in front of Dan, wiped his hands on his apron, and began a new Guinness for one of his bar customers. "So, what brings you in today? Any new information?"

"Yes, as matter of fact that's why I stopped by… I didn't want to call with an update and I hope this isn't an intrusion just coming in like this."

"No… not at all. When your food comes, we'll move to a table in the back room where we can talk. Maggie can handle things for a bit.

44

It gets very busy about 5. So my friend, I have plenty of time for you right now. Let me put a head on your soda."

In less than ten minutes, Dan's meal arrived. He followed Maggie as she carried it to a table in the empty back room and she smiled, "Enjoy your meal," and turned to relieve Tim at the bar.

Dan sat and eyed his lunch. Three large crispy brown pieces of fish, more French fries then he could ever eat, and a small lettuce and tomato salad. *Looks perfect*, he thought and he liberally covered his fish and chips in malt vinegar and was able to take a few bites before Tim joined him.

"This is great, maybe the best I've had in a long time Tim. I know where to come now during Lent."

"Ya don't need to wait till Lent, we serve it just about every day. Now ya know Dan, an Irish cook book is only two pages, so there's not much variety in the menu. Thanks, I'm glad you like it. A cold Guinness would go much better than the flat soda ya drinking. Keep eating your meal and we'll talk when you're finished. No rush."

Dan kept eating while they small-talked about things new friends always talk about. Tim had owned the bar since his father died many years before. Dad was the "Buddy" in the bar's name. Dan said he had grown up in New Jersey, went to St. Peter's College, and had been a NJ state police officer before Homeland Security came along after 9/11.

When Dan finished eating, always the host, Tim asked." Want some coffee?"

"No, I'm good. Thanks again. Be sure I get a check for this. It was great and you'll have me back here again. Off duty... so I can drink a little bit or drink a lot, depending on the company."

"You're always a welcomed customer here. Now what's so important that a big shot like you comes to my humble establishment on this fine sunny summer day?"

Dan grew serious. "Tim, I've got some very bad news. You remember when I told you that you might be in some danger. Well, there's absolutely no doubt about it based on information we just received from the Philippines. They know who you are and a death threat has been issued against you."

Tim sat back in his chair, reached in his pocket for his pipe, filled it and started to puff away. He was obviously surprised but Dan could sense Ryan was not particularly or obviously frightened by this bad news.

He finally spoke. "Well, fuck them and fuck the horse they rode in on."

"Tim, this is serious shit. You know what a fatwa is, it's a death threat that allows any Jihadist to seek you out and kill you on sight. For God's sake, they may already be on the way here. We just don't know. That's why I want you to let me help. I can get you in witness protection until it's safe. What do you say?"

With a few more puffs, creating blue-white clouds of a fine smelling pipe tobacco, Tim finally answered Dan's question after some deep thought.

"Dan me lad, let me tell you a little about Thomas J. Ryan, known as Tim to friends and foe alike. I was born and grew up right here in Hell's Kitchen which is still one fucking tough neighborhood. You might have heard of our local Irish lads, the Westies. They were the official "Murder Incorporate" division of the MIFA. Unfortunately, I ran with them in my youth and did some foul work until my Dad beat the shit out of me one day and made me join the United States army... for which I am eternally grateful. I came out as a machine gun squad leader, buck sergeant with in-country time in Vietnam. I've stood behind this bar for more years than I can remember; beat up more drunks than I want to think about and got beat bad by some of them as well. I'll be seventy-two next November, lost the love of my life a few years back and have lived an interesting and good life. So fuck them. It is what it is. I'm not going anywhere."

"I guess that means no witness protection then?"

"That's what it means... ya sure you don't want a quick nip of Jameson before you go?"

Tully was not surprised at all by Tim's refusing protection. He had expected it from the start. He was concerned, but if anyone could face up to this threat, well, Tim Ryan could.

Maggie walked into the back room. "Tim, small emergency," she laughed. "The Guinness tap needs a gas refill. Could you check it please? I'm sorry to disturb you and your friend."

Tully answered. "That's ok... we're finished up here." He stood and the men faced each other. "Tim, good luck and watch yourself my friend. And I'll be sure to stop by for more fish and chips real soon." He handed Maggie a $20, shook Tim's hand, and left. She cleared the table while Tim went down into the basement to hook up a new Guinness gas cylinder.

Tully replayed his conversation with Ryan in his mind as he headed for the subway. He kept thinking, *Was there something else I could have said that would have convinced him? Probably not.*

His "cop" subconscious registered the young guy just passing him... head down, dressed in a heavy red jacket, hood up in 85-degree heat. Tully was 100 feet past him before he fully recognized the significance of what he had just seen. *This guy could be a suicide bomber on his way to Buddy's Shamrock Tavern!* screamed though his brain. Pulling out his cell, he quickly speed-dialed and alerted his office. They automatically had his GPS location and would react faster than a 911 call for help. He hoped he wasn't already too late. Dan Tully was in good physical shape and with his Glock in hand, raced after the man in the red jacket now only ten yards from the entrance to the bar.

"Stop! Stop! Police. Stop!" he shouted.

The guy was in a trance, just kept walking. *Should I shoot or wait until I can be certain?* flashed through his mind. The red jacket guy had reached the saloon door, turned and saw Tully. His coat opened and the suicide vest was clearly visible. Tully fired. Too late. Dan's last conscious thought was, *Strange, he didn't shout "Allah Akbar."*

Later they recovered Tully's mangled body along with five other victims including Maggie and the kid named Billy from the destroyed bar. Tim Ryan had been working on hooking up the beer gas in the basement and survived the attack without a scratch.

CHAPTER 13
Tim... I'll get by with a little help

I heard and felt the explosion. It knocked me down. My first thought was a gas line blew up and then smoke began to pour into the basement and I could feel heat from the fire that had begun upstairs in my bar. I ran up and had to push the blown off door to the basement to get into the wrecked bar. In Nam I had seen devastation and death but not like this. There was fire starting everywhere and bar stools, pieces of the bar, brass mirrors, and body parts cluttered about. I couldn't see a living soul but I heard low moaning from the back room. I found Jack McGee on the floor back there, his legs gone and blood gushing. I don't remember what I did during the time it took for help to arrive, they told me later I saved McGee's life. How, I don't really know. Besides myself and Jack, there were three other survivors. Two were saved because they were taking a pee and sheltered from the worst of the blast in the men's room, the other, a young lady, had dropped her cell phone and had been close to the floor looking for it when the bomb exploded. She was badly hurt, but thank God alive.

The weeks that followed are still a blur. After we all got out to the street, the cops closed off the block and Buddy's Shamrock Tavern became a crime scene and a major media story. I went to all my friend's funeral masses, stood at their grave site remembrances and thought about what I was going to do with my life now in shambles. I decided to fix up and reopen Buddy's Shamrock as soon as I could. What else could I do? This was the only life I had ever known. I wasn't going to just fade away and die in some New Jersey nursing home.

I was questioned by the NYC Bomb Squad, FBI, Homeland Security, the DEA and I think a lady from the CIA, off and on for weeks after the explosion. The attack was identified as being a genuine terrorist attack and hit the front page, tv and cable news outlets here in the States and most likely the rest of the world as well. I was told not to give interviews and the NYPD kept a 24/7 guard at my house and stayed close by whenever I went out. They offered me witness protection again, which I refused again.

I didn't have many visitors and was surprised when there was a loud knocking on my door. The young cop assigned to watch me was having his coffee in the kitchen and I was taking my morning crap. The cop looked first through the window before answering the door.

"Is Tim available?" I heard the voice of my oldest friend Gerry McGuire ask.

"And who are you sir? May I see some identification?" the cop asked.

"He's ok, Tony, he's an old friend. Come on in Gerry."

Let me tell you a little bit about my old friend Gerry. We grew up together in the "Kitchen", were next door neighbors, the same age. He fell in love with my sister and I fell for his sister too. They both married other guys though. He and I were part of the Westies Mob for a while until I went off to Vietnam. He's retired from crime now, or at least that what he'd have you believe. His youngest son Billy McGuire died in my bar's bombing.

"So what brings you out lad?" I asked while pouring us both a shot of Jameson.

"Timmy lad… to your health. Slainte."

Tony the cop left the kitchen for the front stoop to have a smoke and give us some privacy.

"We didn't have a chance to speak at Billy's wake and if ya don't mind, I have some questions about that bombing but only if you feel like talking."

I poured us another. "It's a long story Gerry."

"I have the time and I need to know why some bastard killed my son."

A red light went off in my brain at that comment. Gerry was old school tough and I knew that someone was gonna pay for his kid's murder, no doubt about that.

We sat talking for over an hour and I told him everything I knew. He asked questions here and there and he was surprised to learn that I was still in some danger.

"Ok Tim. Two things are gonna happen. First, I'm ordering up some real protection for you. Fuckin police can't do shit. My lads will keep you safe until this bullshit Snake has his fuckin head chopped off. Second, I'll be taking a ride over to Brooklyn and discuss this matter with the Snake's people. I'm sure they know where the prick is and how to reach him. I'll find out. Maybe send him a message."

Gerry was on a mission now. He felt good that he could do something and bring justice for Billy. I actually felt good about the Westies keeping an eye out for me. I knew the cops would pull my bodyguard sooner or later. We had a few more Jameson's and Gerry left. On his way out, he said that there was a little surprise coming for me this afternoon. The surprise turned out to be an eight-week-old Rottweiler puppy. There's was a note attached to his collar, "So you'll never be alone."

I named the little guy "Rocky", an abbreviation of Shamrock.

CHAPTER 14
A little payback

Jake Asoph, Paul's dad, was worried. He had kept a low profile when he came to America with his parents all those years ago. Yesterday he had a visit from Homeland Security asking about Paul. The family had lost touch with Paul years before but his wife or his father received an occasional birthday card or brief note, usually from somewhere in Europe. Jake was not loved by his son and he never really loved the boy either. Theirs' had been a rocky relationship. The boy was weak. He could have never lived the life of fighting and killing that he had lived in Beirut. He would never have been able to defend his country and do what was necessary to protect it and his family.

The Homeland Security investigator had visited him a few times over the last four years. Always the same questions, "Where is your son? What do you know about his activities in Lebanon?"

He always answered truthfully. "I don't know. I have no son. He is dead to me."

It was a bright Sunday morning on 76th Street, a little after 5 am when he was taken. Jake never heard the two men come up behind him, one quickly grabbing and tightly holding him and the other placing the hood over his head. He felt the car quickly drive away and he could smell the alcohol on the floor where he had been roughly placed. There was a foot holding him down and not a word had been spoken. He didn't know how long they drove but he could hear the sound of ships horns from the Narrows so he knew he was still somewhere in Brooklyn.

An old soft voice from the front of the car finally broke the silence.

"Good morning to you Mr. Asoph. Ya probably a little concerned right now and wonderin' what's goin' on? Don't worry lad, we're only gonna ask ya a few questions about ya son. Sit him up lads so he can hear me better."

He felt himself yanked up and placed on the seat between two men. "Why are you doing this? I have no son. He is dead to me."

"Ach... ya have no son is it? Well I have no son either but your bastard son is still alive and he killed my boy. Ya gonna tell me all ya know... where he is, what he's doin'. What time he takes his mornin' shit."

Jake felt the power of the fist that smashed his face and tasted the warm blood that erupted from his broken nose. He was truly frightened now. He had known evil men like this in Lebanon. They enjoyed killing and he knew he would die here.

They beat him for a long time. He told them all he knew which wasn't very much. He even told them that his wife and father might know where his son was but he had no contact with him since he left America.

"Ya may be lyin' or may be tellin' me the truth. I was gonna kill you... but I think I'll let you talk to ya family first and see what they can tell me. I'll be in touch in a bit and ya better have some information for me. Do ya understand?"

"Yes," Jake answered. He was crying and in pain. He would find out what he could.

"I think ya will lad. Now let me give ya fair warnin'.... If I don't find out what I need to know, I'll start by killing you, then your wife and kids and finish up killin' ya old mom and dad. Do ya understand that?"

They took him from the car, but kept his hood in place and the wire that still bound his wrists.

"Now ya prick... here's a little something for ya before we leave."

The Glock 23's normal loud report was somewhat dulled by the empty warehouses surrounding the marine army terminal docks on 39th Street. There was no one there anymore and the neighborhood was filled with drug dealers always firing their weapons at each other anyway. Nobody cared even if the heard the shot. Jake Asoph cared. The 40-caliber bullet smashed into his left kneecap and he fell to the pavement wreathing in pain.

A week later Mrs. Asoph tearfully told the caller all the family knew about her son's whereabouts. Six weeks later the Philippines ISIS knew about the attack on the Asoph family and received the message sent to the Snake. "Come home now or your family will die."

Unfortunately, he never got it. He had left the Philippines.

BOOK 2

CHAPTER 15
Snake... A New Life

I was thinking about the concept of truly evil people and their evil actions and concluded that I'm not an evil person. Though I must admit I am strange, not a nice person, dangerous even. I'm very bad of course, but I don't consider myself evil. I have met, lived with, and intimately known many evil people. I have killed innocents, I have killed evil people, and I have killed in war but all my killings, or murders if you prefer, were the result of either my hatred for evil people or uncontrolled circumstances for my killing the innocents and of course I killed for my self-preservation during war. With the exception of that pedophile priest I killed so long ago, I never really planned to kill anyone. In a little bit, I'll tell you about the most evil person I ever met and believe me I've encountered many evil humans. Her name was Sophia and I when I met her and perhaps, I fell in love with her, or something like love, she and I killed together in Beirut and it was in Beirut that Sophia died. I killed her.

I first saw Beirut from the air. In a strange way I was reminded of the costume face mask of the Phantom from Phantom of the Opera... that's how this city looked. Its civil war had left its mark. Beautiful buildings on one street side and destroyed buildings on the other. You could readily see that it was in the process of rebuilding and even with the work in progress appearance, there was no doubt Beirut would once again become one of the most beautiful cities in the Middle East. Surrounded on two sides by the blue Mediterranean, high cliffs, Old and new buildings, wide boulevards, narrow street... trees, colorful plantings... traffic, all lent to my feeling that this was a vibrant city, a good place for me to become a part.

The first thing I noticed when I arrived and departed from the plane was the beautiful weather. I'm a guy from New York City. My city is great but the weather in NYC stinks. Here in Beirut the weather was magnificent. I began loving this place at once. The next thing that became apparent was this city was still fighting a war. The airport was loaded with cops, soldiers all carrying machine guns and checking out every passenger with the clear intention that they would blow you away if you made a suspicious move.

Having dual US-Lebanese citizenship got me through Customs without a problem. My grandfather had alerted my relatives on my arrival time and so, there waiting, were at least a dozen smiling Asoph cousins, uncles, aunts and I'm still not sure who they all were. I really had planned on not having any contact with family but it was out of my control. I smiled, laughed, and answered all their many questions. I wound up staying at the ancestral family farm in the hills overlooking the city. My grandfather's younger brother was the Asoph clan leader and he had three sons and from what I could see about 100 grandkids. It was apparent that my Lebanese family were well off. I knew that my grandfather had owned a Mercedes-Benz dealership in Beirut and lost it during the civil war. I often wondered why he and my father had left Lebanon. I found out they had to get out fast. Both were active leaders in a Christian militia and had participated in the brutal massacre at a Palestinian refugee camp. They were wanted men, murderers, I now knew where my need to kill came from. I spoke with my grand-uncle and he told me he had a wonderful surprise for me. My grandfather had instructed him to provide me with a very large sum of money he had been keeping for grandfather and I would never have a money problem living and working in Beirut. I didn't expect that.

I spent a few weeks living on the farm or better described as an estate. I'm a city guy so I don't know much about farming, taking care of animals, planting, picking and working the land. These people did. They had been farmers for 1,000 years and the Asoph family land was beautiful.

I stayed with my relatives for about two weeks. They had parties for me and we all met at least once each day for a big meal. The food was great. I had eaten with my grandparents back in Brooklyn and Grandma was a good cook, but these people and the meals they created for our get togethers were better. Don't ask me what I had or enjoyed the most. It was all fresh and great tasting. On Sundays we all went to church. I pretended to care. I guess I'm a chameleon because I've found over my lifetime I could fit in anywhere, almost be anything to anybody. My relatives couldn't begin to know what I really thought about them or their religion.

One of my cousins drove me into Beirut and left me at the university that had hired me as an English language instructor. Why they hired me, I didn't know. I had no teaching experience, was not native born so had no understanding of Lebanese culture, manners, or the local norms. They got me cheap though. I reported to Administration and after a bit was taken to my living quarters on campus. A few days later I was part of the new group of instructors who were given an intensive orientation. I found that my French and Arabic language skills were adequate since almost all of the instruction was conducted in these languages. I noticed that many of my new colleagues tended to speak English when around me which made me think, *I must look like an American.* I needed to change that because I had to fit in, not look different, or be easily remembered. Over the next few weeks, I had my haircut, bought local clothes, shoes, I began to grow a beard. I worked on my American accent when I spoke Arabic. This presented a problem. You may laugh, but I never in all the time I was away from America and no matter what language I spoke or no matter how well I spoke it, I still had a noticeable and very distinctive sounding "Brooklyn" English accent. Since I look like a young Al Pacino, many thought I was an American mafia gangster from the *Godfather* movies. Sometimes this worked for me. It made them think I was tough, which I'm not.

I had a suite of three rooms on campus. The apartment building I lived in with a few other unmarried instructors had been built in the early 1900s and had a very elegant European look and feel to it. I liked it immediately. It was on the second floor with a nice view of the university's garden like quadrangle from my living room windows opening onto a small balcony. It was a large roomed, fully furnished apartment and included kitchen utensils, wall hangings, bed and bath linens. Everything a bachelor needed. I had a short walk to the central market and I quickly learned the Lebanese way to shop… haggle.

I studied my course syllabus and realized how little I knew and how much I needed to learn about teaching. Luckily most of my students were freshman and dumb. I had prepared my lesson plans and reviewed them with my department head who was only impressed and grateful to have an American teaching in his department. He hardly checked or commented on the inadequate course material I submitted and so I began my teaching career as an associate college professor.

Most of my young students already had a basic if not an advanced understanding of English. That first year teaching was an education for me. I think I matured and actually had no problem controlling my need to kill. I made few friends but completed my Muslim studies. Let me set the record straight, I didn't care about being a Muslim. I care nothing about any religion for that matter. I had a need to fit in here and this was just part of my disguise.

During school recess I was able to travel. I visited Saudi Arabia, Jordan, and Syria. I was not impressed. Of course there were many beautiful monuments and historical places that were on any tourists must see bucket list. But I found these countries to be backward, dirty, poor, ignorant, and even dangerous places for foreigners to visit. I was happy to get back to Beirut.

I mentioned that I had made few friends. My definition of friend is probably different than yours. A friend to me was someone I could use. Someone who really didn't have a strong personality and I could manipulate. I had a lady friend who did all my shopping, another who made sure my rooms and clothes were clean and one I used for sex. I'm not gay in case you were interested. As an American I seemed to have a lot of admirers. Strange. Back in Brooklyn people just left me alone. Here in Lebanon I was deemed different, someone people wanted to know. I was invited to a lot of social events and always introduced as the "American" professor. This is how I first met Sophia. Immediately, I knew she was different. She wasn't impressed with me. Actually, she was rude.

"Paul, please allow me introduce you to Sophia. Paul is an American and a good friend of mine,"

"I don't like Americans," Sophia answered.

I laughed. "I don't like them either. That's why I'm living in Lebanon. Nice meeting you Sophia. I can see you're very intelligent and charming too."

Sophia was pretty, not beautiful. She had an Arab nose, the rest of her was fine though. I could tell she was rich by the look of her clothes and jewelry. I pegged her for a rich spoiled brat, well educated but angry at the world and with everyone in it. I was wrong. She had an evil soul.

I held out my hand to her and she limply took it in hers. I held it a second or two longer than she expected and she smiled at me.

"Why do you hate Americans?"

"Do you really want me to tell you? You'll be angry. You are arrogant people. You think you run the world. You only care about money and power. You use your army and air force to kill anyone who gets in your way. Oh, and your women are lazy and fat pigs. These are just a few reasons why I hate America. Are you angry now?"

"No."

She seemed surprised at my answer.

"I'm sorry if I offended you. You seem alright even though you're an American," she lied. I knew she wasn't sorry. This was just the way she was.

"I'd like to talk with you more about your reasons for hating Americans. Let's get out of here and go somewhere so you can continue to offend me," I laughed. I watched her eyes. I felt she was looking at me as a potential equal. She would need to discover more about me, so she agreed and we left together.

We traveled a short way from the party to a small café I liked in the Armenian section. The food was always great and the coffee even better. Sophia drove, a new Miata sports car. She drove too fast and didn't seem to care much for traffic rules and pedestrians.

Our coffee was quickly delivered and we chatted while we waited for our meal.

"Have you been away from Lebanon Sophia? Europe perhaps?"

"I've traveled a lot Paul and know a lot about the world outside of Lebanon," she bragged.

"Really, where have you been? What have you seen?"

"Well, I went to school in Europe, lived in Paris for two years and Barcelona for about a year. I enjoyed living away from Lebanon. How about you?"

I would have some fun with her now and switched from Arabic to Spanish. "I've not been to Europe yet but plan to go sometime soon. What did you enjoy most in Paris?" Sophia had no idea what I just said but she tried to answer in incoherent Spanish. I then switched to French. "What did you enjoy most in Paris?" and I added for fun. "You have a big nose.". She laughed, still having no idea what I said. "I guess my language skills aren't as good as yours Paul." She said this in fairly good sounding English so she wasn't a total fraud.

"Would you prefer English or Arabic?" I asked.

"I need to practice my English. You're an English Professor so you can teach me. Right?"

" I can teach you many things. What else do you want me to teach you Sophia?"

She smiled and gave me a coy look. "Perhaps in time I'll ask you to give me private lessons. I am a quick learner. So, it wouldn't be hard for you. You don't like it too easy do you Paul. You look like a man who likes it hard, I think. I enjoy it being hard."

She put emphasis on the word "hard". This woman thought she was intelligent and, in my mind, she was only manipulative and use to being in control. I would change that.

"Hard is a subjective word. Your first lesson will not be hard. But you can make it hard if you don't use your mouth properly and form the words correctly. I'll teach you how to use your mouth. I think you'll be a good student."

She was enjoying our conversation and we continued like this until our food arrived. While we ate, she told me more about herself. I assumed she was still bragging but I tried to appear interested. "My family is well to do here in Lebanon. My father is in government and also has business interests all over the world. I have an older brother and a younger sister. I think my parents are disappointed in me. They love my sister but I hate her."

"Why do you hate your sister?" I asked.

"She's a little pig and a liar. She lies to my parents and tells them things I do which are not true. Do you have siblings Paul?"

"No. I'm an only child and my parents are deceased. That makes me an orphan. All alone in the world." I decided to match her lies. I was enjoying this conversation. "But I was left a substantial amount of money, so I guess that makes me rich too." I could tell she was envious now.

We chatted and lied like this through our meal and finished with coffee and dessert. When it was time to leave, she offered to drive me back to my apartment. I accepted. On the way home she asked if I liked boating. I was never on a boat if you don't count the Staten Island Ferry so I lied and said I did. She claimed that her father's boat was docked in the Marina and she and I could use it anytime I'd like. We made an open boating date and she gave me her cell number. No goodnight kiss when she dropped me off and I was glad to be rid of her. I almost forgot about her until she called me a few days later.

"Hello Paul, did you forget about me?"

Actually, I guess I hadn't forgotten her. She was use to men chasing after her. But I wouldn't play that game. I hadn't given her my phone number but I knew she could easily get it if she was interested in me.

"No, how could I ever forget you Sophia? It just been so busy here that I didn't have any time to call. How have you been?"

"Fine Paul, I've been busy too. I was wondering... Do you think you might be able to meet me tonight or tomorrow for coffee? I really need to practice my English and you said you'd help me."

I decided to string her along a bit... keep her hanging, waiting for me to commit to a date.

"I'm glad you're well... so you've been busy. Working? I never imagined that you worked." I said this with a little laugh to my voice. Sophia was the kind of woman men only wanted to bed, not marry, and she knew how to play the game better than most. I could tell by her brief hesitation that she was just a little surprised by my question and not jumping at the chance to be with her.

"Yes, I work," she answered. "I am in charge of my father's business here in Beirut. That is a very important part of what I do. So Paul, tell me, are you available?"

I suspected she was lying again but agreed to meet her the next evening. I told her the restaurant where I wanted to go which was fine with her but she said she'd pick me up at my apartment so we'd have more time to speak English.

"That's great Sophia. I'll wait outside for you then. See you at 7. I'm looking forward to seeing you. Ciao."

I decided to impress Sophia. She probably knew expensive when she saw it, so I dressed "expensive". I had money to spend and I had bought Versace casual. Most of the world thinks of the US as being the "home of the cowboy" so tonight I'd wear my Versace Leo Chain denim western shirt, my white, slim fit jeans and my Cross Chimer Western sneakers... total cost about $2,500. I'm not a handsome man... but at twenty-four I looked damn good.

I waited until 7:20 before I left my apartment. I knew Sophia would be deliberately late and from my window I saw her arrive at 7:15. She called up but I didn't answer. She was driving a black MB 550 tonight. I wondered where she got it. Probably her father's or maybe she stole it.

I got into the passenger side, no European double cheek kiss was offered or given.

"Hello Sophia. Thanks for coming to pick me up. I hope it wasn't a problem for you."

I deliberately didn't acknowledge the expensive auto she was driving or the elegant apparel she was wearing. She was dressed to impress, just as I had. Her short skirt was already hiked up far enough to almost see her panties. I laughed to myself. *She's really working it.*, I thought. *But then again, so was I.*

I had made 8 o'clock reservations at a very well know restaurant called Al Falamanki Raouche. It's perched on the cliff overlooking the Raouche Rocks. It's an absolutely beautiful location for a restaurant but the food is just ok. I liked it for the view of the Mediterranean and a bowl of their famous almonds soaked in water and always served with my coffee. I had no need or desire to take Sophia to some trendy restaurant. This is where I wanted to go. I had reserved a table by the floor to ceiling windows overlooking the magnificent view. We were a little early so we had coffee together with a bowl of those wonderful almonds while we waited. When you bit into one, almond milk would fill your mouth.

"You look very handsome tonight Paul. I like your clothes. Very American cowboy."

"Thank you, Sophia. I thought you hated America and Americans. Do you like our cowboys?"

I wasn't planning on returning her compliment. I'm certain she took a lot of time to get ready for tonight and expected one. Keep her off center. I wanted to control her, but if I wasn't careful Sophia would control me.

"No, I still hate America but I love Versace."

We were seated at a wonderful table with a magnificent view. Surprisingly our meal was exceptionally good and all in all it was becoming a pleasant evening. Sophia was playing her seductive role. She hung on every word I said… her eyes wide open, laughed when she thought I was being funny. Occasionally, she would reach across the table and touch my hand. To be honest, her game was working. I wanted to bed this woman and I knew it wouldn't be difficult.

When we left Al Falamanki, she suggested we stop at her apartment for coffee and her special dessert. I agreed and actually enjoyed her fast and crazy driving through the Beirut streets. She had an expensive apartment high up in a building known as the "Grudge". It was called that because one brother built it directly in front of his brother's hotel to block the view. I was beginning to believe some of Sophia's claims. It appeared she did in fact have money or perhaps some sugar daddy was keeping her.

"Relax on my balcony Paul while I start the coffee. I'll bring it out when it's ready."

I went to her living room windows and admired the view. If this was New York, the rent for a place like this would be astronomical. I'm sure it was still well beyond the reach of 90% of most Lebanese. The city was spread out before me and I could see the Med as well. She had a wide balcony and I opened the door and sat on one of the comfortable chairs enjoying the view. There was a fragrant Mediterranean breeze and Sophia had put on a jazz album the music matching my mood perfectly. I could smell the distinctive aroma of pot coming from her living room.

She came outside carrying a coffee and dessert tray and placed it on the table between the two wicker chairs and sat.

"Do you smoke Paul?" she asked offering me a black coffee, pastries and a slow burning fat joint.

I took what was offered, toked up, and enjoyed my perfect combination of great coffee, great marijuana, great view, and the possibility of great sex with a willing woman.

An hour later, lying naked on Sophia's bed, totally exhausted from our Olympic class sex, we shared our third joint.

"Would you like to do some coke Paul?"

"No thanks, pot is all I use. But knock yourself out if you want. Just don't forget, you're taking me home Sophia. I have a class to teach in the morning."

CHAPTER 16
Sophia's Problem

Pot was cheap and easy to get in Beirut. It mostly came from the Bekaa agricultural region up near the Syrian border. Cocaine came from there too and Sophia was a heavy coke user. I watched her do a few lines before we left for my apartment. It was too late to get a cab and I don't drive anymore. I have an expired New York driver's license but never owned a car or drove all that much before coming to Beirut.

"Sophia, are you ok to drive?"

I asked her this while she was doing at least 60 mph through the dark, narrow Beirut streets heading in the general direction of my apartment. She didn't answer. All the time my right foot was instinctively searching for the invisible brake to slow us down. I'm sure she saw the old man just stepping off the sidewalk at the same time I did… she didn't slow up. In fact, I felt the massive MB swerve into him and hurl him over the car. He had to be dead after that. She just drove on.

I felt the familiar tingle. I suddenly felt like I did when I had killed back in New York.

Sophia broke the silence. "Old fool, he should have watched where he was going."

After a bit I spoke. "Yes. I agree, he should have been more careful."

We both laughed.

CHAPTER 17
Perfect Storm

For the first time since I discovered that I processed a strange need to kill I felt a sense of contentment. I had found another, somewhat like me, who'd given up on the normal human aversion to take another's life. But Sophia and I were not alike in this. She sought out her victims. I didn't. Killing for me came only with unexpected opportunity. Sophia made her own opportunities. Granted, we enjoyed equally the results of our actions but she was much more driven in satisfying her appetite for killing. I realized that I could only be her partner, never the initiator, waiting for her to take the lead. Which suited me.

I was now in the second and final year of my university teaching contract. I didn't believe I would continue in Beirut afterward and began to plan for an extended stay in Europe. My goal was to live in all the major capitols, improve my linguistic abilities and perhaps return to New York and start my life there…. Marry, raise a family… I didn't really know.

But while I remained here in Beirut, I would take advantage of my new found relationship with Sophia. I wanted to learn as much as I could about her. Who was she? I began with her real name… Sophia Hartom. She was in fact the daughter of a wealthy and well-known local Druze politician. She did work in some minor fashion for him and she did have a brother and a younger sister. Sophia had been in trouble since her teenage years. This was a difficult and dangerous time for her, especially with her family connections, to have had any notoriety considering the state of affairs in Beirut over the last ten years.

She was linked to a young man who had been executed for selling drugs on a grand scale. Sophia was also considered a PLO sympathizer, but the official interest had not risen to the level of "deadly interest" in both the Christian and Druze communities. If it had, she would have been killed. Most thought it was just "rebellious youth" and she would grow out of it.

My real relationship with Sophia began on her father's boat. I would spend all of my weekend time with her, sailing out of Beirut into the beautiful Mediterranean Sea. After a bit of instruction, I was able to captain this 39' yacht as well as anyone. The boat was well equipped... both master and guest bedrooms each with bath, a full galley, and lounge. I had never met Sophia's parents or older brother but her younger sister, Fatima, did come out with us on the boat many times. I liked the kid. She was fifteen, better looking than Sophia, and had a nice way about her. She and I hit it off and I deliberately made Sophia jealous by showing the young girl a lot of attention.

We'd journey about ten miles off shore, anchor, and the girls and I would swim around the boat until we got tired. One lazy afternoon as Sophia lay forward sunning, she went topless... I imagine just to show off or annoy her sister. A bit later Fatima dropped her top as well and when I began to look, Sophia had a fit.

"What are you looking at Paul?"

I ignored her stupid question and just lite up a joint. *What do you think I'm looking at?* I thought.

She adjusted her bikini top and glared at her sister. "Put your top back on you pig!" she shouted.

I thought she was going to attack the kid and I told her to stop. I started the boat and took us back to the marina. I made sure I spoke with Fatima on the way back. Sophia was still fuming when we arrived. That night she and I went to a local club. All the rich, spoiled kids were making this place a favorite hangout. I don't drink but enjoy dancing. Sophia ignored me for the most part and found herself a few willing dance partners. The woman could dance, no doubt about that and she always had most of the guys watching her every sexy move on the dance floor. If she was trying to make me jealous it wasn't working.

After realizing that I didn't care, she sat next to me and in a voice as soft as this loud club music would allow, told me she was sorry about being such a bitch on the boat. Later that night she met a young couple traveling to Beirut from Jordan. She introduced me to them and asked me if it would be alright to invite them to join us on the boat the next day.

"Sure... why not?" I answered. This was not the first time we had guests on the boat but I didn't realize that Sophia had concocted one of her evil plans and that these two nice young people would be dead within twenty-four hours.

The guy's name was Michael and his girl was Sarah. They were obviously in love and this trip to Beirut was their pre-honeymoon. They were to be married back in Jordan in a few weeks. I liked them. Michael offered to pay for the fuel but I told him thanks, but that Sophia always insisted and used her father's credit card when we topped off the tanks. I took the controls and drove our boat about 10 miles off shore, north toward Jounie. Another beautiful day in Lebanon and boating on the Med. Not a cloud in the sky, the sea sparkling calm and not another boat in sight. A typical day boating for us. I anchored and we all went in for a swim.

"Paul, I have a cramp. I'm going back to the boat. Could you swim back to the boat with me?"

When we returned to the boat, instead of going below, Sophia climbed the stairs to the bridge. I followed and she caught me by surprise when she started the engines and engaged the anchor chain lift control. In seconds the anchor was raised and she pushed the throttle full speed, quickly moving the boat away from where Michael and Sarah were still swimming. They were confused at first, but some seconds later I could now hear them shouting after us.

"What are you doing? What's going on Sophia?"

I was furious and she pushed me away as I tried to take control of the boat.

"I just want to see how well they swim. We'll go back for them in a few minutes. It's just a little joke... relax Paul."

"This is far enough," I shouted.

I could no longer see the two swimmers but Sophia just kept the boat moving full speed further and further away. We struggled and when I finally had control and turned the boat back to where I thought the couple would be. It was too late. There was no sign of them. Either I had taken us in the wrong direction or they had drowned. We circled looking for them until it got too dark to see and returned to Beirut. I must admit I was not too upset after all and made very passionate love to Sophia all that night in her apartment.

CHAPTER 18
The end and the new beginning

Weeks became months and soon it was almost the end of my contractual arrangement with the university. They asked me, perhaps begged would be a better way to describe it, to stay on for another two years. I declined. Sophia and I were still exclusively connected but she didn't seem particularly upset when I told her I would be leaving in a few months. I began to wonder if she had plans to kill me. I'm not kidding. Given an opportunity I knew she would not hesitant and I had to stay on guard when we were alone together. We used the boat every weekend and hit the hot clubs at night. Our love making sessions were getting better and once in a while she'd bring another girl or guy into our bed. I didn't mind. Sophia was sexually insatiable and having some help satisfying her was a welcomed relief.

We never discussed what had happened on the boat and honestly neither of us thought all that much of it anyway. But I could see that whatever control I thought I had over her was really a myth. In time, she became more and more controlling and I went along with it only because I knew I'd be gone from her and Beirut in a little while.

One night, after hours of dancing in the clubs around the city and Sophia doing more lines of coke than a Columbian street whore, we lay together on her bed. She had become very aggressive and demanding in our love making. Love making? That's a joke, it was more like personal combat. Anyway, I found myself on top of her and she was demanding that I begin choking her. She enjoyed sexual asphyxiation and to be honest, so did I. Usually, I'd bring her to the point of being unconscious and then she'd experience her orgasm. Simple stuff really. This time and I don't know why, I kept choking her. she never resisted, just passed out. I kept squeezing her throat until I knew she was dead.

I felt a strange sense of relief. She was gone... another brick in my wall. I cleaned up, left her on the bed, and left. I took her Miata and drove close to my apartment before parking it. I had no plan, no alibi, honestly no concern at all. I thought, *If they catch me, they catch me. I don't care anymore.* I got up the next morning, showered, ate breakfast, dressed and went to class. It was just another day as far as I was concerned.

As I was walking home to my apartment, Gabriel, one of my better students approached me and grabbing my arm forcing me to stop. I was a little angry at having my personal space violated.

"Hey Gabe, what's your problem buddy?" I said while removing his hand from my arm. I kept walking.

"Professor Asoph, please... I have something important to show you."

I stopped and he handed me an envelope which I opened, removed two photos and got the shock of my life. The color photos were of Sophia lying obviously dead on her bed and a second photo of me leaving her apartment building.

Gabe smiled. "I have many more pictures here if you want to see them Sir." He handed me a manila envelope fat with photos.

"Where did you get these?"

"I've been asked to give them to you Professor. Someone I know will talk to you soon." And with that, Gabe turned and left me holding the photos and thinking, "I'm fucked."

My plan, if the police asked about Sophia, was to deny that I had anything to do with her death. I figured that it would be a day or two before her body was found. I didn't really have an alibi but I didn't think that they would have held me for her murder. I was a Professor, a guest... an American guest for God's sakes. I knew she had some deadly enemies and I imagined that her murder would give the Lebanese police reason to settle some scores with the PLO and the drug people she had known. I was leaving the country anyway and would be long gone before the investigation got around to me. Obviously, someone knew I had killed her and I could only hope this was just a blackmail effort and not a death sentence.

When I entered my apartment, I had a bigger shock. There was a well-dressed older man waiting for me in my living room. I didn't know him, never saw him before.

"Hello Professor Asoph. I see my young friend gave you those very interesting photos... we need to talk. Oh, please don't be afraid, no one else has seen them. You may call me Jake, just like your father. Perhaps, I'll become your second father. Please sit down and we can chat."

He's not a cop, I thought.

"Alright Jake... you seem to have me at a disadvantage. Who are you?" I sat... thinking, *In for a penny. Let's see who this guy is and what he has to say.* I sat on my couch and gestured for him to continue.

"I'm someone who can help you, and perhaps you can help me. I'm going to put all the cards on the table as you Americans say... you have been observed, actually followed for a while now. My friends and I weren't particularly interested in you... but your late girlfriend, Sophia, well that's another story. I take it you knew she was the daughter of one of our politicians here in Lebanon and the poor misguided girl was a principal source of important State information to the PLO."

He had a kinda British sounding voice and the mannerisms of someone use to being in charge.

"Would you like some coffee Jake? I always enjoy a cup after school about this time of day," I was stalling.

He smiled and I left the living room and started a pot in my kitchen. When I returned, I had composed myself. "

Who are you sir and who do you represent? It seems to me you're not from the Lebanese police." My voice rose a bit. "Who the hell are you and what do you want?"

"Let me begin by telling you that you that I am a friend and I will help you leave Lebanon. I know you plan on leaving but I'll make sure you don't have problems with the police."

"What do you want?"

"Ahh... good, you understand that you have something I need. Well, let me see. You are an American. You're young, adventurous, very smart, speak many languages, and I think, a make-believe Muslim,." He laughed at that. "And, please believe me when I say I know you're a killer. Paul, I work for Israeli Intelligence and we need someone such as yourself to help us gather information in places where it is difficult for us to go. Are you interested in hearing our proposition?"

I thought, *This came out of left field.*

I waited a second before I answered," Let me fix us some coffee first. I may be interested Jake."

CHAPTER 19
The Proposition

You already know I'm not a stupid man... flawed no doubt. Jake, or whatever his name was, had proof that I murdered Sophia. I wouldn't last an hour if it got into the hands of her father, the PLO or the Lebanese police. He seemed to hint that he could get me away from this mess without a problem. At this moment I only had a vague plan about traveling in Europe. In any case, I knew I didn't want to return to the States and I knew I had nothing to lose hearing him out.

"How did you know my father's name was Jake?" I smiled when I asked... I guessed this information was easy to uncover and no doubt "Jake" had done a lot of homework on Paul Asoph.

"I can mention the names of your entire family, where you went to school... actually, whatever you may want to know or had already forgotten about your life Paul."

We sipped our coffee and sat there chatting like old friends discussing the results of a recent soccer match.

"I'm sure you could Jake. It doesn't really matter what you already know about me, I guess. What matters is what you're here to offer me, wouldn't you think?" I finished my coffee put the cup back on the table and gestured for him to begin explaining his proposition.

"Do you have something cold to drink Paul? This will take a bit of time."

Jake was most likely a college professor at some point in his life. I was impressed with his knowledgeable lecture on Middle Eastern

History. He began with the 12th century crusades and carried his lecture through the passage of 1,000 years of history. He described the "tribes" conflict that influenced the region even to the current day. The portioning and creation of countries by the European victors after WWI caused a significant upheaval among the Tribes of the Region... mixing Sunnis with Shia, Jews with Arabs, Kurds with Turks, Muslims with Christians, all creating the powder keg that has erupted periodically over the last 100 years.

It was growing dark when Jake finished.

"Would like another drink?" I asked.

"No thank you. Now let me tell you why I am here and what I hope you'll agree too. Simply put Paul, we'd like you to work for us. We want you to be our spy."

I had to laugh... me, a spy. "Jake, I feel flattered that you think I could be a spy, I'm really a nerd. No James Bond. I hate danger. Really. Why do you want me to be your spy?"

"Paul, my country has been at war since it was founded. The only reason it is still here because we have the absolute best intelligence service in the entire world. We have active agents in most countries that have declared they are our enemies and we have always been a step ahead in whatever they were planning... actually we were sometimes caught lacking but that's another story. At this time Iran is our number one enemy. They will at some point in time be nuclear. We destroyed their capabilities in the past with bombs and computer viruses but we don't really have enough information about what is happening in Iran. Many of our on-ground agents were caught and hung in public squares. Many have difficulties in getting important information to us. Sadly, our American friends don't always share data gathered from their satellite's program. We believe that someone like yourself can be a great help for us."

I stood and began pacing. *This is crazy*, I thought.

"You actually want me to go to Iran and spy. That's nuts. They hate Americans. I'd be caught in a minute and hung. I think you need to find someone else."

Jake stood and walked to my balcony door and turned. "No. We don't want you to go to Iran. We want you to become a member of Al-Qaeda Paul."

CHAPTER 20

The Evidence

While Paul and Jake were talking, a Masoud crew was busy at Sophia's apartment. Her body was wrapped, minus her hands and a vial of her blood, and then carried to a waiting van. In an hour or two it would be weighted and dropped Into the Mediterranean. Her apartment was cleaned and all items that might have been linked to Paul Asoph were removed. Her computer hard drive was wiped clean, her cell phone first disassembled and then destroyed and even her bed was remade and the sheets and bathroom linens that Paul may have used were removed. Her severed hands were then used to place her fingerprints on the apartment surfaces the agents had previously wiped clean and that she would have normally touched. Finally, a small amount of cocaine and marijuana were left in an open location in her living room for the police to find without looking too hard. When they located her Miata, it was also sanitized and then her hand prints were added together with a sprinkling of her gathered blood. Some cocaine was left in the car and it was driven to a location close to the home of a known Beirut drug dealer. Sophia's hands were wrapped in plastic and left to be found as well.

Later, when the police investigated her missing person's report and found her Miata, they concluded that she was murdered during a drug deal and her body had been cut up and hidden. Paul Asoph was never questioned or considered a suspect.

CHAPTER 21
The Plan

"You have to be kidding. I'm not a radical. How the hell could anyone who knows me ever believe that I'd be a member of Al-Qaeda? I think you picked the wrong guy Jake..."

Jake took a few seconds to answer. "You're absolutely correct Paul. Anyone who knows you would never believe that you'd could become a jihadist. But we're prepared to change all that. Let me explain how."

I thought, "This is gonna be good."

"Ok," I said, "Tell me how you're gonna recreate me."

"During the two months that remain in your teaching contract here at the university you will begin to publish papers supporting the radical Muslim position. They will begin as somewhat benign observations supporting the acts taken by the jihadists and then become more and more radical. You will begin to attend services at a known radical Muslim mosque and seek out members who are known to support the views of Al Qaida. After you leave the university, you will move to an area of Beirut that is known for its radical Muslim followers. This might be somewhat dangerous and we'll keep an eye out for your safety."

"Hold on.... I need some more coffee, ice water for you?" I asked.

I had to take a break and try to digest what this guy was suggesting. I returned with the coffee and water in a few minutes. Jake had taken a bathroom break and I turned on the apartment lights. It was a beautiful night and a soft, fragrant breeze wafted through the open living room balcony doors.

"Ok Jake, let's assume that I agree and follow your plan. Jeez, this will take months... "

"Actually, it will take a few years to complete this work. This might be the time to lay out the reward Israel is offering for your help." Jake took a sip of his water and continued. "When you have gathered enough information for us or in the event your safety is gravely threatened, you will be pulled from where ever you happen to be at that moment and taken to safe location. If you wish, you will be given a new face, certainly a new identity and located anywhere you want to go to live the rest of your life. There will be a significant amount of ongoing financial support provided for your entire lifetime and there will be no need for you to ever have to work again. This is a general outline of our offer and the actual details will be filled in over time. But tell me Paul, how do you feel about this now?"

"I don't know. I have no real idea what you expect me to do for you and somehow, I don't think I'll be alive at the end anyway. You need to tell me more Jake. What do you want me to do and how do you want me to do it?"

"Alright, fair enough... our ultimate goal is to have you become a part of Al Qaida management... to be involved with all aspects of its operation. This obviously would include interfacing with Iranian agents and officials at varying levels. We have some agents located in Iran and they might be able to use you as a conduit for transporting their information to us. We believe that you are the right person for this work. Let me continue with describing our plan for you. Do you want to hear more?"

To be honest, I was both intrigued and confused. I didn't envision myself being a spy nor did I image I could pull it off if I was.

"Ok, tell me the rest of your plan."

"Paul it's obvious that you're really not much of a Muslim religion believer... one advantage of living in the radical neighborhood and attending services at the mosque will be to establish that you are a true believer and can be trusted. After living there for a while, you will be approached and asked to consider becoming a jihadist. I will explain how this will come about. Without going into too much detail at this time, we have some our in-place mid to low level agents who will see that you advance within the Al-Qaeda organization. They will vouch for you, recommend you when any position of importance or responsibility becomes available and in general, they will watch over you, keep you safe. You must remember that you are an ideal candidate for higher level work within the organization. Your credentials are almost a guarantee that you will be noticed and in time, given greater responsibilities.

Now let's discuss some unpleasant aspects of your involvement. At some point they will require that you complete basic training at a Jihadist camp... where and when, I couldn't say. After training you would be expected to participate in various military operations... again where and when is unknown. You would have to kill people Paul; you would see killing sometimes done in very evil and brutal ways. Captured soldiers, innocent civilians, religious people... terrible things to see and participate in. Unfortunately, this is the only way to establish yourself within this organization. Becoming a dedicated Jihadist fighter."

I already knew a lot about Al-Qaeda and what Jake just said was no surprise. I didn't have any feelings one way or another about either witnessing or killing. Honestly, I was more concerned about going through intensive Jihadist training. I was young, but I was out of shape. Actually, I was never really in good shape at any time in my life. The thought of jumping, running, doing endless pushups, and the YouTube videos I had seen of these black robed idiots training on playground monkey bars was more concerning than having to kill someone.

"Jake, I don't think you realize that I'm not the best physical specimen I might need to be to accomplish this... also, I know nothing about spying other than the James Bond movies I saw. How can someone like me manage to even get through the physical training and then not get caught attempting to become a spy?"

Jake just laughed at that. "Well put, well put... here's what we propose. Between now and the time you are recruited to become a jihadist, you will train both physically and you will also learn at least the basic spying techniques. I will have a doctor and a physical trainer here as early as tomorrow to examine you and then set up a proper training regimen. However, training you to be a spy will be a little more difficult but I'm sure that at least a crash course could be organized. What do you say Paul? Are you willing to try?"

I had already decided that I would accept Jake's proposition. I wasn't going to play hard to get. I still had Sophia's murder on my mind and I wanted to leave Lebanon anyway. I knew I didn't want to go back to Brooklyn, I really had no idea where or what I wanted to do. Besides... I liked adventure or at least the prospect of adventure.

"Alright Jake, I'm in... now what about Sophia? Can you make that problem go away?"

"Paul, that problem is already gone."

CHAPTER 22
Enemy of the State

Before he left, Jake gave me his contact phone number. I needed to memorize it and never write it done anywhere. I was to call him only if there was an emergency and only while I was still in Lebanon. He also told me that my student Gabe would be his intermediary in Beirut and would usually be available to help if I needed help. He asked my schedule for tomorrow and then made a call to a doctor. I was to have a full physical and meet with a trainer to set up my body building regimen. He left me and candidly I was nervous. *What have I gotten myself into?* I wondered. I was an American. I was a guy from Brooklyn who had grown up believing that I was a citizen of the greatest country in the world. I learned and believed in our laws, our way of life and that we were always good and just in everything we did. Now I was setting myself apart... becoming an enemy of the United States. I knew that Israel would never divulge that I was working undercover for them. I knew that I would never see my family or my country again. I knew that there may even be a time when I might have to kill other Americans.

From a practical point of view, I accepted that I was not a good person and probably would never be one. There was something intrinsically wrong with me that would never change no matter where I lived or what I did for the rest of my life. I rationalized and began to believe that working for Israel was ultimately a good thing for America. I'd be helping America's ally to survive, wouldn't I? Iran was America's enemy too.

But no matter how I tried, the ultimate truth remained. I would become a member of Al-Qaeda... the terrorist group responsible for 911. I knew I was doomed.

CHAPTER 23
Working Relationship

The next day I called a taxi and visited the doctor where I had a through physical. The office was equipped with x-ray and an array of all sorts of lab equipment. I had never been examined like this before and aside from a somewhat unique eye condition, it seems I could see better than most people, everything tested physically anyway, was normal. I wondered if this would be the outcome if Jake had arranged for me to visit a psychiatrist.

The doctor had me wait until the trainer arrived. She was beautiful. Lydia was her name. Probably not her real name, but it suited her. We were alone in his office and before we left, she had me strip naked and poked and probed me like she was buying a cow. She noted my weight, height, and all my body measurements in a journal.

"You have some belly and arm flab and your legs and arms need strengthening too. When was the last time you exercised?"

"You have to be kidding Lydia. Me? Exercise? Probably never."

With that flip comment, she punched me hard in the gut. I doubled over and my breath was gone for a few minutes.

"Why the hell did you hit me?"

She got really close and answered, "I want you to remember that... because when we're done you will be able to shrug a blow like that off. Do you understand?"

Ok, I thought, *And when I kill you, you won't remember anything either honey.*

Lydia told me that she would be my live-in girlfriend until the school year ended… in about ten weeks' time. This would give her a 24/7 opportunity to get me in shape without arousing too much suspicion. She also planned to conduct the "crash" spy-craft course Jake had promised during our time living together.

Live in girlfriend? I thought. *Good idea.* I knew that no one on campus would think anything about her being with me full time. She was the right age and had the right look for someone like me. It would allow us the freedom to interact publicly without arousing anyone's suspicions. I did wonder if she could cook though.

When we left the doctor's office, Gabe was waiting in his car to take us back to my apartment. She sat upfront and it was apparent that he knew Lydia and they chatted, I think in Hebrew, and I'm sure they were speaking about me and no doubt, he would report her findings to Jake.

"Professor, Jake would like you to review this essay written for you. It will be the first that will be published explaining how you began to accept the jihadist movement and why you think it's important. He said you should add or change it anyway you want but we will need it back tomorrow. If that's ok with you?"

I took the large envelope Gabe passed back to me. "I'll look at it later and let you know."

"That's fine Professor, when you have it completed just bring it to class and I'll take it from there."

I was beginning to realize what I had gotten myself into but I still felt ok about it. When we entered my apartment there was another surprise waiting for me. While I was out, gym equipment had been delivered and set up in my living room. There were also cartons of various food items laid out in my kitchen. Lydia apparently had her clothes delivered as well… there were two large suitcases in my bedroom.

"Well what's this all about Lydia? I guess you're really moving in with me and I guess I'm gonna be trained," I was smiling when I tuned to faced her.

She gave me a hard look; she was serious now. "I want to setup our ground rules Paul. I will always call you Paul, not professor or Mr. Asoph. I am not your girlfriend so there will never be any intimate sexual moments for us to share. No doubt you and I will see each of us naked from time to time, but get no ideas about that. We're now living together and sharing what most might consider intimate moments; there's not going to be any. I have no problem sleeping on the living room floor or your couch. I would sleep in your bed only if you promise that I will never have to remind you of our business relationship. Do I make myself clear Paul?"

I took a few seconds to answer. "Loud and clear Lydia. There's no problem at all in what you said. Sleep wherever you want. I just want to get trained and be on with my assignment. Now... do I make myself clear?"

She laughed and stripped naked. "I'm taking a shower Paul. Read your article while I freshen up."

And with that, our working relationship began.

Lydia is a very exotic looking lady. There was no doubt she had Arab blood flowing through her veins, almond shaped brown eyes, long black hair and a well-shaped, hard body. She's a few inches shorter than me and probably would kick my butt if we ever had a fight.

When she had showered and changed, she sat quietly across from me and watched while I proof read and modified the article Jake had prepared for me. It was pretty good. Not too strident in tone, honest sounding but a little skewed in the premises put forth, but all in all... it might be something I would write if I had ever held a belief in the justice of the Jihadist cause.

I finished making some minor adjustments and put the completed article aside.

"Paul, do you drink? Smoke? Use drugs?"

"I enjoy marijuana."

"If there's any here in the apartment you'll have to throw it out, now, today Paul. No stimulants of any kind while you're being trained. Oh, and that includes coffee... only one cup each day, you can pick when you have it. Is that understood?"

"Understood... now who's doing the cooking? I like to go to restaurants and I imagine that's not on your approved list of places for us to go."

"I will do all the cooking and buying our food while we are living together. Paul, you must eat healthy to grow strong and I'll make sure you do."

CHAPTER 24

Training

Lydia did sleep in my bed while we were together. She snores and farts a lot. She sleeps naked but she doesn't move and toss and turn too much. But to be honest when my training began, I usually fell asleep as soon as my head hit my pillow and hardly ever noticed the beautiful woman lying next to me.

As a city kid my exercise came in a schoolyard... stick ball, catch, and mostly basketball was about all the exercise I had. I guess you could count walking too. We did a lot of walking back in Brooklyn. When I began this formal exercise regimen I was not at all prepared. It was difficult. My day began with a 5 am wakeup. We dressed in our running shorts, t-shirts, and sneakers and ran for at least an hour. Lydia wanted to do at least five miles each morning but she started me off with a shorter run until I could build up my endurance. This took about two weeks. When we got back to the apartment I showered and changed for class while she made our breakfast. I forgot to mention our running was always on university grounds. People in Beirut don't run for exercise. If you were on the street and saw a runner, you'd automatically figured that somebody or something was chasing them and you had to get away quick. Too many years of conflict had changed their behavior, I guess.

After returning from my teaching class, she had me on the weight machines for at least an hour. She told me this lifting exercise was to strengthen my upper body. She said she didn't want to make me into looking like a muscle-bound weight lifter, just a guy who was toned and could handle strength challenges. I then did pushups, sit-ups, and stretching exercises. Then we had dinner.

I usually had free time to complete my student class work and work on the latest article Jake had sent via Gabe. I knew that Gabe and Lydia usually met each day or two and she would give him a report on my progress. He'd also deliver our food and other supplies as well. Jake paid for everything.

At night we'd walk around town at a brisk pace to round out the day's physical activity. I was usually in bed asleep by 10 pm. After a few weeks, I was beginning to feel good and look better. I honestly enjoyed the intense training and looked forward to working out each day. When I showered, I'd think, *Another day to accomplish great things.*

Early on, I visited our language lab at school and picked up some Hebrew language instruction tapes which I listened to during my morning run. Hebrew is actually easier to learn than Arabic and after a while and with Lydia's help, I had a basic conversational ability; writing and reading Hebrew was another matter.

A big part of Lydia's assignment was to give me a basic course in spying techniques. We worked at this during our evening walks and any available free time. I found this part of my training to be of most interest. I could use my mind and improvise. I was finally able to codify my natural abilities and came to recognize that I had a genuine talent for deception.

On our very first town walk, Lydia asked, "Paul how would you describe lying?'

"Hmm... telling someone something you know is false or you might believe is false."

"Ok, now since you're now in the lying business we're going to spend a lot of time on learning how to tell lies and just as important, tell when you're being lied to. Remember that all people lie. At least five times each day according to experts. Lying is in our DNA. It's a survival skill. One of a professional liars' problems is that no matter how good they are they eventually will be caught in a lie. A good interrogator knows the liar's secret techniques and will trip them up eventually. Remember that."

"How do they trip them up?"

"I'll teach you the interrogators methods. I might even ask Jake to loan us a lie detector and train you on how to fool it. Now, to start, a liar will memorize a story and will usually work out all the details ahead of time to anticipate the questions they will be asked. A good interrogator will ask questions that force the liar to tell the story forwards and then backwards. Really. This usually trips up the liar somewhere along the way. So, if you create your cover story, make sure you memorize it backwards. Focus on the details, stay as close to the truth as you can but Paul, be prepared because you'll eventually get caught lying but doing this will buy you time. Perhaps enough time to escape."

"What about body language? Doesn't that tell you whether a person is lying? At least that's what I've seen in all the spy movies."

"Body language, the usual stuff, is not always observable and anyway it's not infallible. The subject may be sick and sweat, they may be genuinely innocent but very nervous. And so on and so on. I'll instruct you on what you should watch for but keep in mind the physical signs you might pick up on are not always indicative of lying. But there are body language signs that will tell you if you're in imminent danger. You most likely intuitively know some of them but I'll instruct you on what to look for."

When we returned home that night and just before bed Lydia had a surprise question for me.

"Paul," she asked, "how long have you been drinking coffee at class?"

I figured this was her first test for me on successful lying. Since she asked the question this way, she either knew for sure that I was drinking coffee or she was just probing. I decided that Gabe had witnessed me drinking my coffee in class and had reported it to her.

"I don't drink coffee in class but honestly I have had a cup of tea on occasion. Tea is ok, right?"

She smiled. "Good job liar. You knew I had you cold so you deflected, created probable confusion with your interrogator. You're a quick study Paul. But stop drinking your extra coffee... only one cup a day. And no tea either."

I laughed. "Ok, ok you got me, but how did you know? Gabe rat me out?"

"Hmmm... maybe, but maybe I followed you to class... never give away your information source. Oh, and you blinked and quickly looked away when I asked you the question. Body language failure. Work on it for the future."

We did work on techniques of successful lying over the following weeks and I did fine tune my skills. She told me that I was a natural liar, really just a nice way of saying I was pathological. Lydia instructed me on reading body signs but cautioned again that they were easily misread. The most important ones include possible danger signals, or confrontation... fist clinching, a grimace, changes in voice tone and many others. When I saw them, I needed to be prepared for the possibility of something bad to happen.

During one of our early walks she told me the most important skill I needed was to become a good observer. "Take in everything... use all your senses, not just your eyes. Some call it situational awareness. I call it survival instincts. When we're walking, I want you to heightened your senses. Smell, sounds, things you might touch and things you might have seen. When we get home, I'll quiz you on what was important, something you should have noticed during our walk. Let's see how you do. Ok?"

I worked at it and in time realized most people go through life not noticing their surroundings. We had a dangerous experience one night that proved the value of Lydia's instruction to be constantly observant.

We tried not to ever walk the same route. Again, Lydia's instruction. Habit, behavioral consistency just didn't work well in the spying business. Don't let the enemy predict your actions.

"Paul have you noticed the three teenagers ahead?'

I had; they were about a block away standing together in front of an abandoned apartment house.

"Why, what about them?"

"They will attack us... try to rob us."

"Really? Maybe we should turn back. Avoid conflict, right?"

"I think it's time for me to demonstrate one method of handling a dangerous situation. Here's what will happen. One of them will approach us when we're about fifteen or twenty feet away before the others move. He will be their leader and they will take their cues from him. He will ask us to stop... ask for money, cigarettes whatever to distract us... try to put us at ease. He will be smiling. He will keep his hands in sight and attempt to appear to be innocent and no threat. He will keep moving toward us and the others will circle around... try to get behind us. They may have weapons, possibly knives... no guns. But even fists and feet are a weapon. Do you understand?"

"Yes, but I still think we should turn around."

"That won't work... too late anyway, if we turn now, they will follow. I don't want you to engage them in anyway. I will speak and when they attack, I will handle it, You're just an observer.'

We continued walking. Lydia engaged me in loud idiotic conversion which I realized she was making just to keep our future assailants comfortable. As predicted, when we were getting close, the largest and tallest of the trio came toward us. He had a smile on his face but his eyes were cold. His hands remained in sight and I think he may have stooped over a bit to appear smaller than he was. This was not the first time for this guy. I was nervous.

"Sir, could you spare me and my friends some of your cigarettes please?" He gestured with an open palm for cigarettes. I noticed the other two had split up and were now moving toward us. We had stopped walking. Lydia fumbled in her now open purse. Big guy got closer, less than six feet away.

"Here, here they are. How many do you need?" She pretended to be pulling cigarettes from her purse.

He smiled and inched closer to Lydia. She dropped her purse and as his eyes followed it to the ground her right foot shot out and connected to his balls and dropped him like a sack of potatoes to the broken sidewalk. The other two seemed confused but Lydia didn't wait a second. She picked the closest one and chopped him hard, her hand held sideways shaped like a knife blade, dead on to his exposed throat. She then spun and kicked out at the third guy who actually seemed to be trying to get away. But too late for him. She kicked his knee; probably broke it and he fell beside his two moaning buddies. Her lethal attacked lasted less than ten seconds if that. We left them and continued our walk, me in silence, I was still in shock.

"Ok Paul, now let's debrief... this is our after-action report. First, we anticipated what might happen. We had a plan and reacted as planned. We used surprise and executed with decisiveness in our attack and concentrated on the most dangerous of our opponents first."

I laughed. "You keep saying 'we'... there was no 'we', just YOU, Lydia. I can't believe what just happened. Can you train me to do that? I need to know how to fight like that."

"Paul, first, let me say I always knew you had my back. Perhaps you're not trained yet, but I'm certain you would have served as a distraction in some way while I finished things. Second, no, I will not train you to fight. I might teach you a few basic defensive moves, but your combat training will come later. If you should enter a Jihadist training camp with an advanced hand combat knowledge, they would immediately become suspicious. You're a college professor, not a Chuck Norris. Third, and remember this, we had complete surprise in that action. They were always focused on you not me. Always expect the unexpected."

Another key area of my training was tracking, trailing, pursuing... whatever you want to call following people. Lydia explained that I needed to master this skill because at times I could be either a tracker or I had to be able to recognize when I was being followed. She explained the various techniques of following someone... noting that it usually involved multiple trackers to do the job with any hope for success especially if the subject had been trained in surveillance. During our walks we'd pick someone out and follow them. Sometimes alone, sometimes together. The object was not to be noticed by them, which is a lot harder than one would think. I found tracking women to more difficult. They seemed to have a sixth sense about being followed by a man.

She trained me to be aware of trackers and how to ditch them. It wasn't easy since I knew that there would most likely be more than one following me. I learned how to use storefronts to stop and view the street, how to double back. How to use public transportation and a lot more evasion techniques. In time I felt reasonably sure that I could track and avoid being tracked.

As the weeks passed, I became physically and mentally stronger, more confident in both my abilities, and able to handle my future assignment. Lydia was a good teacher. She knew her trade and gave me the encouragement that I needed to succeed. There were times I became discouraged, times I grew tired, frustrated, even times I just wanted to quit. But she helped me work through them.

On a few occasions I was required to attend social and other school events and it was appropriate for Lydia to accompany me. She was up to the task. She always looked great and always seem to say the just right things in these social settings. I began to realize that some of my colleagues had a problem with the articles published under my name touting Jihadism. I found myself in a few heated discussions more than once and Lydia was always able to defuse the situation. I can't ever say that I was falling in love with her, more of a sense of growing dependence. I would miss our time together.

CHAPTER 25
Becoming a Muslim

My university apartment was put back to the way it was when I first moved in. All my stuff, including the exercise equipment, had been moved to my new place. My goodbyes to university staff and friends had been made and I now stood alone with Lydia. She took a last look around before walking toward the door and out of my life.

"Hey, thanks for everything. I'm going to miss our training sessions. You taught me a lot."

"Sure, and good luck to you for the future Paul."

"Wait a minute. Aren't you forgetting something?" I asked.

She stopped and then turned and came back toward me. "Oh yeah, I forgot. I promised you something when we were done, didn't I?"

She punched me hard in the gut. I felt nothing. She left and I never saw Lydia again.

My new apartment was very nice. Not plush but nice. Beirut is a very expensive town to live in, it's the most expensive city in the Middle East. Jake had set me up in a safe, semi-protected neighborhood in a two-bedroom high rise. I still wasn't paying for anything since I went to work for him. There was extra money deposited to my account each month and all my bills were paid through the bank. He told me that the money couldn't be traced but should anyone ask, just tell them it came from family sources. They wouldn't be able to prove otherwise.

My exercise equipment had been set up in the spare bedroom and the rest of the apartment was tastefully decorated. I had no complaints. My books, papers and other personal items were neatly stored, and my clothes hung in the spacious closets. I already felt at home, but I had not received any instruction from Gabe or Jake on what I was supposed to do next so I just relaxed, read, watched crappie Lebanese tv and waited.

I faithfully kept to my daily exercise schedule. I practiced people tracking and I think began to get good at it. At least no one seemed to take notice of me following them. I found that my daily run was the high point of my day. I started very early each morning, rain or shine, and completed at least five miles or more. My diet was essentially the same as before and I was in the best physical shape of my life.

Each morning upon returning to my apartment from my run, I stopped in the lobby and emptied my overflowing mailbox. Today the university had forwarded a large package of mail to my new address along with the usual flyers and other crap that tends to get tossed upon delivery. There were letters from Brooklyn. My grandfather and mother wrote me frequently, why I don't know since I rarely replied to them. I had already decided not to answer their correspondence any longer and I certainly had no intension of giving them my new address. When I entered my apartment there was a notice that had been slipped under the door advising that the cleaning service would be visiting tomorrow at 7:30. *Thank you Jake*, I thought. I wasn't exactly a slob but like most guys, cleaning was never high on my list of things to do.

The next morning at exactly 7:30, a soft knock came to my door. I opened it quickly and waiting there was a mature lady, dressed in a neat service uniform, carrying cleaning supplies and a vacuum cleaner. She smiled and introduced herself. "My name is Fatima. Good morning sir." She entered and walked through the apartment. "Sir, do you have any special instructions for me? I will be coming each week at this time."

"No, not really, do you have your own apartment key? I might not always be home. But you can let yourself in and do your work."

"Yes sir, thank you. One of your friends gave me a key, so I can let myself in when you're not here."

I was a little confused. *Who is the friend she's talking about?* I thought.

"Alright, I guess. who gave you the key?"

"A nice gentleman. His name is Mr. Jake. And I have something for you today. Something that he wanted you to have." Fatima handed me an unsealed envelope stuffed with money, a lot of money.

"What's this money for Fatima?" I was a little surprised. It seems that Fatima would be my contact.

"I also have a message for you. You are to visit the Mohammad al-Amin mosque and meet with Mullah Abu as soon as possible. You are to introduce yourself as a true believer and ask Mullah Abu for help in becoming a better Muslim. You are to give Mullah Abu this money as a donation. It will ensure that he will instruct you. Do you understand Mr. Jake's instructions sir?"

"I understand and thank Mr. Jake for sending you to me. Do you work for Mr. Jake or are you delivering his message just this time?" I asked. Somehow, I found it difficult to believe that Jake had a cadre of housekeepers working for him.

"Mr. Paul, now I work for you. Excuse me sir. I will begin cleaning your bathroom."

CHAPTER 26

I have to admit I was surprised that Jake was having me study and become a "genuine Muslim" at the Mohammad al-Amin mosque. First, it was a Sunni Muslim mosque. If my goal was to spy on Iran well, Iran was mostly Shia. Second, I knew that thousands of prominent Sunni Muslims from Saudi Arabia worshipped there. Being part of this mosque would never ingratiate me with anyone in Iran. From what I knew, Al-Qaeda didn't seem to have allegiance to either Sunnis or Shia, Maybe Jake had a more devious plan to ultimately establish me with the Iranians. *Were there Al-Qaeda members attending services at this mosque? I don't know. Oh well,* I thought, *I'll just go along with the program and let it play out.*

I called Mullah Abu's office and made an appointment to see him for the following afternoon. I began to plan my meeting. I decided to create a plausible narrative on why I wanted to become a better Muslim and needed his help. I'm a quick study but I knew that I probably wouldn't convince this guy to help me if I didn't sound fervent, a true believer, so I created my background story and worked out questions he would most likely ask.

I kept busy the rest of the day and got up early the following morning, completed my run and readied myself for my appointment with Mullah Abu. The mosque wasn't far from my apartment so I decided to walk. Another beautiful day in Beirut. The Mohammad al-Amin mosque is huge. It dominates the city skyline. Many have complained that it is too big. It's located in central Martyrs Square which had been the center of intense fighting during the Lebanese Civil War. There was still occasional fighting around the mosque which was hated by Shia, Maronite Christians and the Druze. I had heard that Saudi Arabia financed its construction at more than forty-five million. Needless to say, when I entered and inquired where I could find the mullah's office I promptly got lost. When I eventually found the office, I was met by the mullah's young assistant, a real pompous ass. I took an immediate dislike to him and his arrogant manner. He asked me questions that were inappropriate and had a permanent smirk when I refused to kiss his ass and wouldn't answer.

"Please understand, I am not here to speak with you and I have very personal business to discuss with Mullah Abu. So... is he available to speak with me now or not?"

"The mullah is a very busy man and I am his assistant and he has instructed me to sometimes act on his behalf. I will see if he is available to speak with you now Professor, please wait."

He left for about five minutes and seemed annoyed that the mullah was waiting to speak with me. I followed him to a very simple room and was introduced to Mullah Abu. There were just two chairs and a small table that held a tea pot and some cups. The mullah was about 60 years old, short and had a kindly face. He was smiling and when we were seated and offered me some tea which I accepted.

"How can I help you Professor?"

I then began by recounting my religious journey. Born and raised Catholic, receiving mostly a Catholic education, a period of searching for a better way in serving God, studying many religions and finally finding and accepting the Muslim faith.

"My need is to understand my Muslim faith to a higher degree and I had hoped that you in your kindness would help me."

We chatted for an hour. He mostly listened. I liked him. I stayed with as much of the truth as possible and I doubt if he could tell if I was lying anyway. That's just the way he was, honest, trusting. When it was time to leave, he agreed to me visiting him for more instruction and when I went to hand him the money envelope he refused. He told me to speak with his assistant, Rasim and he would schedule another instruction meeting. I left, honestly feeling pretty good for having spoken with this kind and holy man.

Rasim was waiting for me outside.

"Please come to my office Professor. We need to talk."

"I'm busy Rasim... maybe next time." I walked past him and began to head out.

"Mr. Jake asked me to speak with you Professor. Should I tell him you were too busy?"

Unbelievable! I thought. *Masoud has agents in a Muslim mosque.*

I followed Rasim back to his lavish office... no simple piety here. The guy was dangerous and I knew I needed to be careful around him. I sat silently and waited for him to tell me what Jake wanted me to know.

"I think Mr. Jake gave you an envelope for me. May I have it?"

I handed him the money and the prick counted it before continuing. When he finished counting, he took a large envelope from his desk and handed it to me. "This is you next Jihad article. Read it, correct it as you wish and bring it here tomorrow. You are instructed to return here each day for evening prayers. We will meet and I will arrange for you to continue your instruction with the mullah. Now, I want you to understand that studying with Mullah Abu is an honored and prestigious blessing and will bring you much admiration among all Muslims of the world."

I wondered if he knew that Jake was Masoud or did he believe that because I was an American, I was CIA. "I am honored to learn from the mullah. Now what else do you need to tell me, because I really need to leave."

Rasim sighed, gave me that annoying smirk again. "You Americans are always in a rush to go somewhere. Yes, there's more for you to know. As I said you will be here every day for prayers and instruction. I will be sure to introduce you to the right men who will assist you. At some point in the future you will become a member of the Mosque's Protection League and be available to guard the mosque on certain evenings. Other than that, Professor, you're free to leave unless you have questions for me."

I decided then to call Rasim... Ratface. "No, I understand fully and I'll be here tomorrow."

Religion to me was and still is a joke. I fully believe in God and have always believed that there was a Creator. I would be a jerk if I didn't and I'm not a jerk. I approached my Muslim training as another of my life's learning experiences. I now called myself a Muslim but in fact, I had never been anything, certainly not a Catholic. Strangely as time passed and I got into my studies with the mullah, I did come to recognize the beauty of this religion. It was simple and at times poetic. I used my new knowledge in this faith to attain inner peace and at times of stress I found it to be a comfort. Seems strange, doesn't it; a crazy man like me finds solace in a religion. I thought about everything I had been and what I wanted to become. I began to understand.

CHAPTER 27

MMA

My life in Beirut was not boring. I am an obsessive compulsive. I've always overdid anything I had my mind made up to do. This was the case with my daily exercise. Once I began, I couldn't stop. But I needed a better way to gain greater skills and improve my body and mind. I thought about learning judo or Kungfu, nope, no physical contact there... no punching and getting punched. I wanted to learn how to hit someone... hard, make them hurt, so I began MMA training. There were more than a few MMA training gyms in Beirut and I picked the best and most expensive. I could afford a private trainer and I picked the best in this superior school. I finished my daily run at the door of the MMA training school and usually spent the next three or four hours learning my new combat skills. My hard-daily exercise over the last six months gave me endurance. My reflexes were better than average and my superior vision allowed me to anticipate my opponent's kick placements which I learned to easily block. In time my trainer became impressed with my progress and encouraged me to have friendly bouts with other students. I looked forward to actually practicing what I had learned and my trainer arranged for me to work with students more or less at my level. Before each bout we agreed on how hard we would fight... light punching, hard kicks, whatever. It usually worked but there was one fight that I had with another student where things went south.

The guy was a Syrian about my age but much bigger. I'm 5'9' about 150lbs and he was easily 6'2', 200 lbs. He was arrogant and I had seen him practice fight a few times. He agreed to a "soft" fight, no really hard punches or kicks, but the minute they began fighting he went nuts and kicked the hell out of his opponent. Not good. He had been warned and they told him they were going to throw him out of the gym if he didn't follow the rules. He had watched me training and asked me if I wanted to soft fight him. I had had a few bouts already and knew what it felt like being hit. I could take a punch or a kick and not fall apart.

"Sure... now?" I asked.

"Why not... give me FIFTEEN minutes and we'll get it on. Soft is ok for you little man?" he laughed. I think he was trying to psychic me out.

"No asshole," I answered. "I want you on the ground. I will come out rough and stay rough. Is that ok for you asshole?"

He didn't expect that and I could see by his expression that he was thinking about backing down.

I kept at it. "You afraid of me? Afraid I'll break your face?" I could actually feel anger. I never really felt anger and it took a lot to get me angry in spite of what you might think of me. I wanted to hurt this guy... bad. My trainer heard us and stepped in.

"Guys... guys, let's keep it friendly. Ok?"

The big guy couldn't back down now. "No, if little man wants it rough... I can give hm all the rough he wants."

"All right guys," my trainer said. "Just one five-minute round and then it's over. If I see someone getting hurt, I'll stop it immediately. Do you both understand?"

We agreed and the Syrian went to take a pee or something while I waited in the cage.

My trainer seemed nervous. "Paul this guy is bad for you. You're out of your weight class and he has had much more training. Are you sure you want to go through with this?"

"Thanks, but I'm ready... I told you I wanted to learn and fighting this asshole would be an advanced learning experience for me."

I had watched the Syrian fight and knew his style. He'd rush out at the bell and begin with a flurry of mostly right leg body kicks. When he backed his opponent up, he'd throw right and left-hand shots to the head, then he'd grapple and put his guy on the mat and continue to pound the guy's head until he tapped out. Always the same... too predictable. My plan was simple. Make it all happen quick.

The bell sounded and he bull-rushed me. I moved to his left, deflected his now weak right leg body kick and as he passed, I lashed out with a powerful right leg kick to the now back of his head. It was over before it really began. I didn't even bother to press his unconscious body to the mat. The guys watching were stunned. I was calm and left the cage not really feeling anything. I had anticipated, I planned, I executed and I was successful. Lesson learned.

CHAPTER 28
Protecting the Mosque

My Beirut life remained constant. Daily exercise, MMA training, meet with Ratface, evening prayers, home, and bed. My housekeeper brought Ratface's money every other week and occasionally news from Jake which was for the most part always the same: "You're doing well... stand fast. I'll be in touch when you're needed." I didn't have a regular girlfriend but through acquaintances at the mosque, I did have a somewhat limited social life. I met sisters, daughters, cousins, and wives' friends who were all eager to be with the American professor. My Arabic was perfect if you discount my Brooklyn accent and my appearance and manners charmed all I met. I even began to learn how to cook. Not great but getting better.

One day, Ratface announced that I had been accepted to the Men's Mosque Protection Association and two or three times a month I would report for evening guard duty. Of course, there was a regular security service at the mosque and we were just an auxiliary unit, just there to sound a warning should something happen and no armed guard was nearby. Our equipment was a handheld radio and a knife for protection should we want one. I bought my own knife, a WWII vintage US Marine KA-Bar.

"Professor, you will be on guard tomorrow night," Ratface announced while still counting the money Jake sent with me. "But this will be an opportunity for you to become a bit of hero here. Two men will come to your post and attempt to desecrate the mosque.

They will not be armed or pose any danger... you are to shout and alert the armed security force and they will immediately turn and run away. Do you understand?"

"No."

Ratface seemed annoyed. "What is so difficult about this that you don't understand?"

"Why am I chasing away two men? What has this idiot act have to do with me gaining admiration and credibility at the mosque? Was this Jake's idea?"

Ratface sighed. When he spoke, he sounded like he was speaking with a small stupid child as he began answering my questions.

"Mr. Asoph, did you forget you're an American, not a true Lebanese? Most people in this part of world don't trust Americans... many hate Americans. You are not yet considered a true believer. Many here see you as insincere. You're an outsider to us. And no... Mr. Jake does not know of this plan. But I am sure he would approve. Do you want to wait for his approval? For the sake of Allah... you are only chasing away two young boys from using spray paint to desecrate the mosque. Can't you accomplish this simple task? Don't you see that this act of protecting this mosque will convince many that you are committed to your Muslim faith?"

I noticed he wasn't calling me "Professor" anymore. I guess he didn't like me or respect me; old news. I thought, *There's more to this bullshit than he's telling me, but I'll go along with it anyway. It didn't make any sense... I was already well liked and getting known by the right people, namely the Al-Qaeda Saudis, especially for my Jihadist articles. I think Ratface had a different reason.*

The next morning, I completed my run, exercises and workout at the MMA Training gym. I looked though my wardrobe and selected an all-black outfit to wear that night. I had no appointment with the mullah today so I had some free time. I would not see Ratface before prayers and I would just report in to the Protection League's office early. When I arrived, I was given my radio and told that I was assigned Post 18. This post was a little off the beaten path... way at the back of the mosque. There had been a number of incidents there and they usually had two men covering it all night. I noticed that I would be alone. I didn't ask why... I knew why and I would be ready.

Post 18 is at the back of this enormous building. There are many columns along its perimeter and there's a garden like area behind it... bubbling fountains, many flowers, trees and shrubs. People would oftentimes sit in this garden after services to think and pray. I often did myself... but just thinking. It was tranquil. I decided not to complete the usual patrol routine by just walking back and forth under the covered walkway corridor that ran parallel with the columns. Instead, I'd pick a secluded spot in the garden where I had 180 view of the entire backend of the mosque. I now stood in almost complete blackness under a low hanging willow tree and waited. The night was moonless and the only sounds came from the many fountains within the garden. I was calm and I meditated... time passed quickly. I had turned off my radio so no sudden sound would potentially alert anyone who came this way. My deadly Ka-BAR knife was in a sheaf carried on my belt and ready should I need it.

I smelt them before I heard them. Having bad body order is never a good thing when you're planning to surprise someone. There were three men, not teenage boys with cans of spray paint. They came through the garden and were now less than twenty feet from where I crouched, hidden under the low hanging willow tree branches.

I could hear them talking in low murmurs. "Where is he? I don't see him. Do you see him?"

I thought, *Over here boys... come on over.*

They stayed in position for a minute or so and then decided to split up... one to the left one right, and the biggest guy headed dead center. I thought, *Big mistake splitting up like that... you're making it too easy for me.*

I let them separate about twenty yards apart before I ran full tilt toward the guy in the center. My plan was to take him out quick... the other two most likely would hear me but it was dark enough that they probably wouldn't see me all that well. I suspected that when the center guy went down the other two would start running toward me. My thought was to then turn toward the guy on the left and hit him next. With luck, I'd get to my number two target quick enough that the guy on the right would still have a way to run and present no problem. I already made up my mind to kill these three. No prisoners, only one story to tell and it'd be me telling it.

The center guy was big... maybe a little deaf too because he didn't hear me coming up behind him. I leaped the last few feet that separated us pulled his head back and plunged my knife deep into his throat. Surprisingly, he made no sound as he died alerting the other two still jogging toward the mosque. I pulled my knife and started running left. I wasn't as lucky with this guy, he heard me running toward him and yelled to his buddy about 60 yards away. I closed the distance to where he now stopped and stood waiting... I decided he was making himself ready for a blow and he didn't want to be off balance by running. He never imagined that I would use an MMA kick to his chest that sent him sprawling to the ground. I was on him in a heartbeat and with one stroke ended his miserable life with my knife. I quickly stood and turned to take out the last guy who had stopped about 50 feet away. I couldn't see his face but he wanted no part of me and just turned and ran. I laughed. *Run Forest run.*, I thought.

When I caught my breath, I triggered the radio on. "Incident at Post 18. All under control. Send Security."

Security came in about two minutes. I went through number two guy's clothes. He had a wallet some rope but nothing else. No knife, gun or weapon. They were just planning to beat me up, I guess. Apparently Ratface didn't think too much about my ability to defend myself against three thugs.

"What happened here Professor?" asked the security guard.

Two more security men showed up and I described what I did to protect myself. "They attacked me and I defended myself. I told them to leave our property and they refused. The one who escaped had a knife and I assumed that they meant me harm."

"Praise Allah Professor... did you teach knife fighting at your university? They are both dead and deserve to be so. You say there was a third attacker. Did you see his face?"

By now I was surrounded by the entire Security force. Patting me on the back... too dark to see their faces but I imagine they were all smiling and wishing that it had been them who killed these infidel scum.

"Will we call the police?" I asked.

The officer in charge answered. "Not until tomorrow. We will take the bodies away and identify them... I think I already know the big man as a member of the Druze Militia. They have done this before but we never caught them. You said one escaped?"

"Yes, the one that showed me his knife. He ran back through the park."

"Did he see your face Professor?"

"Probably. But it's dark, so most likely not well enough to identify me."

"Then you might be in some danger of retaliation. I will assign two men to escort you home and stay watchful outside until tomorrow. Please come to my office tomorrow morning and we will prepare a report for the police. How do you feel? Were you injured?"

"I'm fine, no injuries." I decided to appear a little shaken though. "I'm somewhat upset... I never took a man's life before. This was a terrible experience for me. Thank you for waiting until tomorrow for my report. I just want to go home now. Please tell the mullah's assistant, Rasim all that happened and that I'm fine and will see him tomorrow after we speak."

CHAPTER 29

After Action Report

It was 3 am when the mosque security guys dropped me off in front of my apartment. They said they would wait out front but if I wanted, they would spend the rest of the night outside my apartment door.

"I think I'm ok but stay if you can, I'd feel better. Thanks," I told them and left them out front. I stripped, took a hot shower, then called Gabe told him we needed to meet... at our usual place, usual time. I never mentioned any meeting names, locations or any other important information since I was never certain that someone was listening to my phone conversations. I needed him to report what had just happened to Jake. Gabe and I arranged that our meetings would always be at noon and at a restaurant we both knew. I hit the bed and fell asleep immediately. I don't normally dream but this one was a dozy. I was back in Brooklyn and I switched constantly from being a kid to grown up. My father was there and he was building something... then he was on a ladder and I think he fell off. He was yelling at me, "Give me the rope." My sister, not sure which one, was eating and wouldn't give me any of her cake. I was hot. The dream was in technicolor... daytime. I woke and at first, didn't know where I was. I had slept late... up at 8 am, dressed and out for my run. I told the two Security men who had waited all night outside in their car to leave and I'd be fine. "Thanks again guys. Tell your Chief I'll see him around 2 this afternoon." I knew he wanted to meet this morning but I had things to do.

My run always gave me time to think. I replayed the attack and felt pretty good about the way it had ended. I don't brag, I just accept my successes and move on. I don't dwell on my failures either. What's the sense? I had been prepared for the attack and I wasn't completely surprised that Ratface had organized it. "Why? What did he hope to accomplish by having me badly beaten or maybe killed? Is he working for someone else besides Jake? Who does he think I really am? Am I a danger to him or someone else?"

I came up with a lot of dumb conclusions that I immediately discarded and accepted that I would have to wait to find the answers to my questions. Surprisingly, when the answer materialized in my head it was a simple one.

Gabe was already sitting and waiting for me when I entered the small restaurant close to the university. "You're looking well Professor." He called to the waiter and we ordered lunch... more like brunch for me. Damn the coffee tasted good.

I recounted all that had happened... the attack... and my theory as to why I was targeted. "You'll need to speak with Jake as soon as you can and ask him for my instructions Gabe."

"I'll do that as soon as we leave here Professor. But first let me recap my report to him and please correct anything that's not accurate."

"Go on," I answered. I continued eating and listening.

"You were instructed by Rasim to stand watch... alone, which was not normal. He told you some boys would come in the night to desecrate the mosque and you would chase them away. There would be no danger. Instead, you confronted three Druze thugs and killed two, while one escaped. You believe that your dead girlfriend's father, who is a Druze politician here in Beirut sent these men to kidnap you and bring you to him for questioning about his daughter's murder. Did I forget anything?"

"Yes, be sure to tell him that I believe that I'm now a marked man and Sofia's father will come after me with a vengeance. I have to leave Beirut immediately. Oh, and that Rasim got a payday from Sophia's father for the setup. He can't be trusted."

"Professor I'll speak with Jake... can we meet later tonight or tomorrow morning with his instructions for you?"

"Call me at 4 this afternoon if you can and we'll take it from there. Actually, call me whenever you have my instructions. Ok? Thanks Gabe.

I have to meet with the mosque security chief now and see how he wants to handle this mess. Oh, and tell Jake I am not going to retaliate against Rasim. That's not going to help matters but Jake probably shouldn't use him for any work in the future, the guy is a rat and sells his soul to the highest bidder."

I paid the check and Gabe volunteered to drive me over to the mosque which was a bit of walk from the restaurant. I agreed and he left while I waited inside. I noticed a young lady standing in a doorway across the street holding a cell phone. I suspected she was following me since I recalled seeing her on my way here. She may have observed Gabe and I meeting or perhaps there was another plant already in the restaurant. I decided to continue with Gabe and he would tell anyone who might question him that he was just my former student and we were only discussing his studies. I figured it didn't matter anyway if they had already connected us.

Gabe pulled his car up out front and I left the restaurant and jumped in. The girl began taking photos of us on her cell camera. When I got settled, I watched the side mirror for anyone leaving the restaurant... sure enough, there was a young guy and he and the girl quickly met up and were animatedly talking... that's all I saw before we turned the corner, but it was enough. Gabe had been followed to the restaurant. My phone was tapped and perhaps his. Either way it didn't matter to me but it did to Gabe. He was outed... compromised as an agent.

"Gabe you have a problem buddy. You were followed to the restaurant or at the least, your phone is bugged. They're watching you and now they can connect you with me. Not good for you Gabe. Now watch for a tail, I don't know if your watcher drove over or not. They may still be following us."

He didn't seem upset. Gabe took the news with a typical Israeli shrug.

"Consider the facts Professor... they, the Druze that is, think of you as a possible murderer, which you are. Rasim thinks you're CIA... and after last night now knows you're a killer too. Kinda funny if you think of it. What does that make me? An accomplice to murder? A CIA agent? But maybe just a former student and friend... the Druze don't care if I'm CIA, but they would want to talk to me about their daughter's killing I'm sure. Me? I only know what I read in the newspaper. That's all I could ever tell them. I can handle a hard interrogation. So relax, don't worry so much. Oh, I was followed here for certain. We never mentioned where we would meet, did we? And the guy was already in the restaurant when you arrived. He had to have followed me in. Looks like one of our phones are bugged. Probably yours Professor. All they did was trace my number from your call and got my address. They must have been outside my place all morning, waiting for me to leave. I suggest that I give you my cell to make your calls. I have a backup waiting at home... the number is in my cell listed under backup number. And please don't call my girlfriend's number or look at her photos." Gabe chuckled and handed me his cell phone and I checked it over before putting it away.

Logical and one smart guy, I thought.

"Thanks buddy. But you're on their radar now Gabe. Maybe it's time for you to think about going home."

Gabe dropped me off in Martyr's Square near the mosque. As far as I could tell we hadn't been followed. It didn't really matter now. Let them follow me to the security office if they wanted. It was after I left the mosque that I'd need to be on alert. I had a thought, *Maybe I should just call or visit Sophia's father. Just get it over with. I believed that he really didn't know all that much about me so why not?*

I found the security administrative office without a problem since I had been there before. The chief was waiting for me. I had never met him before last night; he was never around late at night when I went on duty with the Men's Protection League but I already know a lot about him. He had been high up in the Beirut Police Department before taking this post. He was known as a "hard ass" but his men respected and maybe feared him a little too. I didn't really get a good look at him in the dark last night but he seemed ok when we talked. I announced myself to the man on the duty desk and almost immediately I was brought into the chief's office. Not a fancy office, Spartan even. The chief sat behind his desk and didn't rise to shake my hand when I entered. Not a good sign.

CHAPTER 30

A real interrogation

Without his beard the chief could easily be taken for a US Marine commanding officer. He was crisp and ridged, a no-nonsense leader. I knew that this was not going to be an easy discussion of last evening's events.

"Why are you coming in here four hours late Professor Asoph?"

"Well sir, I was a little shaken and I slept later than usual and had a very important scheduled meeting with one of my former students. I apologize sir."

"That answer is not working for me Professor. Two men were killed and you killed them. This mosque's security and its property are my responsibility. You're telling me that a 'meeting' with a former student was more important than a meeting with me under these circumstances? I want to know why these men were killed, when they were killed, and how you killed them Professor. I have the Beirut Police Department demanding immediate answers and you're off somewhere at what you call an 'important' meeting with your student. What's wrong with you Professor?"

The fact that he wasn't screaming these questions at me I actually found more upsetting and I was not as mentally prepared as I thought I would.

"I was wrong sir. I apologize again. There's no excuse for my ignorance sir. How do you want me to report? Shall I write something up for your review? Or would you rather we discuss it now?"

"Sit down. I'll need both but you can begin with your verbal report right now and we'll discuss it from there. Begin talking Professor. Leave nothing out."

I was on edge, off balance and had to gain better control of myself before I began.

"May I have some water Sir? This will take a while to recount."

I was buying time and I think the chief knew it. I said nothing until I had been handed the bottled water and took a sip. It bought about two minutes delay giving me a chance to calm myself and get my act together.

"To begin sir, I came on duty at 11 pm. I was issued my radio and I already had my side weapon... my knife. I was driven to my post and continued there until I had a need to relieve myself. Urinate. I left my post, walked to the park, found a tree and urinated. While there I heard footsteps and low talking coming into the park. I remained hidden under the tree. It was very dark and all I could tell was that there were three male trespassers. I had turned off my radio to ensure that I wouldn't be heard and I heard one of them say something about spray painting the mosque walls... at least that's what I thought I heard him say. The men split up and started walking toward the mosque. I let them get a bit ahead and then stepped out from under the tree and shouted for them to stop. I heard one of them yell to his companions, 'Get your knives out.' And it was at that moment I pulled my knife and ran toward the largest shaped man I could see. Somehow, I was able to incapacitate him and when the second man attacked me, I was able to incapacitate him as well. The third man shouted something at me when I moved toward him, but then he just ran. It was at this point I turned on my radio and called for assistance. That's pretty much it, sir."

The chief had said nothing as I spoke, he made no notes... his face remained neutral, hands folded on his desk the whole time. I could read nothing from his body language. I braced myself for his questions. True to form as a good interrogator, he began his questions at the end of my story.

"Tell me about the third man... the one you left standing."

"What do you want to know?"

"Start with anything you can recall about his body, voice... anything."

"Well, remember it was very dark... he seemed about my height. His accent seemed Palestinian... I'm not sure about that though. I just had a sense from his voice that he wasn't native Lebanese. He had a light short sleeve shirt and dark pants. I think he had a beard, no hat... oh, he could run very fast. That's about all I can remember."

"How close was he to you?"

"Fairly close... I could smell his bad body odor."

"Really? Weren't you concerned that he was armed and posed a danger being that close?"

"Actually, I think I was going into shock at that moment. I had just fought with two other men and my mind was swirling. I don't recall having any fear."

"I see, but why not? You said they indicated that they all had knives. Why didn't you run... turn on your radio and call for help? Attack this third, smaller man with the bad body odor? Explain your actions Professor."

"Chief, I have never been a fight, let alone a knife fight in my entire life. I'm surprised that I am still alive. At that moment, I think I may have felt that this third guy was not a threat to me. He had just witnessed his two associates lying on the ground, incapacitated. Maybe he was afraid of me. How do I know what I should have felt or done? Would you?"

"So when he turned and ran you decided not to chase him?"

"Yes."

"What did he say to you... you said he said something to you... what did he say?"

The chief's questions came fast. I slowed things down and took some water.

"Not sure... maybe something like "You're a dead man'... something like that I think."

"Did he use your name? 'You're a dead man Asoph'... 'dead man Professor.' Did he know your name?"

"No... how would he know my name Chief? I don't know men like these. Why did you ask me that?" I decided to become a little more assertive, take some control back from the chief.

"Professor let me do my job. If there's a chance that this incident may be personal and not a dumb spray paint attack on the mosque walls, I want to know about it. Alright?"

"He didn't use my name."

"Where did he run to?"

"Back through the park."

"Did you hear anyone else back there? A car door closing... driving away? Anything at all?"

"I heard nothing after he ran... It was quiet until your men came."

"Why did you think he sounded like a Palestinian?"

"Chief, I'm a language instructor and language expert... he sounded Palestinian to me."

"Alright... now tell me about the second man you fought with."

"Well not too much to tell. After the first, bigger guy went down the second one ran toward me... swung at me, missed and I stabbed him and he fell."

"Did you kick him?"

I realized then I was screwed. "Maybe, it all happened very fast. Why did you ask that?"

"There was a shoe print on his shirt and a nasty bruise on his chest. It appeared he was kicked. Do you know karate... kick boxing?"

There's was no sense in lying. "Yes, a little... I think I forgot most of what I learned. I was never very good at it anyway."

"Really? That's not what I heard. You regularly train at an MMA gym here in town and they told me you're pretty good too."

"They're much too kind Chief. I barely know what I'm doing."

"So then you actually have some fighting experience?"

I laughed out loud. "If what I know about kick boxing qualifies me as having experience fighting then I guess the money I spent at the gym was worth it. Chief don't forget... I didn't go looking for a fight with three guys. I'm the victim here. They guys came onto the mosque property at 3 am to do what? I was just doing what I was supposed to do."

Something was beginning to bother me. Why was the chief on duty last night? He was never there at night. His questions seemed spot on in many ways... did he already debrief with the third man? Is he in on this... working with Rasim?

His hard questions kept on coming. I really couldn't deflect many of them... I attempted to just confuse the issue... let them chalk it up to me being just a teacher, a frightened civilian, not a trained killer MMA fighter.

An hour later we were more or less finished. I was drained and now understood what it was like to be interrogated by someone who knew how to do it. I had discovered that deep preparation for an interrogation was essential. The chief saw right through my crappie answers. The facts didn't support what I claimed and it was plain to him that I had attacked and killed these two guys and more importantly, I was pretending to be someone I wasn't.

"I'm going to need your written report by tomorrow Professor. I'm still not sure I understand why you stabbed to death two unarmed men who may or may not have been planning to desecrate the mosque. This matter will need further investigation. Thank you for coming in and someone from my office and the Police will get back to you soon. Probably later today or tomorrow. You're free to leave."

CHAPTER 31
Jake

I didn't bother to visit Ratface after I left the chief's office. I wasn't angry at him. Actually, he may have done me a favor. He proved that he had no loyalty... well, he was always loyal to money. Jake now knew he couldn't be trusted... but Jake most likely already knew that. On the upside, when the word got out what I had done, I knew that many of my fellow Muslims would think of me as some kind of American super hero, defending the mosque.

Gabe believed my cell was bugged. I had read somewhere that you needed fifteen minutes to installing bugging software. At first, I couldn't figure out how they had access to bug my phone and then I remembered that I usually kept it in my gym locker while I trained... plenty of time for someone to get into it and install bugging software. Oh well, another lesson learned the hard way. I wondered how long they were tracking me. I had always tried to remember to turn my cell off when I didn't need it to avoid GPS tracking. I guess I didn't think about tracking software. Dumb but learning.

I was still inside the mosque when Gabe called. I knew it was safer to wait there and not be out somewhere alone on the streets.

"Hello Professor. Are you still at the mosque?"

"Yes... just waiting for your call... I liked your girlfriend's photos. She's hot," I laughed.

Gabe laughed. "She has an older sister if you're interested."

"Not at the moment buddy... not at the moment. What have you got for me?"

"I spoke with Jake. He wants to meet with you. Now. Since they already know we've uncovered their tail I'm just driving over and will pick you up. Maybe 10 minutes. I'll ring you when I'm almost there. Come out the street side and run like hell to my car. If they're on foot we'll lose them, if their driving I'll lose them. You ok with the plan?"

A few minutes later the phone rang and I didn't bother to answer... I just took off running for Gabe's car now waiting, passenger door open, thirty yards from the front of the mosque. There's a busy traffic circle there and he drove around it three or four times before picking an exit and turning off to his final direction.

"Your cell had tracking software installed Professor. I killed it so it should be safe, but I'd get a new phone in any case. Just sit back and relax, we have a bit of a drive. It'll be dark when we get there."

We had both shut down our cells... no GPS tracking anyway.

I didn't ask where we were going nor did I relax. Gabe handed me a pistol; a Glock. I don't know anything about guns but there was a chance we would need to shoot our way out if we were stopped along the road. He told me the gun was ready to fire... no safety. I kept it in my lap the entire ride.

"How did your meeting go with the Security Chief, Professor?"

I filled Gabe in and told him that was only round one with the Chief and I flunked... I'd be in for more questioning.

"I think you'll need to leave Beirut... soon from the sound of it. Maybe Jake has a plan for you leave by now."

"How much did you tell him Gabe? Did he say anything to you?"

Gabe thought before answering.... probably deciding how much he should say. "Well, I told him everything you told me. He took it well but I know him. His mind was running a million miles a minute working out a plan. He doesn't want to lose you Professor."

We continued on with Gabe occasionally doubling back to uncover any tails we may have picked up. We were good all the way. A bright moonlit night arrived and for the last two miles we were off the paved roads, traveling somewhere deep in the rocky hilly terrain surrounding Beirut. It was desolate... the land was poor and not many farmed this area. Good for goats, olive trees and not much else. But a perfect location for a secure meeting.

The dirt track ascended about a mile before it ended at a large ancient farm... the one-story stone farm house had to be 300 years old, maybe older. It had been added too over the centuries and was substantial... there were a few white-washed out buildings glowing in the bright moonlight and I could see endless stony fields surrounding the hilltop house. Two road dirty Range Rovers were parked in front. A very large, Uzi carrying guard was posted at the front door and readied himself as we came to a stop. When he recognized Gabe. he broke into a big smile. We left the car and I left the Glock on the front seat.

"Gabe my friend. You need a haircut. You look like an American hippie."

They embraced. "And you're still fat Saul. Too much potato kasha. Is Jake inside?"

"Yes, he is, probably drinking his ninth cup of tea and waiting for you and... so this is the Professor we've heard so much about?"

The farm door opened and a tough looking unsmiling middle-aged lady also armed with an Uzi walked toward us. Gabe and Saul stiffened as she joined us.

"Let's get on with it gentlemen, if that meets with your approval." Her voice was deep and commanded authority.

I thought, *She's at least a general.*

No introductions, she abruptly turned and Gabe and I followed into the semi-dark farmhouse lit only by soft glowing yellow light lanterns and some candles spaced here and there. A young man sat seated at a table in the hallway, he had an Uzi at side and a radio headset fixed to his ears.

Jake stood at the end of the long hall waiting.

"Ah Professor. So good to finally see you again... come in here... come in." He motioned for me to follow him and spoke to Gabe and the lady general. "I will speak privately with the professor now. Everyone keeps watch."

We entered what might be called a library room... lots of books tucked neatly on wall shelves and two comfortable looking leather chairs set near the very small shuttered window. There was a fireplace with a small smoky log fire. Considering this location was in the middle of nowhere the décor was quite pleasant and a bit surprising.

"Please sit Professor. Would you like some tea?"

When we were settled with our tea, Jake sighed and gave me a stern look. "That wasn't the most intelligent thing you did last night Paul... killing without provocation two important Druze militia men. There will be retaliation. But you already know that don't you?"

"I guess it seems that way."

"Oh, and it also appears that you've acquired some deadly hand to hand combat skills as well. Weren't you instructed to avoid learning too much about combat techniques?"

"Jake, forgive me saying this but... it is what it is. I can't change anything now. What's next? How do I get out of Lebanon with my skin?"

"Bear with me a bit. Let me first tell you what you don't know and what I have planned for you. Alright? Some good news... some bad news as they say."

I smiled. "Start with the good news... I need some right now."

"To begin... you're still alive, not held by a grieving Druze father in some basement and beaten nearly to death. Just as important, your actions last night attracted the right people to your cause... many have read and supported your jihadi articles, many more were impressed that you became a student of Mullah Abdu and even now more are impressed that you killed two infidels attacking the mosque. In a nutshell, you've become accepted by Al-Qaeda here in Beirut. Tomorrow afternoon a Saudi prince has arranged for his private jet to take you to Pakistan and there you'll begin your training as a Jihadist. But ultimately, they want you to become a leading member of their European recruitment team. Now the bad news. You're finished in Lebanon. You'll never be able to return here. Even now the city is being searched and perhaps they may even know you're here, that's why I brought my security team with me."

"Jake... I don't understand. You recruited me to spy on Iran. I'll never be able to do that if they have me recruiting in Europe. How is that going to help Israel?"

Jake chuckled. "And I thought you were a smart boy Paul. Don't you see... if Israel can provide intelligence to the French, English, Germans, Belgians, Dutch, and Spanish about international terrorists, that will bring money, weapons, and returned intelligence to my country. Having you at the center of Al-Qaeda recruitment in Europe is much more valuable to all of us. Even the Americans would pay for this information. Your information would be a gold mine."

I thought about what he just told me. "Jake, it's all well and good but if I'm traveling all over the world how do I get information back to you? I'll never know where I'm going to be and whom I'm meeting with. How do I communicate."

"When you have an assignment Paul, either before you leave or after you arrive, I want you to use a pay phone and call ***-555-5555... ask for extension 518 or dial it in. You'll be connected to a special desk that is on duty 24/7 and is charged with monitoring you. I know, I know, don't laugh, the 555-number thing is the universal fake number they use in the movies but we figured out how to use it for real. My people will know where you are and when possible, send backup to monitor you and your contacts. When you want to give us a detailed report, just call and ask for instructions. You'll be met by someone or they'll tell you how to get a report to them."

"Ok, I feel a little more secure now... I like the idea that someone may have my back. I'm still learning my trade Jake and I hope I don't screw things up." I really wasn't all that confident.

We had another cup of tea and Jake began to tell me about this mystery Saudi prince who was flying me out of Lebanon tomorrow.

"His name is Prince Nayeb bin Abdullah and he is probably one of the dumbest of the 50 or so current princes. He travels the world, spends a fortune everywhere he goes and thinks he's a desert warrior. We've embedded a guy in his entourage whom he listens to and have fed him a lot of cockamamie crap over the years, which he usually falls for. Our guy put you on his radar a while back and the Prince has read all your jihadist articles from what I heard. This morning he was told that you killed infidels attacking the mosque and our guy told him you needed to escape Lebanon. The prince called his sources at Al-Qaeda and approved transportation to Pakistan for you. You've been set up to meet with some big shots in Pakistan and if you pass muster, they'll send you to Afghanistan for combat training."

"What happens if I don't pass muster?'

"I imagine you'll be killed... but don't worry you'll be accepted. They're desperate for foreign fighters and important guys like you, an American with a brain."

I mulled that over and was about to ask Jake some questions when the "general" ran into the room.

"Sir... there's serious trouble coming and we have maybe twenty minutes to prepare for an attack."

CHAPTER 32
The Siege

She was carrying two bullet-proof vests which she threw at Jake and I. I never put one of these things on but I quickly learned. Heavy.

"Moshe reported at least thirty soldiers, most likely Druze, in three trucks, and an armored car with a heavy machine gun just drove past his position on the road and are heading this way. No chance to run sir. We'll need to fight it out." I have to admit she was calm about the whole thing. This was not her first barbecue; but it was mine, I was scared.

"Move the cars out front. We'll need at least one later. Get the boys in position." Jake then turned to me. "Professor, did you ever fire a rifle?"

"Only at the Coney Island shooting galleries." I wasn't trying to be flip.

"Were you any good? Win a stuffed animal for your girlfriend? Gabe, come in here. I need you to give the Professor a quick lesson in shooting a sniper rifle."

I have to say none of them seemed particularly concerned about 30 or more armed men with machine guns coming up the hill to kill us. It was quickly decided that Saul, the radio operator, the "general" and Jake would man the front of the building... Gabe and I would be positioned in the back and act as snipers when the flanking attack came.

Gabe took me to rear, to what would have been the kitchen except there was no kitchen, just a big empty dungeon like room. No windows... thick solid stone walls. This building was a fortress. He handed me what looked like a WWII rifle and a bandoleer of ammo.

"Ok. This is very simple. In your hands is a German Mauser sniper rifle, equipped with a very high-quality German sniper scope. Just like mine. It has already been bore sighted and calibrated for 200 yards. I'll give you everything in yards since you Americans don't understand the metric system. It loads five rounds on a stripper clip... let me show you how to load a stripper clip. Nothing to it. You have 200 rounds in your bandoleer, god forbid you have to use them all. Are you ok so far?"

"Gabe you have to be kidding. I'm ok but scared out of my mind right now. I've never had a real rifle in my hands before and you really expect me to be a sniper... I'd be better help just loading your rifle then me shooting at someone."

Gabe seemed to be enjoying himself. "You'll be fine. It's volume fire power we need here and an extra gun, even an inaccurate one helps. Don't worry so much. The odds are right... only three or four to one. We're in a fortress. We have two guys outside who are trained snipers in the enemy's rear and they don't know it yet. Come on let me show you your shooting position and what to do."

He pointed to the concrete floor. There was a black painted steel plate built into the wall at floor level about fourteen inches square. It was on some spring lever and pully system and I quickly realized I was supposed to lie down in front of it... pull the lever that controlled the pully that raised the plate, look through the opening, site a target and shoot and then maybe lower the plate. I told Gabe what I surmised and he said, "Perfect Professor. And I didn't even have to tell you."

He had me lie down and get comfortable. He brought a sand bag for me to use as a rifle rest and had me remove about ten clips of ammo from the bandoleer and place beside me. I practiced raising the plate and looking though the rifle scope. It wasn't too bad seeing objects out there because of the bright moon and barren ground, but I didn't think I could really accurately site a target beyond 120 to 150 yards.

Gabe placed a full canteen of water near me and a clean rag too.

"Use the rag to stop the bleeding," he said.

He turned off the lantern, blew out the candles and then went over and prepared his firing position which was to my right. We covered 180 degrees from our two firing positions. There was a dead spot in the center where the ground dipped... about 100 yards out. This might be a problem.

"Ok Professor let me give you some important information. We are in a genuine fortress. It has been a defensive position since the Romans. Jake had this part of the building reenforced with concrete and steel. It can take an RPG hit and survive. When you begin shooting, you'll go deaf on the first shot. The room will get smoky and you'll feel the rifle recoil on your shoulder and after a while it might hurt. Watch me for hand signals. We may need to leave at some point. There's a trap door and a tunnel over there... the tunnel leads to one of the out buildings. Oh, I forgot... squeeze the trigger... don't pull it. Always be surprised when the rifle shoots. Ok?"

"What about the others? Do we help them?"

"If they need help, they'll ask for it... but probably not. Professor, we are all highly trained Israeli soldiers. All of us have been in situations like this before. My guess is that the Druze guys out there haven't... they'll make mistakes and we will kill them. But some probably know what they're doing... maybe the people in the scout car, the guys on the RPG's are the biggest threat. I think you need to know and understand... we won't surrender... we won't be taken alive. You still have the Glock I gave you?"

"Nope... left it on the car seat... hahaha." I began to laugh, maybe a little hysterical... nerves I guess... I'm not prone to nervousness. Probably good I feel like this once in a while. Gabe just ignored me and I opened the steel plate and peered through the rifle scope. He had his opened as well.

"Professor, remember, you stay left... I'll cover whatever comes on the right. Call if you need help. Got it? They're going to surround us but the shooting will start out front. Hold your fire until you have a target. Ok? This is just like the cowboy movies when they surround the wagon train."

"Got it Clint Eastwood... hold fire until I can see something to kill."

"That's the spirt. You can close the plate when you're reloading or if they fire an RPG at us... your call Professor."

The waiting was the worst part. It was 15 minutes before they began shooting out front and there was still nothing that I could see moving out back. I felt myself calm down though... I constantly moved my scope over my field of fire looking for anything I could kill. So far nothing. Same with Gabe. It was dark in our position and he was humming some folk song or something. The Druze laid down some heavy fire... a couple of RPG rounds hit our little fort but I could tell by the dull sound didn't do any damage. I also heard distant firing and assumed it was our guys sniping away at the rear of the Druze. They were taking casualties. A heavy machine gun opened up... probably the armored car... still all the action was in the front.

"What's that moving?" I called to Gabe. "There at nine o'clock... something moving... I have it fixed clearly in my scope. Should I shoot?"

"How far"

"Maybe 200 plus yards... "

"You have good eyes Professor... good night vision. If you think you can hit him go ahead and shoot him."

I centered my sights on the figure crouched and slowly moving toward our position. I remembered to squeeze the rifle trigger and was surprised when the gun fired. I saw the figure fall and lost my hearing at the same time so I never heard him scream as he died out there. I chambered the next round and looked for another target. I heard the muffled sound of Gabe's rifle as he took out another Druze soldier.

They were probing the back now and Gabe and I took out at least six or seven guys before they retreated.

It got quiet... no more shooting front or back. Maybe they gave up and left. "Wait Professor while I see how Jake and the guys are doing. Shoot anything out there that moves. I'll be back soon. Ok?" He had to shout and give me hand signals at face level because my hearing at this point was maybe twenty percent. I motioned a thumbs-up "ok" and he left. I was extra vigilant while he was gone, maybe just three or four minutes at the most. All I could see out there in the dark were the heaps of dead or maybe wounded Druze. I chanced a quick sip of water. Damn that tasted so good.

When he returned, he closed both our plate covers and lite a candle. It was still very dark in our room but he motioned for me to stand and relax a bit. I felt weak, unsteady on my feet and he grabbed me by the arm to stop me from stumbling over. I just laughed. Gabe did too. Maybe it was because we happy to be alive. I was still mostly deaf. I jumped on one foot and banged my ears like you'd do if you were swimming and got water in them. It didn't do any good but I kept at it.

CHAPTER 33
Lebanon Farewell

We met in the library room to debrief and complete the after-action report. None of us had received any injuries. All indicated that they were certain that they wounded or killed at least one or more Druze. By our collective count there were as many as forty attackers and half that number were most likely killed or wounded. Most of the Druze dead had been removed, and all their wounded were gone as well.

It was decided to leave the remaining four bodies where they lay for the returning Druze to remove. Since the farm was usually vacant, we discussed the possibility of Druze revenge destruction when they returned. Jake said he would have a third party contact their leadership and inform them about the location of their remaining dead and offer them a blood money tribute for each of their wounded and killed. This was the custom. He said that they would be told that I was under Al-Qaeda's protection now, that I knew nothing about the unfortunate death of Sophia Hartum and that I was leaving Lebanon for good. They would be warned that any further violence against my friends would only result in terrible revenge.

The farm house had some structural damage which Jake would have repaired and reinforced. He said that he would add some more defensive capabilities as well based on our experiences. I suggested that a "higher" portal or two be added to the kitchen wall defense. Also, I pointed out the problem with the ground depression and the cover it provided to attackers. I mentioned night vision scopes would have helped too.

The Druze had one retreating truck and their attacking armored car destroyed by our RPG fire and the hulks would need to be removed. Both of our Land Rovers were also hit by RPGs and were no longer operable. Gabe's car had some body damage but mechanically was fine and he would be able to drive me to the air field. Jake had requested evacuation by helicopter to Israel for the team. It might create an international incident should the Lebanese government discover their air space had been violated but there really was no other choice for Jake. The chopper was airborne and now on the way. The team would be home for lunch.

It was getting light as Gabe and I readied to leave. I was exhausted... a natural coming down after my adrenaline rush, I guess. I noticed that the others remained alert and animated and I wondered how they did it. Jake motioned me aside for one last conference.

"Paul you did well today. You may well imagine that I've always had some concerns about your character considering the incident that brought you to us. I know I'll never understand why you did what you did. But in all the months you've been under my care you have given my country your complete commitment. You now have a difficult road to follow... you may not finish your journey, but I want you to know it has been an honor to have had you on my team." He embraced me then backed away a bit, looked me in the eye and said, "Mazel Tov... Shalom Paul Asoph."

I answered in Arabic, "Bil tawfiq."

A few minutes later, Gabe and I began our drive to the airport and the start of the long journey that would take me to Pakistan, Afghanistan, then Iraq and Syria... most of the countries in Europe, Asia and finally back to the United States.

There were no problems driving to the local airport, about twenty miles to the north. Gabe stayed alert in the event some of the Druze might have set up an ambush. It didn't happen and we arrived in about thirty minutes. The prince's Lear jet was parked on the tarmac waiting... Gabe just drove out to it and we stopped close to the lowered boarding stairway. We left the car and he went to the trunk and pulled out one of my suitcases.

"Here Professor, this contains your personal documents and some clothes I thought you might need when you arrived. Jake asked me to pack some things for you but not to tell you. I guess he wanted to surprise you."

He handed me the suitcase and quickly embraced me and kissed my cheek before stepping away.

I was touched... really. I never had a real friend in my life and Gabe was now my friend and a brother in arms. We had fought side by side and I knew I'd always remember him.

"Thank you for all you've done for me Gabe. I will think of you as my friend and will always remember our friendship."

With that I just turned, climbed the stairs and took a seat in the empty airplane. I watched his car pull out of the airport as long as I could still see it... we climbed into the clouds and away from Lebanon.

CHAPTER 34
Rasim

Adama Mizrah had been a successful secondary Israeli mole working in Lebanon for over ten years. She had volunteered, trained and been imbedded by Mossad into the chaos that was Lebanon following the Israeli invasion and had established herself within the Beirut peasant community where she worked in menial jobs but always for high-end targets.... politicians, generals, business leaders and such. Her reasons for being there were simple. Her entire family had been slaughtered in one of Israeli-Arab wars and she wanted revenge and spying for her country was her best opportunity for accomplishing it. She grew up in Israel when it was still called Palestine... she spoke perfect Palestinian Arabic and looked Arab.

She was sixty years old, somewhat overweight, plain looking and hardly ever spoke to anyone whether at work or home. Early on, Jake had gotten her a cleaning service position and she was never out of work. Many would be surprised at the information that an astute, "in the background, hardly noticed" cleaning lady could uncover in the course of her daily mopping and dusting.

She was now called Fatima and she worked cleaning administrative offices in the Mohammad al-Amin Mosque. She carefully checked the small spray bottle containing a minute amount of the world's deadliest poison... VX. She knew it was fatality lethal when it came in skin contact or sprayed into nasal passages. She also knew it would kill her as well if she didn't protect herself when she used it. Jake had provided the little spray bottle with the yellow liquid earlier this morning before she left for work. Fatima had done "wet work" for him before but this was the first time she used VX. She knew about it from the killing of Kim Jong-nan, Kim Jong-un's estranged older brother in the Kuala Lumpur Airport in Malaysia. She also knew that one of his attackers had been affected by the volatile poison as well. This was why she had always worn a nose and mouth face mask and heavy rubber gloves starting at the day she was hired and began working at the mosque.

No one noticed her or asked why she was working late. Now after evening prayers, she was cleaning the mullah's assistant's office. She was just a cleaning woman, a ghost, someone ignored.

Fatima had carefully observed Rasim comings and goings over the last month. He always returned to his office after prayers and would be alone until he left the mosque for the evening. The door was locked but she had the master key and let herself in. She began cleaning and deliberately removed many books from their shelves so she could appear to be dusting and ensure that she would not be asked to leave immediately when he returned. No doubt he would like her gone, but she would have to stay and finish her work because of the mess she had created.

The office door opened. "What are you doing here? My office is cleaned in the morning... not now. Get out."

Fatima lowered her eyes and humbled herself. "Please forgive me holy one. I was told to complete my cleaning of your office tonight and not tomorrow morning. Let me return your books to their shelves and I will finish tomorrow."

Rasim was angry. Someone would hear of his displeasure in the morning. Let the old woman finish and leave. He sat and began to examine the papers stacked on his desk. He never noticed Fatima moving behind him or felt the wet spray of VX on his face and then up into his nose. He immediately felt an intense burning and then quickly died, his head falling to his desk. Later it would be diagnosed as death by seizure.

Fatima cleaned up the office, hid the small VX spray bottle in her cart, carefully removed her face mask and gloves, wrapped them in a secured bag and then waited ten minutes before leaving the mosque. No one noticed her. She was fine afterward.

CHAPTER 35
A new beginning

The captain greeted me as I entered his jet.

"Take any seat sir, you're our only passenger today. There's food and drink in the galley, help yourself. Our flight to Islamabad will be 7 hours and 20 minutes. Please relax and enjoy your flight. We'll be taking off in five minutes, so please be seated and fasten your seat belt."

This was my first time on a private jet and I was impressed. I got comfortable, took off my shoes and relaxed in one of the oversized lounge chairs. There would be plenty of time to sleep and time to think. I had really no idea what awaited me in Islamabad. When we were airborne, I opened my suitcase to see what Gabe had packed. My two passports were there, other credentials and my shaving gear which I didn't plan on using for a long time. My beard was substantial now and since long beards were always in fashion with Al-Qaeda, I had to look like I was part of the boy's club. Gabe included some light weight clothes and my running shoes and thank God he didn't forget my Ka-BAR. I'd buy a back pack when I could and ditch the suitcase. Oh, I forgot to mention, there was $20,000 tucked into the suitcase too.

I slept, really went out light a light. I hadn't slept for two days and I needed it. When I woke, I got myself some coffee and fruit from the galley. I was feeling better and had some time to plan my next move. I knew it wouldn't be easy when I got to wherever I was going in Islamabad. I had no idea what the Al-Qaeda management had planned for me. I decided that I would play humble and very religious. Go along with their program, not act stupid. I figured if they believed I was 100% committed to jihad they'd accept me and I could get on with what Jake wanted me to accomplish. I knew these guys weren't dopes and would see through any phony BS. I had to win their confidence and work my way through the program they put new recruits through.

The captain came back and told me we were twenty minutes out and he would let me know when to buckle up. He said we were landing at a private field and there would be a car waiting. I asked if there would be immigration or customs checks and he just laughed. It pays to be a Saudi prince, I guess. In my mind I could see the big sign at this airport... probably read, "Terrorists Welcomed".

I got my first look at Islamabad and I was impressed. It looked pretty good. I could see tall office buildings, wide streets, lots of traffic and what looked like classy neighborhoods. There were shanty sections of course, but it looked good from 3,000 feet up.

It was a perfect landing and we taxied up to a large hanger. I could see a black Land Rover waiting nearby.... probably my ride. I have to admit I was a little nervous. I kept thinking that they were going to kill me although I knew they would most likely want to see and talk with me before they took me on my last ride. I picked up my suitcase, squared my shoulders, said so long to the captain and walked down the flight stairs to the waiting car and driver who would take where, I don't know.

"As-Salam-u-Alaikum, sir. I am here to take you to the house. I trust your flight was a good one."

The driver was a big guy. All in black, very polite and speaking perfect English. He took my suitcase, opened the rear door of the Land Rover for me and we were on our way.

Funny. I thought as I sat there looking out the car window at this new unknown city and thinking I had lived a strange life. I know we all have flashes from our past. I had an explosion of memories... nothing in particular, just everything.... all at once. I became sad, grief stricken. In fact, I really wanted to cry at that moment.

The drive took about thirty minutes... mostly through very nice, upscale neighborhoods. I noticed armed guards at every mansion gate and high foot traffic on all the streets. I saw mostly BMW's MB's and very expensive cars moving around us. My impression was from what I saw that Islamabad was a rich city... maybe, maybe not.

When we arrived at the "house" as the driver had called it, I thought, *This is not a house... it's a palace.* You really couldn't see the house from the street gate, where four armed uniformed guards were stationed. It was surrounded by a high brick wall topped with an iron fence. There was a guard house at the entrance and the guard there waved us through the opened gate. I'm guessing, but the house was about a quarter mile, maybe more from the front gate. The grounds were magnificently maintained. I knew that it belonged to the Prince and he spared no amount of money in establishing this terrorist base in Islamabad.

We stopped in the front and the driver exited, opened my door and escorted me into the palace... I'm calling it a palace because that's what it was.

"Please wait here sir while I announce your arrival." He pointed to a lounge and I sat and waited to see what came next. I reminded myself that I was going to be humble and religious with whomever I met here. No snide remarks and none of my "Brooklyn" humor.

In a few minutes the driver returned accompanied by a man dressed in the traditional Pakistani manner. He was about my size and perhaps in his late thirties. He was smiling as he came toward me. I stood and waited his move.

"Greetings, welcome Professor. We have been waiting for your arrival. Please follow me."

He took me to an office and had me seated while he closed the door and sat at an enormous desk. "What language would you prefer? English?"

"Thank you, sir, I'm fluent in French, Spanish, and speak Lebanese Arabic.

"Yes, of course. Shall we speak in Arabic then? I find it more expressive. You may call me Doctor. I am in charge here and you must know that I will be a member of the committee that evaluates you. If you're successful, you will move on to your combat training which is conducted in the Afghanistan mountains. Should you fail to meet our standards, we will send you back to your home in New York, I think. You come from New York... right Professor?" His Arabic was definitely Saudi.

I thought, *Sure you will... I doubt you'll be sending anyone home. More likely a bullet in the head if you don't pass.*

"Yes, Doctor... I grew up in New York City. And please Allah... I will be worthy and successful here. May I inquire about the makeup of the committee?"

"Of course. Myself. A learned mullah, and our physical instructor will observe and grade each candidate's progress. You will meet them presently. Now allow me to describe the purpose of this training... or school, if you wish. We have found that most of our jihadist candidates that come to us from Europe, America and other locations where they have had no physical preparation, do not do well in the combat training atmosphere. In other words, they are not use to physical hardship and most fail in the rigors of the mountain setting. Our principal task here is to make them ready and better disciplined to succeed when they move on. Also, many only think that they are true jihadists. Many aren't... I concentrate on determining the true mindset of our candidates. Lastly, our mullah determines the depth of the candidate's belief in our faith... and their commitment to serving Allah. The candidate must be successful in each evaluation in order to progress."

It appeared that I would have to prove myself to the committee if I wanted to move forward to the next level.

I nodded my understanding and the doctor continued. "We maintain strict discipline... you will not leave our compound without my permission and accompanied by one of our staff. You will wear our uniform, and adhere to a monastic life while living in a common dormitory with all the other candidates. There are 13 others who will be completing their training with you. You will eat, sleep and perform domestic duties to maintain your dormitory. Your communal meals will be halal and there is never any smoking, foul language, fighting or any disruptive behavior tolerated. There will be hash discipline enforced to any who do not follow our regulations or fail in performing the duties assigned to them. No one will ever question any instruction given from myself, the others on the committee and our training staff. We follow strict Muslim practices at all times and attending prayer is mandatory. A daily schedule of mandatory work and training assignments will be posted in your dormitory. After two weeks training one of the 14 candidates will be made senior and be responsible for the actions of the others. Do you have any questions for me Professor?"

"No I don't Doctor. You were quite clear. I understand. Thank you for explaining... I will do all in my power and ability to become a successful jihadist and I welcome the opportunity to complete this essential phase of my training." I said this with great sincerity and hoped it didn't sound like BS which it was.

"Fine... fine. Now before I take you to your dormitory there are a set of questionnaires, I would like you to complete. This is not a test. There are no right or wrong answers. But your honest responses will aide me in my evaluation. Please sit at that desk and begin the questionnaire. I will return in an hour. There is water and some fruit on the table should you wish." And with that, he left me alone. I was pretty sure that they had a camera somewhere in this room and I played to it... I moved with purpose, tried to appear thoughtful as I answered the mostly phycological questions that I had seen countless times on countless questionnaire over my educational career. I fluffed a few... just to make me seem human but all in all I answered in such a way to help me secure the jihadist recruitment position I wanted.

I finished and I began to think about Saudi Arabia. Before 911 we all believed that they were allies of the US. Now here they were, training jihadist, bombers, airplane hijackers... crashing onto our buildings and killing Americans. These guys were the true enemy of the World and I needed to find a way to tell my Israeli buddies about this school and the assholes running it. This would be a challenge. But I promised myself that I'd find a way.

CHAPTER 36
Boot Camp 1

The doctor returned and brought me to the supply room. There was a barber waiting who shaved my head bald and trimmed my beard to a more reasonable length. I was issued six sets of uniforms, underwear and two pairs of running shoes. My clothes and suitcase had already been taken and I had no personal items left. I missed my knife. I quickly dressed into my new black uniform and followed the doctor on a tour of our training facility. All my extra uniforms were now packed in a large laundry bag which I carried it over my shoulder as we began the tour.

All I can say was the training areas were impressive and expensive. There was a dining hall, the dormitory and a fully equipped gym. We walked past a lounge which the doctor told me was off limits unless invited by one of the faculty and a communications and computer room currently manned by a uniformed and armed radio operator. He then showed me a large classroom and finished the tour with a quick visit to the shower room facilities. Everything was spotless.

"All candidates are required to shower daily and are responsible for washing their own uniforms and caring for equipment. There are daily inspections. The candidates are also responsible for the cleaning of each of the facility rooms... which are also inspected daily. Do you understand your responsibilities Professor?"

"Yes Doctor."

"No real names are ever given or used here. Your new Jihadi name will be Snake. No one will know your real name and you will not know theirs. I will take you outside to meet your fellow candidates. Please follow me Snake."

We went into a hallway and exited through a door that led into a garden. We walked about 25 yards past the garden and out into an open field where my new buddies were seated under some shade trees. *Damn, it's hot*, I thought.

"Brothers... this is Snake. He will be joining you as a candidate in training." The doctor seemed to like being in charge. I could tell by his voice and the "I'm superior" way he held himself in front of these poor bastards. They seemed afraid of him as well. Why, I didn't know. The doctor motioned me to find a place to sit among the group.

I sat and looked around at this sorry group of would be jihadists. All were young. I saw at least five guys who were Caucasian. The rest were brown or black skinned and from what I could tell, most were not in great physical shape. Here we all sat in the blazing heat, bald, sweating in our new uniforms, nobody knowing anyone else listening to a self-important asshole who would control our lives for the next eight weeks and worst... not knowing what was planned for us.

"You are now ready to complete the first part of your training. You are here to praise Allah and destroy the cowardly Crusaders who have killed your mothers your wives and your blessed children with their bombs and guns."

I noticed that many of the recruits had no idea what the doctor was saying... they didn't understand Arabic and just sat there with dumb looks on their faces. I realized that I had an opportunity... I would instruct the non-Arabic speaking recruits in at least the basics of the language. I'd win brownie points for sure.

It was beyond hot and the doctor went on for another half hour with his pep rally speech. It wasn't working for us and I think he finally realized it. He motioned to one of the cadres and just turned and walked away from our group. We sat there and wondered what's next? Then our mullah arrived and it was his turn to pump us up. He was young and had a lot of fire in his speech. Again, he spoke in Arabic and it was totally lost on some of the trainee troops. I had heard the BS that he spewed a thousand times before and actually used a lot of it in the phony jihadist articles that I allegedly wrote. He looked directly at me from time to time and I got the very distinct impression that he thought I was his soul brother. It occurred to me that he knew who I was and I'd most likely get his vote to continue the next training camp. We'd see.

Half way through the mullah's lecture a thug like, battle scared cadre arrived. He stood behind the mullah and I could tell he was sizing up the trainees. His eyes met mine and held... I wouldn't look away as the others had and after a while, his gaze moved on. *Maybe that wasn't a good idea to stare this monkey down*, I thought.

The mullah finished and immediately the thug moved into his place. "I am your trainer. I don't speak Arabic so I will instruct you in English. If you don't understand English it's too bad, you're stupid... learn it. You call me "Boss". I will only tell you I am Chechen and I have been killing infidels for twenty years. That's all you need to know about me. You, there in the back... the Chinese guy... come up here."

The man he was signaling out was Asian... but definitely not Chinese. I could tell the guy was scared but he hustled up front and stood stock still before the Boss.

"Yes Boss."

"What is your name trainee?"

"Sparrow, Boss."

"Well Sparrow you were sleeping while our mullah was speaking. Why were you sleeping Sparrow?"

"I am sorry Boss. It won't happen again. Sorry Boss."

The Boss's fist caught the Sparrow square on the jaw and knocked him to the ground. He began to sob. The Boss then kicked him in the ribs. "Get up fool, get up!"

The Boss turned to rest of us now. "This is what to expect if you don't obey and follow rules. You are here to learn discipline and I will give you discipline. Now... get on your feet fools."

We all stood and jumped to attention.

"There is water there." Boss pointed to a tub of iced bottled water. "Drink fools."

The guys ran to the bucket and most finished their water without stopping for air. Me, I'm a runner and I know the danger of drinking cold water and especially too much cold water when you're dehydrated. I rinsed my mouth and swallowed a few small sips before recapping the water bottle.

"Now fools... form a line of twos. We are going for a little run before you have your dinner."

This was the worst thing you could do to someone who just gulped down a full bottle of ice-cold water. We hadn't run 100 yards before the puking began. He kicked the ones who slowed down and yelled constantly. "You are weak... you are weak fools. Run fools... run until I tell you to stop running."

We ran around the compound for an hour and honestly, I was beginning to feel the heat. But I was one of the few that kept up the pace which I'm sure annoyed the Boss. He got behind me a few times and yelled in my ear. His breath stunk. "You, tough guy... tough fool. We see later how tough you are fool."

The boss must have decided we had enough and had us run to our dormitory. "You eat in fifteen minutes then we give more exercise for you fools. You all like exercise? It will make you tough like Snake fool here."

He knew who I was and made me stand out amount the trainees... not good for me. *They'd probably begin to hate me*, I thought.

Boss left us and most of the guys just flopped on the floor, breathing hard and sweating harder. I stood in the middle of the dorm. I decided to change any ill will these guys might develop for me. I would become the de facto group leader. I also needed to uncover as much information about each of them to include in my report.

"How many of you guys speak English, raise your hands," I shouted.

They gave me some dumb looks but most of them raised their hands.

"Good. The ones that don't, I'll give English lessons also I can help anyone with basic Arabic too. My name is Snake and I am no different than any of you. We need to help each other if we want to get through this training." I actually got a few smiles and a few came over and introduced themselves.

"My name is Wolf. Glad to meet you Snake." The guy was definitely American or maybe Canadian. He was brown skinned and I guessed one of his parents was Middle-Eastern. He was tall, younger than me... about twenty, I'd guess. I met a few more before Boss came back to hustle us off for dinner. The food was pretty good. Lots of calories and second helping were always available.

Let me start by mentioning I don't really know anything about being a soldier. All I know I learned from TV and the war movies I saw when I was a kid. I reasoned that the goal of this training was be break us down; make us little robots that would follow orders. All these trainees had come to the conclusion that dying for Allah was a genuine goal and they willing accepted their fate. I figured that while dying was ok getting hurt, beat up, yelled at, generally treated like shit for eight weeks was not on anybody's agenda. I also reasoned that some of these "fools" would eventually rise to leadership roles should they survive and I needed to learn as much as I could about them. I needed to gain their trust.

Boss returned to the dining room and hustled us into the gym for another hour on exercise bikes and weight lifting equipment. I had no problem and actually enjoyed the workout.

"Now fools, you will wash your filthy uniforms, clean the dining room and then you may sleep. Organize yourselves into work parties and when you are finished, I will inspect. Go!"

We all stood by the latrine wash sinks naked and cleaned our sweaty uniforms. Some guy actually began singing. We liked it. It showed we could take it and most realized, maybe for the first time, that together we'd get through this. I asked any guys that wanted to learn some Arabic work with me in cleaning the dining room. We changed into clean underwear and began to organize work parties and get the dining room and the latrines in shape. I had three Anglo guys join me and as we worked, I taught them simple Arabic phrases. I'd say the phrase in English and then in Arabic and had them repeat it. I decided to have some fun and told them I was going to teach them "Victory" phrases first.

I began with "hands up". I figured it would probably save their lives when they were captured. An hour later Boss returned, inspected and of course we had to do everything again. Finally, he allowed us to sleep. I knew sleep deprivation was a significant tactic in breaking someone's spirit and the Boss had read the same book. We never had more than five hours sleep. The day began with our dormitory clean up... run... breakfast... gym... lunch... religious lecture... run... political lecture... dinner.... gym... Religious service.... clean up assignments... inspections... sleep. By the way, no monkey bars... I worked in English and Arabic language instruction and I could tell that these guys thought of me as their leader. I had no run ins with the Boss... he yelled at me of course but I never got hit. At the end of the second week I was made Senior Recruit Jihadist.

My new position was a blessing. The doctor and the mullah met with me every day and soon I was asked to speak during the religious and political lectures. I was given some freedom and the doctor praised my work in teaching basic languages. "So many of our foreign fighters get killed because they don't understand what's being told to them. Your instruction will help save lives Snake," he told me one afternoon. I thought about mixing up my teaching to screw them up but decided that I'd get caught. Just an idea.

In the seventh week of training the mullah asked if I'd like to visit the Faisal Mosque with him. This was one of the largest and most beautiful mosques in the world... built by the Saudis of course... and I actually was interested in seeing it.

"Thank you Holy One. It would be an honor and privilege," I answered. I was allowed to wear my civilian clothes and shoes... but not given my id's, money or any other personal items. We drove with an armed driver and actually I was happy to get away from the palace even for an hour or two. I thought there might be a chance to make a telephone call... might not happen without money and accompanied by the mullah and a guard, but I'd try if I could.

We parked in a VIP lot and walked to this massive and beautiful building. I have already told you about my feeling about religion but I was impressed. I've often thought about the shame to all Muslims who honor their faith and the perversion of the faith by radicals and Jihadists. I'm not apologizing but in some ways the West created this conflict. Oh well, I'll save my thoughts for another time.

We washed, removed our shoes and entered for prayers. I noticed an old man watching us and felt he knew me. After prayers the mullah left me and the guard to speak with other mullahs gathering nearby and the old man came up to me. The guard ignored him even when he put his hands on my shoulders and came close.

"Your friends are near," he whispered, turned and walked away.

"What did he say to you?" the guard asked

"He gave me his blessing."

"Don't speak with anyone... it is not permitted."

The mullah returned and we drove back to the palace. There was only four more days of training and I thought I was home free... soon I'd be somewhere in Afghanistan learning how to use weapons... was I wrong. My biggest test came one morning when the Boss announced that he would be making an example of two recruits who had blasphemed and dishonored Allah.

"Snake... come up here. Now. Sparrow and Wasp, you too."

I noticed that Boss had a pistol holstered at his side which was unusual. The three of us walked to the front and stood before the Boss. He was barely controlling his rage.

"Snake are you not the Senior Recruit? Are you not responsible for the actions of all the recruits?"

"Yes Boss."

He came close and without warning slapped me hard on the face... twice. In spite of myself I winced. It hurt. I was in shock. *What the hell was going on?* I thought.

"Last night these two vermin committed an unspeakable act in your latrine Snake. A homosexual act! They are filth." Boss spit the words and removed his pistol and without a second's hesitation shot both Sparrow and Wasp through the head. Blood gushed and they fell dead to the marble floor. We were all in shock. Most had never even seen someone killed before and all were deafened by the loud report of the Boss' pistol.

"Clean this mess." The Boss turned and left us... mouths open, still not able to comprehend what had just happened. It was then that I vowed to kill the Boss.

We finished our training in the next two days. The Boss had disappeared, left... we didn't see him again. The doctor conducted a graduation of sorts, but honestly all the recruits were still in shock. I imagine some might have been having second thoughts about becoming Jihadists. Each recruit was told what his next training assignment would be. Most, myself included, would be going to Afghanistan for weapons training. Some would become bombers... suicide or just learn how to make them... we didn't really know. Transportation was arranged and we told we were leaving the next day. The doctor called me aside and said he wanted to speak with me.

"You have done well here Professor and I've decided to include some recruit language training from now on. Thank you. I was informed that you will train, then fight somewhere... most likely Iraq and then you will travel to Europe to recruit and perhaps conduct training there as well. I wish you success and please only remember that you are serving Allah at all times. as-Salam-u-Alaikum."

I was tired... truly tired. I lay on my cot that last night and fell into a deep dreamless sleep. I never heard the Boss; I never even woke when he beat me and left me for dead. I remained in the hospital for six weeks, two of them in intensive care.

The doctor and the mullah visited me often and when I was discharged, allowed me to convalesce at the palace. I learned that the Boss told them he hated me because I wasn't like the others and he couldn't break me. They had explained to him that I was going to be very important to the cause and not interfere harshly with my training. He saw me as a potential rival and finally and without any approval tried to kill me that night.

In time my strength returned and I became a member of the cadre. I ran, exercised and taught language to the new recruits. I also enjoyed much greater freedom and was allowed to leave the compound alone on occasion. I made a few telephone reports when I could... I didn't really have too much information but I was told to gather as much as I could and that what I reported was useful now and certainly would be useful in the future. This Limbo life continued for almost six months. I keep thinking, "Why the hell am I doing this? I'm not helping anyone, not even myself. Maybe I should just pack it in and hitch a ride to Europe or even settle in Israel." I was sure that they'd let me go. I was a wounded warrior who had proven himself. All that changed one morning when the doctor told me I was leaving for combat training in three days. He met me in the hallway and told me to follow him to his office.

"Professor you'll be leaving here in three days to complete your training, you will also be completing an important assignment as well."

"Really? Good news, thank you Doctor. Praise Allah. I thought this day would never come. How may I serve?"

"You are taking a supply shipment to the camp by truck and you will also spend some time in Kabul interviewing new recruits. You will determine their fitness and decide if they are worthy."

"Thank you. How will I transport this supply shipment and meet the recruits? I don't know the country and I don't drive very well."

"A very old and trusted brother will be driving. He will drive the truck containing the supplies and assist you when you reach Kabul and when you are finished with the recruits, he will take you on to the training camp. You are not to tell anyone here these plans. You will be given transit papers from Saudi Arabia, Lebanon and Pakistan. You will identify yourself as Lebanese if questioned. You must be aware there are many American troops and government officials based in Kabul and you are to avoid contact with them. To everyone you meet, you are an official representative of the Suni Muslim faith and you are visiting mosques to learn what might be needed. Is that clear?"

"Yes Doctor, but what do I do if any of the recruits are not worthy to serve?"

"You will tell your companion and he will handle it."

CHAPTER 37
Khyber Pass

In preparation for my trip to Kabul, the capitol of Afghanistan I was immunized against smallpox, hepatitis, tetanus, flu and malaria. I had had some of these shots two years before in Lebanon but I needed boosters. I packed my few belongings, my knife, passports and the twenty thousand dollars in my new back pack. I was ready to go. I met the doctor outside the palace and there waiting for me was the most colorful truck I've ever seen. It had been painted every color of the rainbow and then some... together with the usual fringe roped around the windshield it was for all the world, a typical Pakistani over the road truck.

"Snake this is Abdul your driver, listen carefully to all he tells you. He has made this trip many times and is our most trusted brother. Abdul this is Snake. He has proven himself here and he will welcome any instruction you may have for him."

My new friend Abdul weighed about 300 lbs., stood about 5'5" and with his snow-white beard he could have played an Arab Santa if they ever needed one. He had come over to where we stood and unlike most Arabs, immediately greeted me and shook my hand. I instantly liked the guy.

"Snake? Snake... please don't bite me." And he laughed... a big belly laugh. Abdul spoke in an Arabic dialect I never heard before.... I'd have to ask him where he came from.

"Abdul have you checked your cargo? Plenty of mosque decorative tiles and cases of the Holy Quran? And the camp supplies... are they well hidden?" The doctor seemed nervous.

"Please don't concern yourself Doctor. Even a mouse couldn't find where the supplies are hidden but I don't think the Afghanis will use mice to check it... rats perhaps." And he laughed at his own joke.

The doctor acted like a nervous father seeing his little girl off on her first date. "Remember Snake... you are expected to do great things for Allah and our cause. Learn your lessons well."

Finally, I was able to get away from him and climb into the truck. Abdul had already started it up and the engine sounded pretty good. I knew we would have to climb along mountain roads and this well-tuned engine would be alright. I settled in... no seat belts needed in Pakistan... and looked the cab over. A large basket of food was placed behind the seat, along with blankets and water jugs. We'd be ok on this trip.

"Do you know how to shoot a pistol Snake?"

"I never shot one but I think I'd be able to handle it. Why? Do you have a pistol for me?"

"Sure and hand grenades, RPG's and there's even an atomic bomb in the back too." He just loved to laugh. "Yeah I have a pistol for you. The doctor's gift. I'll give it to you later."

We chatted a bit and I asked him how long will it take to drive to Kabul. "If we drove 70mph it would be about five hours. Now you know that this truck won't go that fast... so about eight hours... maybe ten. It's in the hands of Allah. Oh, I forgot to include stops for food so maybe longer. And of course, there will be security stops and heavy congestion in the towns we drive through. How old are you Snake? Maybe you'll have your next birthday with me... here in my truck."

I was enjoying this drive with this happy man. You don't meet happy people in Al-Qaeda very often.

"Where did you learn your Arabic? I can't place your accent. Forgive me for asking Abdul, but I'm a student of language and your speech is interesting to me."

"Well... I was born in Afghanistan and at a very young age my family moved to Nigeria. It was my father's business that took us there. I went to a native madrassa Muslim school and that is where I learned my strange sounding Arabic. So, you could say I'm a Nigerian-Afganistanie."

He continued telling me his life's story. When he returned to Afghanistan, he became Taliban to fight the Russians. At some point he joined Osama bin Laden's unit and stayed on to fight for Al-Qaeda. He had a wife and kids in both Pakistan and Afghanistan and when he got too old to fight, he started driving trucks and helping any way he could.

"Abdul... why didn't the Taliban and Al-Qaeda join forces? They had a common enemy?"

"Well, the Taliban really only wanted to kick any invader out of Afghanistan, the Russian the Americans... anyone.... As you already know, Al-Qaeda has a more global view. We want the whole earth to embrace the true faith so for now, the world is our enemy until they convert. Also, our immediate goal is to remove the Crusaders from all of our lands."

"What is bin Laden like? Do you know him?"

"Haha... I was part of his body guard for almost two years. Yes, I know the Sheikh and he will remember me and if you meet him Snake, tell him I said hello." We both laughed. "he's a tall, skinny man... doesn't eat much and really, it's true he only eats the leftovers from other's plates, except mine of course. I don't leave leftovers. He's very religious, very quiet... you have to listen hard to hear his voice. He's very brave in battle... I know because I saved him a few times. He speaks only Arabic and he'd be amused by my Arabic when I spoke with him. He told us many times that he wants all the Infidels out of our holy Muslim places. We all admired him and pray he lives a long life."

"Do you think the Americans will find him in Tora Bora?" I asked.

"How can you find someone when they're not where you're looking. The Sheikh has left Afghanistan... he's living in Pakistan now. We passed the road to his new home an hour ago. If I had known your interest, I would have driven us over to his house for tea."

I had to be cautious... not ask the wrong questions. Abdul was an open book, a very friendly guy but would become suspicious if he thought I was overly interested in bin Laden.

"Abdul I am honored to know you even more... a brother who is a personal friend of the Sheikh. Have you seen him since he returned to Pakistan?"

"I deliver reports and messages to him now and again. I will see him when I return from Afghanistan. Is there anything you want me to tell him Snake?"

"Tell him I said it is my great honor to serve our cause and for the greatness of Allah and I hope he lives 100 years."

"Snake, he has four wives with him and many, many children too. I'm sure the Sheikh would like to be at your side in the coming months... get away from all the noise at home... replace it with the happy sounds of battle." Abdul was laughing when he said this.

This was no doubt that this was the most important information I had ever gathered... the current whereabouts of Osama bin Laden. I had no idea how I would be able to communicate it anytime soon. I'd figure that out when I could.

We drove on. The two-lane road was better than I thought it would be. It was in good repair, but without marked dividing traffic lines of course, Pakistanis' and Afghanis' don't much care about staying in their lane. The danger of a serious or fatal accident was constant... dangerously passing cars, trucks, guys on horses, motorcycles. It even had many "I don't care" drivers passing each other on blind curves. At first, I was scared we'd crash and fall off this high mountain road... but after a few hours I got into the rhythm of driving with this crazy truck driver among equally crazy drivers. When we reached one of the many towns along the way we'd be boxed in huge, totally disorganized traffic jams. People just didn't seem to care about rules of the road, especially the many pedestrians. They'd just walk out in front of moving cars. Then there were the street beggars and countless vendors that attacked the stalled vehicles like plague of locust.

The scenery was magnificent. Barren... different shades of boulder strewn brown earth, snowcapped mountains, grand vistas. The air crisp... the bluest sky I had ever seen. Welcome to the Hindu Kush. I must admit I was enthralled by it all. We drove through long dark mountain tunnels, on a road that wound around and around. Past isolated houses, some mud brick others plastered rock... pastures filled with sheep, goats and cattle. There was abundant timeless life here in all its splendor and glory. It had been so since the beginning and I knew it would remain thus long after mankind ceased. This was a journey I'd long remember.

We stopped to eat at a roadside stand and give Abdul a break... I had to pee so I was happy to get out of the constantly bouncing truck. The food was very good... lamb stew I think and fresh pomegranate drinks.

"So Snake, you speak Dari?"

"No, I don't."

"Well then you must speak Pashto, right?"

"No my friend, I don't speak either of the Afghani languages."

"Then how will you question the young men we are going to meet in Kabul?"

"I thought they would speak Arabic. Was I wrong to assume this?"

"Most likely... no matter I'll be your translator. This might work out better anyway. They can help me unload the truck. We will stop first and pick them up and drive to the warehouse, unload the truck of the religious cargo, you can interview the kids and then we'll drive on to meet our brothers and unload the camp supplies."

"What's the timing on all this? Tonight? Tomorrow morning?"

"Most likely tomorrow morning. We still have a long way to go... our next stop is the border check point at the Khyber Pass. If there's no problem, then it's about a three hours' drive to Kabul."

"Could there be problems?"

Abdul laughed... "Yes, my friend... we may have a problem with our papers and the Afghani's won't let us continue. Then there's the tribesmen who may stop us or shot us somewhere along the way to Kabul. We may run off the road or get hit by lightning... It's all in Allah's hands. That reminds me... let me give you a pistol shooting lesson now. It may be useful if we run into trouble on the road."

Abdul opened the box the Professor had given him and removed an American Army issue Colt .45 along with three boxes of ammunition and a leather holster and web pistol belt. His eyes lit up. "Ah, a fine weapon... Snake you will be envied in camp. Here, let me show you how to load the clip and then you can fire it a few times."

He handed me the now loaded .45, showed me how to cock it and the safety features. "It only holds seven rounds... but if you hit your target anywhere on their body they will go down. Very effective at close range."

It was heavy, but felt good in my hand, very solid. I aimed at some boulders about twenty feet distant and squeezed the trigger. The recoil surprised me a little but after firing two clips and taking time to aim over the iron sites, I felt confident that I could use it properly. I put on the pistol belt and holstered my new toy. There was a holster compartment for the now loaded extra clip and I filled my pocket with fifteen rounds. Heavy weight, I felt my pants sag.

"Is it alright for me to wear this? I don't want to have a problem at the boarder."

"My friend, understand that carrying weapons openly is the birthright of all Afghanis... no one will say anything."

We got back on the road and out of nowhere Abdul asks me, "Would you like to take revenge on the Boss for what he did to you?"

I was more than surprised at this question. Abdul knew the Boss and he knew about the terrible beating I suffered at his hands.

"Abdul, I dream about meeting him again and taking my revenge. Do you know where I can find him? Is he at the training camp?"

"No. He's somewhere in Iraq the last I heard. I don't like him Snake. He was with our group in Afghanistan during the Soviet invasion. He bragged about how many Russians he already killed in Chechia. I never believed him... I watched him in battle. He was a coward. The Sheik didn't notice and I never said anything. We heard about his treacherous and cowardly action against you. I will locate him and advise you when I discover where he is. Inshallah."

The road continued to climb higher into the mountains and Abdul seemed to grow tense. "We are very close to the pass and the checkpoint. Let me do the talking. I know some of these guards on both sides of the boarder. They will ask you to step out of the truck, perhaps ask some questions while your papers are being checked, most of them speak English. Remember you are staying with me at my home in Kabul when they ask you. Don't show fear or nervousness... Sorry, I should have not said that. Oh, I have money in case they ask... but do you have any money with you?"

I pulled my back pack open and removed five twenty-dollar bills and handed them to Abdul. "Will this due?"

He smiled and nodded his approval. "Keep your money hidden at all times."

We continued on and up... mostly up. I'm not a history student but I couldn't help thinking about all the history of conquerors that this road had seen pass through... Alexander the Great, the British Army, and on and on. The Khyber Pass... Gateway to India... and here I was, a guy from Bay Ridge Brooklyn, living an adventure I would have never dreamed possible ten years ago. I knew I would never tell my kids about my life. I knew I'd never have children. I knew my life would end quickly and violently but I would live it and enjoy it while I still could.

The Pakistani check point was just a formality. We didn't even leave the truck. Abdul presented our papers and we were flagged though. It was a short drive and just a few minutes to the Afghani check point. Abdul turned off the engine and he and I exited the truck. I was immediately approached by two machine gun carrying guards. One seemed to be very interested in my holstered .45 and remarked to his companion who nodded his head. The older one said something in a language I didn't understand so I answered in Arabic.

"No speak Arabic... English?" he asked.

"Yes English," I answered. "Allah Akbar."

I received no friendly answer... just a scowl. "Your papers." He seemed annoyed at me.

Why, who knows? I imagined that this was his way to establish his authority and dominance. Kinda like all the cops I encountered back in Brooklyn. Ok, I'd be pleasant and show him that he was the boss.

"Here sir. Thank you." I was acting meek and compliant. He seemed to like that and I noticed his underling smile a little. He took my papers and walked to the guard shack for examination while I waited. Abdul was going through the same process on the other side of the truck. I couldn't see him but I heard them questioning him in Afghani. In five minutes, my guy returned holding my papers. During this wait they had Abdul open the truck and they were still searching it.

"Why are you visiting Afghanistan?"

"I work for the Muslim Mosque Society and I am visiting mosques in Kabul to learn what supplies they need?"

"You are an American... but carry a Lebanese passport. Why?"

"Yes sir, I was born in America but have lived my life in Lebanon. That is why I have a Lebanese passport sir. Is that a problem?" He didn't answer but just handed back my documents.

"Thank you, sir." And I got back into the truck and waited for Abdul. *That wasn't so bad*, I thought.

Abdul was chuckling when he hoisted himself into the driver's seat. "They were very happy with your American twenty-dollar bills, Snake. The captain is giving us an armed guard to Kabul. Here we go."

He started the truck and slowly pulled away. A military pick-up now led us with two guardsmen in the cab and a machine gunner positioned in the truck bed.

"I guess you don't get security very much do you Abdul? Does this make a difference in keeping us safe on the road?"

"Safe? No... if the Tribesmen want to stop us, they will. The Afghan Army has no authority here. This is mostly for show. But this seems strange that they gave us security. I hope it isn't some kind of trap. Stay alert Snake. Stay alert."

Unfortunately, it turned out to be a trap. The pickup stayed in place for about ten miles, then pulled to side of the road and the driver waved us on. Abdul smiled. "We will have trouble. I'm certain now. Stay calm. If there's shooting it's in the hands of Allah. They may just want to rob us.

We'll see."

Two miles on, three pickups blocked the road forcing us to stop. They were at least a dozen fierce looking well-armed tribesmen standing there... watching... guns ready.

"Stay here, I'll talk with them."

I ignored his command and exited the truck... he walked to the group, hands up and spoke with them while I waited. If there's was shooting, we'd be dead in seconds. He spoke with them for five minutes. I could tell he offered them money but they seemed to want something else. Finally, he returned and seemed upset as he spoke. "Snake my brother they want your .45. The guards at the check point told them and that weapon is highly prized. They offered to buy it but if you don't want to sell it, they will fight."

I was mad... insanely mad. I would not give my pistol up without a fight. "Tell them I'll fight one of their men. If he wins, he gets the pistol. If I win, we go in peace."

"Snake... this will be a fight with knives. To the death. Do you really want this?"

"Yes. Even if I sell it to them, they may kill us anyway so let's go down fighting. I'm ready my friend."

"Do you know how to fight with a knife? These men learned in childhood."

I smiled. "I've read some books. I'll be fine."

In spite of himself, Abdul laughed out loud. "Oh, you read some books! Why should I worry."

Abdul went back to the group and told them I would fight. He must have said I learned the "knife" reading books because they all began to laugh. It broke the tension. I decided to use my MMA skills and make this as quick as I could. I would try to disarm my opponent, get him on the ground but not kill him. I would give him a small cut and hope that this would satisfy the honor of the tribesmen and we could get the hell out of here.

They chose a teenage guy about my size, wiry looking and seemingly eager to be my opponent. He carried a longish knife which he held in a stabbing position. I dropped my web belt, pulled my Ka-Bar and got ready. I figured I'd let him make the first move. He rushed me like I thought he would. I side stepped and lashed out with a high kick to his knife hand. I think I may have broken it... he dropped his knife and I was on him in a heartbeat taking him to the ground. I slashed at his face; it began to gush blood. And immediately I stood over him. I could have killed him if he tried to continue but he didn't.

The tribesmen seemed stunned. Abdul told me later that one shouted, "What is the name of the book this man read?"

Apparently, honor was served, we were accepted and they made us follow them to their village where they prepared a feast... we were treated as honored guests and I have to say I enjoyed the experience. Abdul had new respect for me and told me that the doctor was right when he said that the Snake would be marked great among our brotherhood. Oh, the kid I cut came up to me and was very friendly. Abdul translated and said the kid never lost a knife fight and was arrogant in thinking that I would die at his hands. His face would be his reminder that he must practice humility in his life. I guess I made a new friend.

We were back on the road. Not a problem for the rest of the trip. Abdul told me about his wives, kids and grandkids. How he loved them and hoped someday that Afghanistan would find peace. He is a good man and his country deserves better. I only thought how I would be able to find a phone and call in Osama's Pakistan hide out.

I smelled Kabul long before I saw it. It's a city of over five million and all the sewerage dumps directly into the river that flows through it. It is one of the most dangerous cities in the world. Daily car bombings... assassinations... crime, poverty and total despair. As my mother would say "This city was the pits." I would be glad to leave and we drove directly to the pickup point for the would-be kid jihadists. Thanks be to Allah it was not far.

There were four of them... all teenagers... waiting patiently, probably all day, outside a mosque. Abdul got out of the truck and began to speak with them.

He motioned for me to join him. "They agreed to come with us to the warehouse and help unload the truck if that's alright with you."

"That's fine. Where are you going to put them?"

Abdul went to the back of the truck, opened the door and had them move boxes to make space. He had to leave the door open as we drove to the warehouse. I hoped nobody would fall out.

I told Abdul and he just laughed, "Less time for your discussion then."

We reached the warehouse and I asked Abdul if I could talk to them before they started working.

"Sure, why not. What do you want me ask them?"

I wanted to know their names, age and why they wanted to join us for starters.

The oldest was eighteen and there was a fifteen-year-old kid too. They all had family killed by the Americans, and wanted to get revenge and kick them out of Afghanistan. They said they loved Allah and believed it was their duty as Muslims to fight for Him. I was satisfied with their sincerity and told Abdul we could begin to unload the truck. It took two hours to pack the boxes of tiles and Qurans against the warehouse walls and we all were sweating when it was completed. We gave them water and the food left in Abdul's food baskets. I think these skinny kids didn't eat very often and were delighted to have something to eat. Abdul told them to rest and he asked me, "Snake we have a little time, would you like to come with me for a quick visit to my wife's house?"

"I am honored that you would ask me but I think I'll stay here and rest. I'm exhausted and it has been a difficult trip... knife fighting... driving with a crazy man and unloading a truck. I hope I haven't offended you." I was laughing and so was he, "No... No, my friend. Rest easy I'll return in an hour or two and we can move on to meet our brothers and unload the camp supplies."

Abdul left and I waited ten minutes before going in search of a public telephone. I was a foreigner in a foreign land. I didn't speak the language and had no idea where I was. I didn't dare roam too far... I couldn't afford to get lost in Kabul. I used my spy skills to ensure that one of the kids or some curious citizen wasn't following me and after about thirty minutes of looking, I found a pay phone that worked. I had to make this quick and I did.

I dialed, asked for extension 518 and told the operator, "My grandfather's lost afghan which our friends have been looking for so long is now safely hidden near the place I just left. Look to the south to find it."

I hung up. There was a very real chance that the public telephone lines were monitored by the police and I hoped I wasn't being too cryptic. I did speak in Spanish, if the cops were in fact listening, I doubt it would have held them up very long in making the translation. But the Israelis are smart, they'd figure out what I was saying. That intelligence was worth a couple of free American jet fighters to them I'm sure.

I found my way back to the warehouse; the kids were still sleeping and I dropped to the floor to join them. I woke, fully alert the second Abdul shook my shoulder. He then woke the kids while I peed against the far wall. I felt pretty good. Ready for whatever came next. Actually, I was looking forward to Boot Camp and the weapons training. Who knows, maybe the Boss would show up there and I'd enjoy killing him.

We were back in the truck, on the road... the kids now safely in the back but with the cargo door closed this time.

"So how was your visit with your wife Abdul?"

"The same... complaints. My children, the neighbors, she needs more money and all the usual women nonsense a husband has to bear. No time for love making but she did cook me a good meal, so I guess it was worthwhile seeing her. I told her I'd be back soon and she said she'd think about more things she could complain to me about while I'm gone."

"Abdul my friend, would I insult you if I gave you a small gift of American $20's?"

"You could never insult me with such a gift Snake, I promise you that I will pray for you." We both laughed at our lives and the normal things that makes us happy. I would give him a hundred and I knew it would help him and his family. I asked him about the training camp.

"I think you will find it pleasant for the most part. There are good men there, none like the Boss. The instructors are true believers, dedicated fighters who know how to fight and have seen much and learned much. There are many foreigners too... maybe you'll meet an old friend. Who knows?"

After an hour or so we went off road and followed a dirt trail higher into the mountains. I was surprised the truck could make the steep incline but it did. At a desolate and empty place Abdul just stopped and turned off the engine. "We are here Snake. Let's begin to unload the camp supplies and wait for our comrades."

The supplies were off loaded and the six of us just sat and waited. It grew darker and darker and nothing could be seen. Abdul was the first to hear the sound of approaching car and motorcycle engines. He picked up his AK and told me to be ready just in case. They came in without lights, five men on motorcycles and two Toyota pickups. All were armed and alert. Abdul stood and greeted them.

"Allah Akbar. It's my old friend Red Beard himself. This is an honor, a surprise visit from my old comrade in arms. Greetings. Snake come here and meet your new commander, the famous fighter Red Beard."

It was really too dark to clearly see the large man that Abdul called Red Beard so I didn't know if his beard was red but he seemed friendly and happy to see us, especially Abdul. We greeted each other in Arabic and he gave instructions for the two pickups to be loaded with the camp supplies. It didn't take long and Abdul came over to me and said goodbye, thanked me again for my gift and wished me luck and Allah's blessing. He also told me that there wasn't room for two of the kids and they would be returning with him to Kabul.

Red Beard asked me to ride with one of his motorcycle warriors and he got into the lead pickup and off we went, higher into the mountains. We had only traveled a few miles when we heard a huge explosion and stopped to see a ball of fire off in the distance. Red Beard got out of the truck and yelled something to the men. We then drove as fast as we could. I didn't learn until we reached the camp two hours later that the sound we heard and the explosion was most likely Abdul's truck being hit by an American drone Hell-Fire missile. We were fortunate that the drone most likely used its last missile on Abdul and didn't come after us. These almost silent and invisible drones were everywhere and had night vision capabilities and anything that moved, day or night, in these mountains was attacked. Hard lesson learned.

CHAPTER 38
Boot Camp 2

My ass hurt. Two hours hard riding on the back of a motorcycle over super rocky terrain took its toll on my butt. Also, as we climbed higher it got colder and colder. I wore a mid-weight jacket but this couldn't keep me at least semi comfortable in the freezing mountain air. There was plenty of snow on the ground... not deep, but slippery and my driver had a hard time keeping us from toppling over. He was a kid by the way... maybe eighteen. We didn't have much conversation because of the wind, combined vehicle noise and the language barriers. Honestly, all in all this night ride to camp was a lousy experience. It would have been worse if I had known for sure that Abdul had been blown to smithereens. I'm still a heartless son of bitch but I can have positive feelings especially with people I like and I liked Abdul.

When we arrived, I stepped off the back of my ride waiting for someone to tell me what to do. The guys in our party began to unload the supplies and I could now see that Red Beard's beard was in fact a bright orange color. In a little bit, with me jumping up and down to keep warm, he came over, smiled and told me to go to a close by cave for food and warmth. He said he and I would meet in a little bit and I thanked him and ran to the cave he had pointed out.

Caves by their nature and not healthy places. Dark, damp, dirty and in the case of this cave, very smelly and smoky as well, but it was warm. There was food cooking and the smell of whatever it was made my mouth water. I had forgotten how long since I last ate and I just helped myself to a bowl of whatever this stew was, probably lamb. I picked up a spoon and dug in. Damn it tasted good. There was a fat guy, most likely the cook, who asked me something in a language I didn't understand, but I assumed he was asking if I liked it. I smiled and nodded appreciatively. I helped myself to a big hunk of fresh bread and I was in "fat heaven". I forgot the miserable ride to the camp, the miserable time I spent on the road, the knife fight and all the other crap I had been through the last week. Red Beard came in and loudly greeted all the people gathered in the cave. He filed his bowl and began to eat, smiling all the time. I think he might have been cracking jokes to his troops because they all seemed happy to have him there and were laughing at whatever he was saying to them. I had a feeling this guy was a good leader.

I was sitting against the cave wall when he had finished eating and came over. "Don't get up... rest my friend. Welcome." He sat down next to me and lite a cigarette and offered me one.

"No thank you. I don't smoke. Thank you for the hospitality. The stew was very good and I was very hungry."

He got serious. "That explosion we heard and the fire ball we saw most likely signaled the death of our brother Abdul. I don't know if anyone explained that American drones are a constant threat and there is no defense against their Hell Fire missiles. You're driving somewhere, talking with someone and suddenly you're dead. You never hear or see them. They have killed many... also, killed many innocents as well. They attack day and night. They fire on anything that moves. I'm told the drone pilot controller is stationed hundreds of miles distant. I wonder if seeing the killing has any effect on them. A regular bomb dropped from a plane kills, but the plane's pilot doesn't see the death. A drone pilot sees before and after what his work has accomplished."

"Yes, that's true, but is that any different that close combat. We see our enemy and we kill them. We see the blood, hear them scream and understand that we have taken a life."

Red Beard thought a moment. "Yes, that's also true. But remember the drone pilot is warm and safe at all times. He may be drinking some tea when he kills and leaves his post at 4 o'clock to go and drink alcohol. We don't go anywhere. We are frightened, dirty, maybe wounded. Ground fighting and killing is very different."

We continued our conversation about warfare and Red Beard explained his wartime philosophy. "Our Muslim beliefs tell us that dying for our faith is not important. I agree but I make every attempt to protect the lives of my warriors. I subscribe to the tactics used against the Americans by the North Vietnamese. The Americans are impossible to beat when the have the use of their artillery and air force. The North Vietnamese learned this quickly and suffered too many casualties learning it. Their goal and motto were "grab the Americans by the belt buckle" don't fight them army to army. The American will always win. They choose the ground to fight on and were patient. I do the same. We practice ambush, selected bombing and infiltration whenever possible. I have lost many but have killed more."

We spoke about war, religion and the World's condition. This guy impressed me. He had been a university professor in Saudi Arabia and like myself had travelled... spoke English and the Afghan languages and a little Russian as well. He been in Afghanistan for many years. First fighting the Russians, now the Coalition forces but mostly Americans.

"Snake my brother, you are tired and we have much to talk about. Rest here, there are mats in the back and tomorrow I will explain your training program and introduce you to your new comrades."

I thanked him and found a place to sleep and quickly nodded off, it had been a very long day. I didn't dream much, honestly, I had forgotten about Abdul's death and the two kids in the back of his truck. I could only dream about what Red Beard had planned for me and what training he would give me. I was anxious to move on and see an end to this life. I didn't like the uncertainty of not being able to control any aspect of my life and although I didn't want to die, but I did have some positive anticipation of being in combat. Crazy, right?

I woke early. The cave was alive with men and some women too. The cooking pots were boiling and I ate a kind of mush and drank some strong tea. About an hour later Red Beard came in and greeted me. "Did you sleep well? Not too cold? How was your breakfast?" He sounded like a concerned mother talking to her favorite child.

"Thank you, I enjoyed a wonderful rest. I'm ready to begin my training... what have you planned for me?"

He had a very serious look when he told me my personal 10 commandments in training. "Snake, you already know that we have big plans for you in the future. You're taking this training only to enhance your presentations during recruitment efforts for new warriors. I have been asked to see that you receive special instruction and be protected as much as possible. So, I want you to know from the beginning that you will never be included in any action against the American or Coalition forces. We have had too many deaths and captures when we fight them. They are strong and have combat assets we don't have. You will be included in some minor action against the Afghan Army so you understand our methods of fighting and you can describe them with authenticity to potential jihadist. I hope you're not disappointed, but this is the way it must be."

I don't know how I felt when I heard that I'd never be in real combat. At this point I guess any combat for a neophyte like me would be real enough. I never liked the thought of killing American soldiers anyway, I'm not sure what I would have done if I had to.

"I understand and accept my role Red Beard. I will work as hard as I can to learn all that you can teach me here and then begin my work of increasing the number of dedicated fighters for Allah."

We moved to the back of this cave to the camps command center. There was communication gear, maps, computers, video equipment and other administrative support material including a large black flag affixed to the rear of the cave wall. The lighting was good. I imagined a large generator was running all the camp's electrical needs. We sat at an eight-seat conference table and Red Beard asked one of the men there to find us some tea.

Red Beard stood and went to a large area map. "There are twelve active training camps, each with a commander like me. I am the senior camp commander but do not have any responsibilities other than this camp. There is a six-man senior group that is responsible for all twelve camps. They move around from time to time and will be here in a few weeks. You will meet them and our overall commander at that time. At this moment I estimate that there are between 2,000 to 2,500 jihadists in our camps. Our military action plans are made by the control group and coordinated among the twelve camp commanders. I might note there are no major actions in place at this time, but I expect there will be one or more in the next month. Snake, I am presenting this organization to you first, because I know who you really are and second, you may need to understand how are our military organizations operate when you're recruiting. Do you have any question?"

"No... but tell me about the camps. Are they all like this? Do they have unique operations? Operate independently?"

"Ah, the camps. When a new recruit enters a camp, they are evaluated and their skills are determined. We have various departments, if you want to call them departments, that each recruit will be assigned to. There's Supply, Engineering, Medical, Communication and Propaganda, Recruit Training, Administrative, Combat, Logistical such as cooks, drivers and so on, and Leadership... you might think of this as an American Officer Training Department. There's even a department that is responsible for gathering intelligence, and within each department there are various subsets. For example, right now we have too many volunteers for suicide bombing training, so some of them are trained to only make bombs.

When you begin your recruitment operation you may find individuals who have extraordinary skills in one of our departments. You'll be given a full orientation on the work of each so you'll be better able to recruit. Not every jihadist is a suicide bombers or crashes planes into buildings. Does this make sense to you so far?"

"Yes, but how is all this financed? It must cost a fortune to keep an army in the field and pay for the training."

Red Beard briefly described the al-Qaeda funding sources... foreign governments like Saudi Arabia, Iran and China, taxes gathered in conquered lands, sale of stolen artifacts, confiscated money, other valuables and so on. He then described how friendly banks held funds and distributed them through to the field operations. I realized that I was becoming privy to highly important and critical operational information that Israel would be able to exploit.

Red Beard switched gears. "Snake can you drive a motorcycle or what we call a machine?"

I laughed. "I can barely drive a car. Are you going have me learn to ride a machine then?"

"I will teach you skills that will be useful in your ultimate assignment. Driving all kinds of vehicles would be useful, trucks, autos, machines.... How proficient are you with that beautiful .45 strapped to your leg? "

"Not very. I fired it ten times.... at a rock... I don't know how to use it or even clean it."

"You will be an expert when you are finished here in many types of hand guns. You'll also learn the rifle... perhaps other heavy weapons as well. We shall see as time goes on. You must also learn basic bomb making and perhaps the use of poisons too. There are skillful trainers here that you will learn from. All you learn here will be of great importance in your work in foreign countries. Now it is time to begin." He stood and I followed and was ready to learn my new profession.

"Could I get some warmer clothes first?" Red Beard laughed, but I was issued warmer clothes.

I didn't train with the other new recruits. I was already in great physical shape but I did run with them whenever I could. These were mostly foreigners...

One early morning at breakfast I was approached by a man I thought I recognized. It was Wolf from the palace training camp. "Snake is that you? We all thought you were dead. How did you get here my friend?" The Wolf seemed awed that I was still alive and that I made it to this camp. He was speaking to me in English.

"Allah Akbar Wolf and yes, I'm still alive."

He sat with me and chatted. He told me that he had already seen combat. He told me that he was frightened all of time he was in it. He had been wounded and that was why he had been sent back here... to recuperate. He said that the Coalition Forces had awesome fire power... they were impossible to fight when they used all their combat assets. He had been bombed and in many fire fights. He had witnessed his friends blown up, shot dead and captured and then shot dead. He said he was afraid to go back and thought about leaving Al-Qaeda. He told me that all the men we had trained with were dead. The Wolf was no longer useful to the cause in my opinion... he was burned out and probably should leave. He asked me what I had been doing since we last saw each other. I gave him an abridged version of my experiences after my near death beating from the Boss. I left a lot out of why I was here and my training regimen, he didn't need to know about that.

"Snake, have you seen the American woman soldier we hold captive here?"

I had heard something about a captive American soldier but not that the soldier was a woman. "No, but I've heard about a captive soldier. Where is she being held? Have you seen her?"

Wolf had seen her. He said that she had been badly treated; she had been regularly sexually abused and beaten. She was sick and perhaps would die soon. She had been one of three American Army truck drivers who had been captured during an ambush. The other two soldiers had already been beheaded and a video had been posted on the internet of their execution. I was curious but not to the point I wanted to see her. We spoke about the Boss. Wolf had not seen him since he left the palace that last night.

I had a lot to do that day but I promised Wolf that we'd talk more. I said goodbye and left for my daily training duties. Red Beard wanted me to learn how to drive and for the last three days I spent time learning to drive the pickup trucks used in supply transportation. They were all automatic drive so I didn't have a problem learning to shift. You couldn't go faster than 30mph here in the mountains and that was even pushing it but the main objective of me just driving something was accomplished. Obviously, I'd have a problem driving on city streets and in traffic but at least now had some idea of what to do to get a vehicle moving.

Learning to operate a motorcycle was much more of a challenge. They called motorcycles "machines" in the camp. I called them death traps. The kid that drove me to camp was my instructor and spoke no language that I understood. It was all demonstration and hand gestures. He'd demonstrate, get off the machine and I'd try to do what he did. Sometimes it worked, mostly I had to try many times before I got it right. Shifting was a problem at first but in time I mastered it. After a while he'd be my passenger and I drive us over the rocky terrain at slow speeds. Occasionally, I skid out and we'd both topple off. But I was getting better each time I rode. I was beginning to enjoy driving machines.

My weapons instruction began with hand guns. I learned how to handle my .45 and maintain it. I still enjoyed it over most of the pistols I fired except the Makarov .380. It had a nice feel to it and good stopping power. It was small compared to the .45 and I decided I'd carry both pistols at all times. My instructor praised my shooting. He said I had a natural aiming ability and was not only accurate but fast too. I understood that pistols were always the last resort in combat. If you had to use your pistol you were already too close to your enemy and most likely would be killed or captured.

Just as Red Beard promised, the Al-Qaeda Camp Control Chiefs showed up one day. I thought of them as the General Staff but they looked no different than any of us. One thing I can say about al Qaida jihadists, they are a very democratic society. Warriors needed to have full confidence and respect for their leaders. If a leader didn't have the hearts and minds of his unit he was quickly removed and put back into the ranks.

One morning, Red Beard interrupted my pistol training and took me into the Command Cave to meet with our visiting local leaders. They were gathered around Red Beard's conference table reviewing a map and engaged in an animated discussion. No one seemed to notice me standing there until Red Beard asked for their attention and introduced me. They all stood and he introduced me to each one. They seemed interested in me and asked many questions. I was given a seat at the table and a cup of tea.

"Snake we have a very important assignment for you. I will describe it and then answer your questions."

I thought, *This sounds interesting... an important assignment? I still don't know my ass from my elbow and I'm given an important assignment. Why?*

The commander continued. "You know that we have an American soldier held here in this camp. She is wounded but valuable to us. An arrangement has been made with the American military to exchange her for three of our most senior leaders who were captured in Iraq. We want you to be an important part of the prisoner exchange with the Americans."

"I am most honored and will do all I can to make this a successful operation. What do you have planned? What is my part?"

He laid out the plan. Simple but cunning as well. The exchange was scheduled to take place in one month. We had chosen a location that gave us the best advantages. High in the mountains, lots of caves and very windy which was important. Drones had problems maintaining position in high winds and losing GPS signals in mountains. The American's would want a drone, probably armed, on station at all times observing the exchange. There were many more details I'll go into later but my first assignment was to get the American soldier well enough to travel.

Red Beard and I left the meeting and headed to the cave where the prisoner was being held. He told me about her and said my first goal was to asses her physical state and create a plan to get her as healthy as possible in one month's time. Her name was Paulina Boyd she was a Spec 4 truck driver with a US Army National Guard from a New Jersey transportation unit and she had been captured three months earlier. She had received a minor wound to her left hand which had not been treated and was now infected.

The back of the cave where she was held was pitch dark. I needed to change that. The first thing I noticed was the stink. She had not been allowed any provision for her waste removal and even though caves by nature are dirty places, this cave was beyond dirty. I carried an electric lantern and it lit up a scene of great human tragedy. It would have been more humane to have just killed this girl then keep her like this... tied hand and foot and lying in her filth like some animal. Her uniform was in shreds and she wore no boots. I am not easily moved. I've been accused of having no soul but I felt pity for the woman and honestly, if I had come upon her in other circumstances, I would have used my knife and put her out of her misery.

"May I move the prisoner to a different location? I need to asses her condition, treat her and this location will always be a problem."

"Of course,... I'll have some of the women help you. We have a small stone Shepard's shelter about a mile from here. It has water close by and can be kept warm. Do you want to use it?"

"Yes, that would be perfect. Can I have the doctor's help too? She is wounded and her hand needs looking after. There may be other injuries that require treatment and I am not a medical person Red Beard."

"Yes, after you get her cleaned up, I'll have the doctor visit her. You understand that we don't have much in medical supplies but she'll get whatever is needed and available. Snake, make sure she doesn't die."

Red Beard left to organize my women helpers and the stretcher bearers who would transport her to the shelter. I looked at her. She was unconscious and at first, I thought she might be already dead. I knelt next to her, touched her face and she moved and moaned. I spoke to her in English.

"You'll be going home soon soldier. Fight hard now and don't die. Do you hear me?" She didn't respond. Two hours later we had gotten her to the stone shelter. The women had started a fire and the single room, while primitive, was a vast improvement over the cave she had been kept in. I waited outside while the women cleaned her and removed and discarded her useless uniform. They brought a simple wool garment and had her dressed. She already appeared in much better condition when I came back inside. She was still unconscious and I waited by her side for our doctor to arrive.

The women cleaned the shelter as much as possible, gathered fuel for the fire and I could smell something cooking. Perhaps she might live. I could only hope.

The doctor came, treated her infected hand wound and examined her. He told me that she had serious injuries to her body. Her vagina, two broken ribs, a broken jaw and other head injuries as well. Her mouth contained many broken teeth and she was most likely deaf in one ear from a blow. He said hospital care would normally be required to restore her to some semblance of health but he would visit her each day and do what he could. I could ask for no more than that. I thanked him and he left me alone with her. The women had returned to camp and also promised to return in the morning. I ate and sat outside until it got too cold.

She seemed better... her color was better and her breathing normal. She hadn't eaten and I wasn't certain she could eat with a broken jaw anyway. I'd let her sleep and see what happened. The women had set her up on a sleeping mat and had left one for me to use. There were a few heavy blankets and I used one to add cover to her and took the other for myself. I quickly fell asleep and woke the few times I heard her moaning. I asked if she needed anything but she didn't answer.

The women and the doctor arrived at daylight. I waited outside while they administered to her. The doctor came out first... "She's conscious but can't speak. I couldn't wire her jaw obviously but I did set it and held it in place with a head bandage. She can only take liquids for the next week or two. Her infected hand will also heal... I've given her antibiotics. The rest of her injuries such as her ear, vagina and the many cuts and bruises will get better. But it will take time and need the more intense care that I am not able to give her. I suspect her mental state is bad. Most likely deep depression from the treatment she's been subjected to. You will need to speak kindly to her while she remains here. It might help."

I thanked him and he promised to return each morning. I went into the shelter. The women had her sitting and one was trying to feed her goats milk with a spoon. Most of it was running down her jaw. She looked bad.

"How are you feeling... nod if you feel better. Don't try to speak. You will be going home soon. Do you understand me? Just nod if you do." I imagined this was the first English she heard in a long time and I think her eyes brightened at the sound of my voice. She nodded that she understood and I left the shelter. One of the women would stay all day while I trained. I'd spend the night with her and I could only hope for the best.

During the next few weeks, I trained by day and played nursemaid by night. I learned how to use an RPG... not very well I might add but I was superior with a sniper rifle. I had a gift. My instructor told me snipers were suicide warriors. They were always left behind to slow down the enemy advance and were usually killed. I vowed that if I ever did any sniping it wouldn't be a suicide mission. I'd snipe, kill and move on.

The soldier was getting back to a semblance of health. The doctor was pleased with her progress.

"She's young and strong. I think she'll be physically alright in time," he told me one morning. I still wasn't so sure. She had cried the entire night before and I didn't even try to console her. She knew or at least possibly believed she was going back to her US Army but it didn't seem to have the positive effect I had hoped it would have. She still couldn't speak but she understood me. I told her to stay strong and she'd be alright. I asked her questions... "Do you come from New Jersey?" a nod yes. "Are you married?" a nod no. "Did you like the Army?" a nod no. I laughed at that. Perhaps she smiled too, I couldn't tell. One-sided conversations are difficult at best. But I tried to raise her spirits by talking with her. I wanted her alert and interested in living. It would make it easier when we had to transport her to the pickup location.

Our "Generals" returned and we had serious planning discussions on how we would execute the prisoner transfer. Our planning covered transportation, security and reacting to surprises. We didn't trust the

Americans. Some thought that as soon as the girl was safe, their circling drone would launch a Hell Fire and take us out. We devised a plan to prevent this from happening. I would play a key role in the transfer and honestly, I wasn't sure I could pull it off.

We had stationed two men at the transfer cite a week before the actual date. There were many caves surrounding the high plateau where the American helicopter would touch down. Our guys constantly tracked the sky's for drones and reported back that there was air activity... no doubt the American military had concerns about us too. Our plan called for us to arrive two days before the transfer. We would bring the pickup that would carry our three senior guys after their release to the plateau and park it. The girl soldier and I along with the pickup driver would camp overnight and I would handle to actual prisoner exchange.

The long drive to the transfer site was uneventful. We barely spoke and I could tell that she was excited about the prospect of being set free. I didn't engage her or our driver in any conversation. She couldn't speak anyway... her jaw was held in place by a head bandage. I played and replayed what I was going to do during the transfer and I still didn't believe it would work. We reached the transfer site, set up camp and rested. It was a long, cold night. I was in radio contact at all times with Red Beard and he kept up an encouraging dialogue that all would be well and we would succeed.

The next morning at the appointed time the driver ignited a red smoke flare and the sound of the big Huey Helicopter could be clearly heard. It landed about 50 yards from our pickup, the engines shut down and after a few minutes the door opened. Two men in military uniforms jumped to the ground and I met them about half way to the Huey. I had already pulled down my black full-face mask so only my eyes showed.

"As-salamu alaykum," I said in a more formal Arabic to the officer who was clearly acting as interpreter. He was about my age, a captain, probably Afghani, and had an intelligent look about him. I decided to try him out and see how he played the game. "You fools are late. We were about to leave." I kept my voice tone neutral... no anger.

"What did he just say captain?" asked the American colonel.

"He said it's a good day for the exchange and wants to get on with it."

Gotcha, I thought. *This guy wants no problems. Perhaps I could use that.*

"We suggest that you bring the girl here and we bring the three men here as well. We will each take our people and leave. Is that acceptable to you?"

"No," I answered. "You will bring my three comrades here and I will determine that they are acceptable and only then I will have the girl brought here. This is not to be debated. If you refuse, my comrade and I are prepared to die right now and the girl and possibly yourselves will be killed by the troops stationed all around this area. Now tell your colonel what I just said." The captain may have suspected that I spoke English but couldn't sure. All he could do was relay my message to his colonel.

He smiled at my masked face and turned to his colonel. He more or less translated what I said and I could tell the colonel was not pleased. The colonel began to look around at the surrounding mountains for hidden Al-Qaeda troops. He spoke into his radio and a minute later my three guys exited the helicopter... all in handcuffs and foot chains, accompanied by two weapon carrying soldiers. In a minute the group stood before me. I greeted my comrades.

"Captain, have your guards remove their bindings," I ordered in a loud voice while pointing to the hand cuffs. The colonel understood what I had just said without translation necessary and ordered the two guards to remove the bindings. He told them to be ready for any trouble and kill the lot of us if there was. I walked up to the first man.

"What is your name brother?"

He told me and I asked him a personal question that only he could answer. Our Generals suspected that the Americans might send less important captives and wanted to be certain that we were exchanging the right men. He answered correctly and I repeated the process with the other two, who also answered correctly. The captain continued to interpret my questions and the prisoner's answers to the colonel.

When I was satisfied, I told the three to strip naked, remove their shoes and begin to walk to the pickup truck, I also signaled my driver to bring the girl forward. The driver carried three simple robes and sandals which our guys would wear. We were concerned that their clothing may have been bugged and we would be tracked back to camp. I noticed that the captain smiled at my instruction to strip. I'm guessing that they had been bugged. The girl arrived and to her credit and bravery, saluted the two officers. She really couldn't speak but nodded and smiled.

The Americans turned and began to walk back to their helicopter. My guys were already in the truck and the driver had started it.

"Wait!" I loudly shouted at them. They stopped and the captain turned back toward me. The colonel and the two guards then continued on to the helicopter which had already started up.

"What do you want?" the captain asked, obviously annoyed.

"Your girl soldier is wearing a suicide vest. Tell your drones to leave now and I will disarm it."

He seemed shocked but quickly turned and shouted to the colonel what I had just said. They stopped and the colonel opened the girl's heavy jacket reveling a modified vest that the driver and I had installed the night before as she had slept. She had taken drugged tea and with the heavy coat she wore, hadn't noticed it. The coat itself held the bulk of the C-2 explosives; her body rig was mostly the detonator assembly. It was much smaller but much more sophisticated than a normal suicide vest. It could only be deactivated by entering a four-digit code into the firing mechanism. Any attempt at removal would cause detonation.

The colonel ran toward me with his pistol drawn. I wasn't concerned. He knew what would happen if I was killed. Brandishing his weapon was his frustrated attempt to intimidate me. "You son of a bitch," he shouted. "You son of a bitch."

"Tell your colonel to calm himself. We will not detonate unless our jihadists are attacked and that includes removal of your drones. Dismiss your drones and all will be well."

The captain relayed my message to the red-faced colonel. The colonel shouted "Fuck you!" at me, but I could tell he was considering my instructions to end this standoff.

"Alright, alright... the drones go. Now tell this masked monkey to disarm the god damn vest. Pronto. I want to get out of this shit hole place now." The captain translated and I pretended to consider his order.

"Tell your colonel the answer is no at this time. We do not trust you Americans. I will travel on your helicopter and disarm the vest when we land and I have been told that our jihadists are safe. Please tell him that captain." The captain chuckled... "He will not like to hear that my friend, I'll tell him. He might just shoot you now."

The captain translated my instructions and I was surprised that the colonel accepted it without having a heart attack. He was upset no doubt but he could see that there was no alternative. He had to chance it and take me to his base. He knew he had bomb squad technicians that could disarm the vest and he saw the value of at least bringing me back as his prisoner. Of course there was a constant danger that the vest would explode while we were airborne but he calculated that that would not be good politically for either the Americans or Al-Qaeda. When I climbed into the helicopter, he had me cuffed, hands in front, and searched, but not too thoroughly. I was unarmed and that seemed to surprise him.

We took off and began the return trip to the American Army base. One of his sergeants spoke to the colonel," Why don't we just toss this monkey out the door. We have guys on the base that can disarm the vest."

I answered his comment in English and I think the sound of my voice was like a bomb going off. "I don't think that would be wise sergeant. You missed the C-2 strapped to my balls." I grabbed at my crotch. "It's not a lot but enough to take out this helicopter. I have to be certain that your drones are not following my men and will kill them... so there's a change in plans. We are not flying to your base, take off these cuffs and I'll give you the coordinates of our new destination." I held my hands out. "Oh, and don't come any closer or I'll detonate the charge... blow up my balls and all of you too." I laughed for effect.

The sergeant said, "He bluffing sir. Let me take him out."

The colonel only took a second to answer. "Take off the cuffs sergeant. Give me your coordinates asshole." I knew he couldn't take a chance that I was bluffing. My cuffs were removed and I gave the coordinates to the colonel who sent them to the pilots. A minute later the co-pilot came into our space. He was ashen faced. "Colonel sir, these coordinates take us into Kabul... do you really want us to go there?"

The flight to Kabul only took forty minutes but that was the longest forty minutes of my life. These guys hated me and wanted to kill me. The tension and potential of me getting thrown from the helicopter was real and when we finally reached our destination, I breathed a sigh of relief. The coordinates I had given took us into the very heart of an Al-Qaeda-controlled neighborhood section. There were a dozen pickups, armed with machine guns, and a hundred jihadists waiting for us to arrive. We touched down in the designated open area and the jihadists surrounded it. The pilot kept the rotors turning. Without a word, I stood, went to my girl American soldier and entered the four-digit code disarming the vest. I helped her remove all the belt gear and the coat containing the C-2 as well. I took it with me.

"It's been a blast guys," I said as I headed to the now open door. The colonel rose and came to me one last time. "Did you really have C-2 hooked to your balls?"

"What do you think?" and I jumped out of the helicopter and was immediately rushed by a horde of fighters to a waiting pickup.

My boot camp training was complete.

CHAPTER 39
The Escape

I was taken to a safe house, fed and then took a long nap. I was mentally and physically exhausted at this point. I needed to recharge my batteries. Red Beard sent congratulations and said I was now thought of as kind of miracle worker among the rank and file. "Everyone speaks of the Snake who struck the hearts of the American dogs. Allah bless his name." apparently this was the hue and cry at my training camp.

In a few days, I was moved to a secluded building complex mile outside Kabul. I was given a new uniform and had an opportunity to actually take a bath and have a barber trim my wild growing beard. I ate well and watched some television. I was even offered the "services" of a woman from nearby which I refused. I enjoyed just hanging out, nothing to do. Doing nothing.... This was my first down time in a long time. I vowed to enjoy it while it lasted.

I thought about my strange success in moving up into the hierarchy of Al-Qaeda. I honestly didn't work at it. I had no religious fanatism and aside from my homicidal streak, I thought of myself as pretty ordinary. I tried to understand what these guys saw in me that I didn't. Yes, I was a foreigner and they liked foreigners to embrace their cause. Yes, I was well educated, had been trained and accepted by a renowned religious leader, had defended the faith by killing mosque desecrators, tweaked the noses of the American military and survived a near death experience in my basic training. My service, equally "heroic" to the Israeli Mossad would not be included in this mix. Maybe I was something special. If I was well, I never felt special even now or most certainly never in my former life. My loyalty was to myself and getting done with this life and reaching my goal of settling down and raising a family someday. I had no illusions about my chances of surviving but I did have hope.

I had settled into a daily routine of relaxation when a big shot came to see me. I knew he was a big shot even before he arrived when the women in my house began cleaning. And I mean really cleaning up this otherwise dump. My clothes were washed and washed again. I was told to bathe each day and keep myself and my room clean. No explanations were given. I just thought it strange and perhaps indicative of someone important visiting us soon.

When he finally came, I was taking a nap and they had to wake me up. I dressed and went into what passed for a kitchen and there he was, the number three or four man in Al-Qaeda. Not particularly impressive just sitting there, drinking tea and reading a week-old newspaper. He stood when I walked in and smiled. "Salam Alaikum Snake" His voice was deep and rather pleasant. His Arabic was Saudi; no surprise there. We were alone.

"Are you well my brother?" he asked. "Do you need anything?"

"No sir, I am fine and appreciate what you have done for me. I am praying and contemplating the greatness of Allah each day and looking forward to my next assignment in His service."

Wow, could I lie or what? I thought.

He liked my answer and we sat. A woman, I guess waiting outside the door entered and served us tea.

"Are you Lebanese, Snake? You sound Lebanese but not Lebanese," he smiled.

I knew he was lying now. He knew who I was and that I was born American. I'd have to be careful with the guy. Maybe he saw through my bullshit answer and this was his way of evening out the liars playing field.

"No sir, I was born American but of Lebanese heritage. I spent years living and working in Lebanon but sadly, I still speak with an American accent."

"Yes, yes... that explains it. Otherwise your Arabic is perfect. I understand you speak other language fluently. Is this true?"

"I am equally proficient in French and Spanish as well as English of course. I've begun to study the Afghani languages but haven't progressed well enough to be fluent."

We chatted on and on about bullshit and then he got down to business. He was here to debrief me. He asked about the details of the prisoner exchange. He was deeply interested in all the details. From the very beginning of the prisoner exchange to the very end. What was the colonel's name, what was the interrupters name, and so on? Did you recognize the unit insignia on their shoulders? Were there any civilians on board the helicopter. Do you recall any of their conversations in English? Did you see any maps? Could you recognize the weapons carried or mounted on the helicopter? How were you treated, were you harmed in anyway? Did they photograph you or any of our fighters?

We went through this debriefing for three hours, going over and over the same details. He took no notes. I was surprised that as we spoke, I remembered more and more... seemingly unimportant stuff but he was interested in everything I said. I realized he was filing in his image of the American enemy. I was sitting here learning from a master debriefer. I would use this investigative skill whenever I could. Details, details... that was what was most important in a debrief or even an interrogation.

Our session ended with the call to evening prayers. He would stay three days and it was the most significant time of my life as a jihadist in Al-Qaeda. I think Americans don't believe that these terrorist organizations are well structed. They are and I learned how well during my time with this top guy.

He began by affirming that I was going to become a European recruiter, but there would be other responsibilities as well.

"Young Snake, what do you know about our supply chain?"

"Nothing much. When we need something, somebody in the camp brings it to us. That's all I know."

"Your new duties will eventually bring you into an important role in gathering and then distributing supplies... perhaps all over the world. We will discuss this activity and what you will be doing to help us accomplish our supply goals. We receive support from China and Iran... and of course Saudi Arabia and other countries as well. Our weapons are diverse as you know, and having replacement parts and ammunition available is at times difficult. Then there's our continuing need for medical supplies, uniforms, tents, personal equipment for our fighters, food, supporting our propaganda work and on and on. Thousands and thousands of simple and complex supplies are required daily for us to continue our fight. These goods must be secured, centrally gathered, shipped, delivered and finally distributed. This is a monumental task accomplished by hundreds and hundreds of our followers."

He then described elements of the supply chain focusing on Europe where I was to be assigned. I would work in France, Belgium, Spain and the Netherlands. Initially I would be working with an experienced supply agent who would introduce me to our sources and contacts. At some point when I was deemed ready, this agent would leave and I would conduct all supply activities in these countries. I would also recruit when time permitted.

"How long will I remain in Europe?" I asked.

"That is difficult to say. Perhaps a year, perhaps longer. But always remember you are performing a valuable service to our cause. Be proud of what you will do. Your work is essential. Are you ready to begin your new work Snake?"

I gave him a long and windy speech about my commitment to the cause... how I would lay my life down for Allah and a lot of other crap. He seemed impressed. Oh well, this was a fantastic opportunity. I'd be able to uncover all the major supply sources for Al-Qaeda in Europe and I knew this was perhaps the most important position and best information I could ever hope to attain while part of this group of freaks.

He spent the rest of his time with me going over information about the locations I would visit, the suppliers, my contacts and what I'd be tasked with. Honestly, it seemed complicated and dangerous. The European secret services were not stupid and most likely had their own agents embedded in Al-Qaeda. I'd have to alert my Masoud friends as quickly as I could so they'd get word out to all the government agencies and I wouldn't be arrested or killed by James Bond. There was always a danger that Al-Qaeda had its own double agents embedded in the European Counter Intelligence Services and I'd be turned out.

The plan was to get me to Turkey and from there onto my first stop in the Netherlands. It would be a difficult journey and require time and luck. I would use both my Lebanese and American passports to accomplish easy entry into Europe. My back pack had been delivered and most of my $20,000 was still intact. Obviously, I wouldn't be able to take my knife or pistols with me but I was told there were weapons available when I reached my final destination. My credentials as a former professor would be a perfect cover. I would be traveling on sabbatical and this would most likely allow me easy entry through Immigration wherever I needed to go. Some letters of introduction from my former university were forged and would give me additional credibility. My hair was cut into a European style, I was fitted with a Western wardrobe and the beard I had worked so hard growing, was cut and shaped into a "professor-like" trim. Actually, when I saw myself in a mirror I was impressed. My skin had darkened, I had a fit, youthful body and I even wore a pair of fake eye glasses to round out the disguise. I was ready...

CHAPTER 40

Europe
Amsterdam

I was physically drained from my eight days of difficult travel. Amsterdam was the first stop on my itinerary and I looked forward to meeting my Al-Qaeda contact and reaching out to the Mossad. I had a lot to tell them and needed a lot of help.

This was my first time in the Netherlands and my impression was not a good one. The city had no charm. The streets were teaming with cyclists who would run you over without a second thought should you step off the street while they were peddling toward you at 100 mph. There was a grey coldness hanging over everything, the building, canals, people, and I found myself depressed. I needed to kill.

I tried to exercise daily since this activity helped me maintain my sanity and I had always been diligent in maintaining my physical training since leaving Beirut. I ran each morning and completed my exercises in my hotel room. Since I had a few days before I could meet my contact, I decided to explore this city and perhaps come out of my deep depression.

I walked and walked through cold, grey streets. Apparently, my effort to look like an American tourist was working. Two different assholes came up to me on the street and offered to sell cocaine. This always seemed to happen to me.

I growled, "Fuck off." at them and they quickly moved away. I tried to enjoy Amsterdam and learn something about the history of the Netherlands. I visited a few museums and headed for the Anne Frank House Museum as someone suggested. I gave up after seeing the long line of tourists outside waiting entry and I eventually wound up at the Spui Square and stopped for coffee and pastries.

Of course, I remained on constant alert for danger. As far as I could tell, I was seen as just another American tourist looking to get laid in Amsterdam's famous Red Light District or smoke pot until they puked. I used my skills to be sure I wasn't being followed and no one had seemed overly suspicious during the train ride in from the airport or since.

There's a difference between a "coffeeshop" and a "coffeehouse". You can get coffee and something to eat at a coffeehouse. They only serve coffee and marijuana, pot, at a coffeeshop. I paid my check and left the coffeehouse and walked to a nearby coffeeshop. There seemed to be dozens of them in the Red Light District and they were marked by green and white stickers affixed to their front window. I knew they were tourist traps, Dutch people rarely visited coffeeshops.

The shop was filled with old, and young smokers some talking, some just staring into space... quiet background jazz playing, pot smoke so thick I needed to cut through it to find a small empty table jammed into a space with a dozen other mostly occupied small high top tables all placed in front of an array of pot showcases backed up with a marble counter holding a large expresso coffee machine. I waited for a server for a minute before the sandy haired 20 something girl sitting at the next table with her boyfriend said, "You have to go up and get your own shit. Nobody comes over." She smiled at me. She spoke New York City English and I suddenly I felt at home in a strange place.

"Go ahead," she added, "We'll watch your table." They were both burning fat joints and most likely not their first ones of the day.

"Thanks. You guys need anything while I'm there?"

The young guy smiled and pointed to his empty coffee cup. "Maybe a refill if you don't mind?"

I returned to the table with our coffees and a rolled joint. The counter folks were super friendly and made some suggestions. They advised that their pot was most likely stronger than I was use to so I let them make my selection.

"Thanks sir, what do I owe you for the coffee?'

"It's on me buddy, my name is Paul," I answered, holding out my hand to the young guy.

"I'm Connor and this is Alice."

We shook hands and I lit up. "Where are you guys from?"

Connor answered, "New York. Queens. How about you? Sounds like a Brooklyn accent."

"Good ear... Bay Ridge Brooklyn. You guys tourists? First time in Amsterdam?" I felt the pot begin to take hold. *Nice shit*, I thought.

We chatted about New York and our impressions of Amsterdam. They were on an extended European trip and their next stop was Berlin. She was a singer with a band and he was a horn player between gigs. They were friendly and funny too. I told them I was there on business and that seemed to satisfy their curiosity. I had another joint and coffee while we talked. Nice couple but I had an overwhelming desire to kill them.

Mellow, that's how I would describe us after an hour chatting and smoking. They invited me back to their hotel room. "We have some better shit there Paul, come on." I accepted the invitation. As we walked over to their nearby hotel, I gripped the handle of the hunting knife I had bought now waiting in my jacket inside pocket... it felt cold against my hand. *Just like my heart*, I thought. I was pretty certain that the customers at the pot shop ignored us leaving and the counter people were too busy to care. Surprisingly, there was no one working the hotel lobby desk and we saw no one riding the elevator to the third floor. I decided to make this a quick kill. No hanging around. Just do it and get out.

Their room was typical third-class hotel. Not big, but just big enough. Alice needed to use the bathroom and I took the opportunity to stab Connor in his throat. I was careful to avoid blood spatter and he died before he fell silently to the floor. Unfortunately, Alice had just come out of the bathroom just as he fell and she stood petrified as she realized what I had just done. I was on her before she could scream and try to get away. I had to stab her three times before she died and I was covered with her blood.

I undressed, took a quick shower and rummaged through Connor's suitcase for something I could wear. My pants were still good, so I put on one of his shirts and a sweater. Just a little too big for me. I wrapped my shirt and jacket together with the bath towel I had used into a ball and placed them in a hotel laundry bag.

I scoured the bathtub, wiped down any surface I may have touched and opened the door to take a peek into the corridor. It was clear. I found the exit stairs and walked down the three flights. There was a security door leading to the street at the ground floor landing. I hoped it wasn't attached to an alarm as I opened it. It wasn't. A half hour later I reached my hotel. I had already dumped the laundry bag in an alley behind a restaurant that was filled with smelly garbage cans and boxes.

I slept like a baby that night.

I had called the Mossad the same day I arrived and they said an agent would be in touch. As I finished my breakfast the next morning, the old waiter handed me a slip of paper. It had an address and was signed "Uncle Jake". I inquired with a policeman on the street outside my hotel the location of the address on the note. We spoke English... most of the citizens of Amsterdam spoke some English I had pleasantly discovered.

He laughed, "Sir, that's easy to find. Just follow this street to our famous Red Light District. I'm sure you'll find it without a problem. Enjoy yourself."

"Is it far? Can I walk?" I asked, thinking about the crazy bicyclists teaming on the streets I'd have to cross.

He pointed in a direction, "Not far at all, about half a kilometer."

I walked. I only had to risk getting run over two times and I found the building without a problem just as the cop had said. As expected, the address was to a store front prostitute tourist trap. Looking out the big glass window was a 20 something girl. She was pretty, just sitting there half dressed, bored waiting for a customer. I caught her eye and she smiled and beckoned me in. She opened the door, asked me how I was and closed the drapes to her picture window. She began to take off the little she had on and I stopped her midstream by raising my hand.

I smiled, "I'm here to visit with my Uncle Jake." I spoke in English and she answered in English.

"Ah, he's here and has been waiting patiently for you. Please sit, have some coffee and I'll get him for you."

I helped myself to my third cup of coffee that day and reminded myself that I needed to drink less coffee. But the coffee in Amsterdam was so damn good. I had only taken a sip when the door opened and I was shocked to see my old friend from Lebanon... Gabe. I'm not an emotional guy but I was more than happy to see him. Perhaps he was the only real friend I had ever had.

"I'm sorry Professor, but I'm not here for sex." And he laughed as he embraced me.

We laughed and chatted as old friends do... I told him some of what had happened since I saw him last. He was concerned when I described the palace and my near death beating that put me in the hospital. After a bit we got down to business.

"Professor I'll be your contact while you're in Europe. For our future meetings you'll be approached by a prostitute or perhaps one of our female agents who will tell you that she's a friend of Uncle Jake. You will go with her or meet at the location she gives you. We believe that even if you're being watched, your meeting with a local prostitute will be perfect cover. Now let me fill you in. As soon as you tell me where you're going, we will advise that country's National Police and in turn they will provide whatever protection they can. We know there's a danger in sharing your identity. Some of these organizations could have double agents embedded. But we'll stay at the highest levels in sharing your information and pray for the best. We've given this a great deal of thought. But many of these internal security organizations have their own agents embedded in Al-Qaeda and we didn't want you swept up in some local operation. Now tell me all I need to know about your assigned tasks here in Europe."

We needed to be quick in this debrief. Nobody ever stayed more than hour with these prostitutes and someone could be tracking me, so I cut out all the non-essential stuff and got to the meat of my assignment. Gabe took no notes, just listened and waited until I was finished.

"Have you met with your contact here yet?"

"No not yet. I'm supposed to get a call today or tomorrow at my hotel. My contact is in transit somewhere in Europe and we couldn't coordinate my Amsterdam arrival with his schedule. How do you want to handle it?"

"All we can do is wait. Make the contact, do whatever you have to do and, in a few days, when you'll need to have sex again, we can debrief then. Now if for some reason you can't meet or don't have anything new for me, just tell the girl who approaches you that you're gay and not interested. Ok?"

Fine with me. I told him I had some names of suppliers and shipping methods but he said hold onto them and at some point, we'd create a written report but not yet. He asked if I was scheduled to do any recruiting in Amsterdam. I told him that I didn't know yet. Gabe was concerned about my safety and told me he had a small team of agents who would shadow me as much as possible. They would record my meetings and gather whatever initial intelligence they could. He said if I wanted to meet just call my control telephone number. He would get a message to me when he needed to see me. That pretty much finished all we had to go over and he left first and I followed about ten minutes later and returned to my hotel. I checked for a tail... seemed ok but I did get a dirty look from an old American tourist lady who saw me coming out of the prostitute's room. I smiled and gave her a wink.

I waited in my hotel room for a call but none came. I got hungry and left for a local restaurant. While I was eating a skinny guy about 30, dressed nice came over to my table... it was in the back. I always asked for a table in the back of the restaurant. At first, I thought he was coming over to ask me if I needed some cocaine. But it turned out he was my Al-Qaeda contact, my new buddy, the guy who was going to teach me the supply procurement ropes. Strange how appearances can be deceiving. I had actually expected I'd be working with a Saudi or an Egyptian... turns out this guy was French, a native-born Parisian. I would have never given him a second look... "Bon nuit Monsieur Snake." He said as he just took an uninvited seat at my table.

I looked at him like he was nuts. This asshole used my nom-de-guerre in a public place. I wanted to smack him. Obviously, I couldn't... I couldn't even yell at him. Maybe I'd hit him a few times later. I glared at him and he shrugged his shoulders. He continued in French. "Is there a problem my friend? Have I offended you in some way?"

"You're an asshole. Never use my code name in public. Call me Professor or Paul. Do you understand? Or is that too complicated for you?"

"Ah... of course. Forgive me... Paul. Do you want to sit there angry with me or are you prepared to get on with what we have to do?"

The waiter arrived and Frenchy, that's what I'd call him... ordered a Scotch and Soda and I knew that this guy wasn't a Muslim and was in this business for only the money he could make or steal. I decided that I'd kill him at some point but would need approval from my Control

Group back in Pakistan. His drink arrived quickly and he began to sip it and smack his lips in obvious enjoyment.

"Good, good."

"Are you ready now? We can't talk here. Meet me outside in fifteen minutes," I told him.

Frenchy gulped down his drink. Stood. He made intense eye contact. "No, I will pick you up outside your hotel tomorrow morning at 10. Be ready to spend a full day with me and oh, dress comfortably. We will be visiting some very dirty places. Eh, Mr. Paul. Is that too complicated for you?" He turned and walked out of the restaurant. I had made an enemy. But more importantly, how did he know I was here? I must have been followed.

The next morning, I got up early, did my run and exercises. I felt good. I had breakfast in the hotel restaurant and went outside about five minutes early to wait for Frenchy... not his real name which he told me was Claud Arnot. He was already there... waiting for me in his new shinny BMW. The guy loved money; this was his only motivation. Honestly, I didn't care what he loved, in fact his obsession with money I viewed to be a weakness that could be used against him. I walked over to his car and got in. Nice car. I remembered the old NYC joke about assholes who drive BMW's.

"Good morning Paul. Did you have a good rest my friend?"

"Yes, I did. Let's get on with it. I'm not your friend. I'm here to learn what you know. So teach me and that will keep things simple for both of us."

"Ah... so you're not a morning person. Didn't you have your coffee yet?"

I ignored him and he pulled away and headed for the dock area. I wondered if Gabe had a tail on us. Get this guy's license plate and let's figure out who he is. I knew I'd be working with him for a while and I wanted to know as much about him as possible. I already knew he was hard to insult.

We parked on an empty street filled with warehouses of all sizes. Frenchy shut off the car engine. He made a quick call and then we sat and waited.

"Alright Professor or Paul, which do you prefer to be called? We have some time for your education."

"Either name will do."

"Ok then it's Professor. I like the sound of saying Professor. We are waiting for our middleman. He's got the shipping contacts here in Amsterdam and we have supplies ready to ship stored in one of these warehouses. He will show us where and when they will be shipped and I will pay him. We never work directly with the sources in the supply chain. No manufactures', no storers, no shippers. It's all done through middle men... the only exception is the banks. I have my contacts with banks all over Europe and at some point, I'll introduce you."

"How do you get the supply orders?"

Frenchy began to laugh., "From you of course. You'll also pay me my commission when I ask for it. Always in cash by the way. I don't trust banks; even Swiss accounts can be cracked when it comes to terrorists' activities. But of course, you already know all this... don't you Professor? Are you playing with me?"

I was surprised. I hadn't been told any of this. How would I get the information on supplies needed or the money to pay this asshole? I guessed I'd find out. I decided to play along with Frenchy and pretend that I already knew about the arrangement.

"Of course not. I just want you to be sure that you know that I'm the boss. You'll get your orders and payment the usual way. Now where is the jerk we're waiting for? You called him a half hour ago."

At that precise moment a flaming red classic Mustang convertible, top down, driven by a young blond girl came barreling down the deserted street. She stopped her car, parked facing the wrong way and got out. She was stunning. About my height, porno star figure and dressed in tight jeans and a see-through blouse. Her makeup wasn't over the top. Just the right look and when she got close to our car, I was almost lifted off my seat by the intoxicating fragrance of her expensive perfume.

Frenchy was laughing and couldn't contain himself as we both exited the car. He kissed both her cheeks and I think held her hands a tad too long because although she was smiling, it was obvious, she didn't like him. *Welcome to my club lady*, I thought.

"Madelaine, dear Madelaine.... What a total delight to see you. What happened to your father? Is he alright? Why did he send you to meet us?" Frenchy was speaking English.

"Who's your friend?" she asked.

I had come over to their side of the car and stood close by to get a better look at this goddess. By the way she looked at me I could tell she liked what she saw. She smiled and unconsciously touched her long blonde hair as she gazed into my eyes. *She's flirting with me*, I thought. I smiled and held out my hand.

"My name is Paul." She took it in hers and it felt soft and warm to the touch.

"I'm Madelaine and I'm here on my father's business. It is very nice to meet you Paul."

Frenchy abruptly ended the magic moment. "Paul is working with me now and I wanted him to meet your father. Will you be able to show us our goods in the warehouse? I want to find out when you'll be shipping and the route they will take. Is that ok? Can you help me with this?"

"Of course,... but you forgot to mention our payment. Do you have it with you?"

"Certainly, but let's wait till we're inside before I give it to you... is that alright?" Frenchy patted his jacket pocket as he said this. "Maybe a check? Maybe a receipt for a wire transfer" I'd have to find out later. Madelaine nodded her approval, turned and we followed her to a green painted warehouse about 100 yards away. She had keys and opened two heavy duty padlocks on the single door of the windowless building. We entered and it smelled bad. Dusty, dirty... maybe they had stored bananas or some fruit that went bad at one time. She found the light switch and I saw that the immense space was filled with stacks and stacks of freight boxes. We walked down aisle after isle until she stopped and pointed to our supply boxes. The words "Medical Supplies" was printed in large letters on each of the many boxes.

"In a few days these crates will be loaded into shipping containers. Sometime next week they will be then be loaded onto the ship that will take them to Istanbul. They will arrive on or before June 15th. What happens to them after that is your problem."

"Excellent... excellent as always. Thank you and please thank your father for me Madeline. I have something here for you." Frenchy handed her an envelope which she opened. I could see it wasn't a check... probably the bank transfer information I had wondered about. She glanced at it quickly and put it into her purse.

"Then our business is finished?" she asked.

"Yes... I'm taking Paul back to my office. Would you care to join us in an early lunch?"

"Thank you for the invitation. But I can't. I have important business to attend to right now. But I was wondering... Paul. would you care to join me for dinner? I'd like to welcome you to my wonderful city and I have an exceptional restaurant in mind. My treat. Say 8 tonight? I'll even pick you up... where are you staying?"

I accepted not only because I wanted to see more of this exceptional woman, but I wanted to tweak Frenchy's nose. He'd go nuts thinking about me and Madeline being somewhere together and maybe getting intimate. I gave her my hotel information and we agreed to meet in the lobby at 8. Done deal.

Frenchy was quiet for a change during the drive to his office. I had nothing to say or ask so I just sat back and enjoyed the scenery. Amsterdam wasn't so bad after all... I liked the look of the tall houses, canals and old-world atmosphere that seeped out at every corner. This was a busy city... lots of office workers... lots of hustle on the immaculate city streets. I noticed there seemed to be an absence of police... I wondered why?

"I shouldn't care but be careful with Madeline Professor," Frenchy said out of the blue.

"What? What do you mean?"

"Her family is mafia. They come from Sicily and her father is a big shot in the international mob."

"That doesn't seem to be a problem with you. You work with them. Are you mafia too?" I laughed.

"Don't be crazy. I work for myself. I work with anyone who can help me get what I want. That's why I'm working with you my friend. The only reason."

There was no more conversation and when we arrived at a large mid-town office building, Frenchy parked in the basement garage. I noticed he had two spaces assigned... probably didn't want his BMW dinged. His office was on the top floor and from its windows there was a spectacular view of the city. He had spent serious money decorating and his gold office sign announced that this was the "Crystal Import Export LTD". He had a good-looking receptionist who said nothing just handed him a bunch of message slips as we passed. There were three or four offices, all with closed doors. I guess his business was good. We entered his lavish office and he pointed to a seat in front of his huge desk.

"All right Professor. I think it's time for us to have our "come to Jesus" talk as the American's say. Your French is excellent. But you speak French like it sounds in an American gangster movie. We will never be friends, just business associates for the time being. You're terrorist scum and just knowing you could get me killed. But that's never going to happen. Don't ever count on me to save your ass when you screw up and you will screw up. Your bosses are paying me to train you... a lot of money. Then I'm finished with your kind. If it wasn't for the money, I would have never worked for you people. You will listen carefully to me from now on and do what I tell you to do. When you're trained, I disappear from your Al-Qaeda cesspool. If you ever get caught and you will get caught, should you tell them anything about me I will have you killed. Do you understand Professor?"

I smiled to myself. This guy was a bigger jerk than I thought. What made him think that he'd still be alive after I was trained in his job. I knew how my associates worked and there was some C-2, a knife or a bullet coming somewhere in his future. But for now, I'd play his game. Let him think I was frightened by his toothless threat. Let him act like my "boss"... I'd go along for now, cooperate, and wait for the end of his story and life. Maybe they'd let me be the one to kill him. I'd enjoy that.

"Alright. Train me."

He got up, closed the window blinds and fixed himself a drink. He didn't offer me anything.

"We'll start with an overview. Ask questions whenever you don't understand or want more details. My work includes selecting suppliers, warehouse and shipper middlemen. I told you earlier, I don't work directly with anyone other than middlemen. When you tell me what you need, I get the wheels in motion and coordinate the supply chain from start to finish. By the way, you owe me $100,000 American dollars for handling the medical supply shipment. I want that, in cash, in two days. I will introduce you to my contacts and you will handle the transactions at some point. You will need to organize the banking since the middlemen want bank transfers for their services. That's it... Simple, not complicated."

"I will need names and methods of contact... all information and so on for working with the middlemen. Could we begin with Madeline's group.?"

"Certainly. Here is a written report for you to take with you. Don't lose it. It identifies the supplies that Madeline's father normally gathers and ships for us. It contains all the information you'd need for ordering these particular supplies. His group is unique since that handle both the supply gathering, warehousing and shipping. A single source. Most are not this simple. But you'll find that out as we go along. Now, if you don't have any questions we're done for the day." Frenchy dismissively waved his hand... like, Shoo, go away.

I was going to remind him that we were supposed to have an early lunch... that's what he told Madeline but I imagined that asking him that would set him off. So, I just left and taxied back to my hotel. There was a short message waiting for me shoved under my room door. *Nice penmanship*, I thought. *Must have been taught to write by the nuns.* The note was from the front desk: "Please call the Front Desk. You had a visitor and many telephone calls while you were out. Thank you."

I did one better, got back in the elevator and walked over to the Front Desk, serviced by an attractive middle-aged blond lady. *Is everyone a blond in this country?* I thought.

"Good day sir. How may I help you?" she asked.

"Good day. I'm Paul Asoph, Room 921," I handed her the message slip.

She read it, smiled at me and retrieved four missed call messages... all from the same telephone number. She said a gentleman had also stopped at the desk about an hour before looking for me. He left you this card. She handed me a business card that read, "John Bowman United States Consulate, Division of Immigration. On the back there was a note. "Please call when you can. Thanks." I wondered what this was about. I had used my American passport at Immigration when I arrived at Amsterdam. "Oh well... I'll call him later."

"Thank you. Oh, by the way did you write this?" I pointed to the message placed under my door. She looked a little confused.

"Yes, I did. Why do you ask?"

"Did you attend Catholic school; taught by the nuns?" I laughed the question.

She laughed her answer. "Of course. Good handwriting, yes?"

"Of course you have good handwriting. Me too... but not so good."

I found a simple sidewalk restaurant close to the hotel. I didn't think anyone followed me, but who knows? These "trackers" were usually pros and I might be ok at spotting one tracker but I could never really be sure. They worked in teams and had great skill in going undetected. My table was outside and I could keep track of comings and goings of passerby's. I ordered a salad and skipped the coffee... had a fruit drink. I looked at my missed calls and thought I could safely use my cell out here.

"Salaam," was the greeting on the other end. I had reached a Muslim woman.

I answered her in Arabic, she responded in Dutch. I tried English. That worked.

"Yes, hello. How may I help you sir?"

"I received a number of telephone calls from this number this morning. But no name was left. Could you help me?"

"I'll try. May I have your name?"

"It's Paul Asoph. Sound familiar?'

"Not to me but let me check with the others here in the office. May I put you on hold?"

I only waited about 30 seconds before a male voice came on. "Hello Mr. Asoph. Welcome to Amsterdam. My name is Joseph Kazem. I am the senior staff coordinator here at the al-Quozah Mosque. I wanted to invite you to evening services today. I hope you can make it. I really want to meet you sir."

It didn't take me long to understand that this guy was my Al-Qaeda contact here in Amsterdam. I had to see him and soon. But tonight was out. I had a date with Madeline and I needed to find out as much as I could about her, her father and their organization. I might not have another chance.

"Would it be possible for me to come now? I have an important meeting tonight but I'm free for the next few hours."

"Certainly... that would be perfect." He began to give me directions but I stopped him and told him I'd be coming by cab.

"Fine. When you reach the mosque, our office is located in the white two story building next door. I'm on the first floor. Just ask our receptionist and she will call me. When do you think you'll be arriving?"

"In about an hour if that's alright?"

"Perfect. See you then Mr. Asoph." And he hung up.

I had time and continued to finish my lunch. I decided to call this guy at the American Consulate and see what he wanted. I knew if I didn't contact him, he'd only make a pest of himself and keep trying to track me down. *Who knows?* I thought. *Maybe it's important.*

I placed the call and after answering the same dumb questions as to why I was calling three times, John Bowman finally came on the line.

He wasted no time with pleasantries, "When can you come in to see me Mr. Asoph?"

Ok, I'd play along. "Hmm... what's this all about Mr. Bowman?"

"I'd rather discuss the matter in person. When can you come in?"

"Tomorrow morning." I was abrupt. I tried to sound annoyed.

"Be at my office at 10 am." And he just hung up. I guess he was having a bad day.

I wondered what this was all about. No sense in thinking about it... I'll find out tomorrow at 10 am.

I finished my lunch, paid the tab, and took a cab to the mosque. The office building was right next door and I went in and announced myself to the receptionist. She asked me to have a seat and she called Mr. Kazem. I didn't have to wait long and a young man wearing an agal or traditional headdress, came to where I was seated and greeted me. "As-Salaam Alaikum Mr. Asoph or would you prefer Professor?" He was soft spoken and slightly built. His English was perfect. Big smile and friendly face.

"Alaikum Salaam. Paul would be fine. Very nice meeting you too Mr. Kazem."

"Thank you, Paul,... please call me Joseph. Would you please follow me to our conference room? There's some wonderful tea there and we can speak privately."

A short walk down a hallway and we entered his conference room. I noticed that the walls and ceiling were covered in acoustic tile for soundproofing, very thick carpeting and the door was made of heavy steel. This room was secure from eavesdroppers, maybe bomb proof too. Joseph locked the door after us and fixed us some tea before sitting across from me at the large conference table. I wondered if we were under surveillance or being recorded. I'd be careful and wait for him to take the lead.

"So, Paul, are you enjoying our city?"

"Yes, I am... are you from here Joseph?"

"No, no... I came to Amsterdam with my family from Istanbul when I was a child. You may already know that Turks have been coming to Holland since the 16th Century. This country has been kind to Muslims, even Christians too. Your American Pilgrims left on the Mayflower from Holland after they were forced out of England. More than five percent of this country is Muslim by the way."

"Really?"

He began to laugh. "I didn't invite you here for a history lesson Paul. Forgive me. There's another more important purpose in meeting... I needed to introduce myself as your contact here in the Netherlands. Whatever you require I will secure for you. Also, it is my responsibility to coordinate our supply needs with you. I wonder if you might tell me what you saw today concerning the medical supplies we procured."

"I saw stacks and stacks of boxes that had the words "MEDICAL SUPPLIES" stenciled on them. I didn't open any to verify the contents. From what the shipper said, they will be shipped to Turkey early next week. Other than that, I know nothing more. If you need more information I could find out."

"Yes, you're just beginning in this responsibility and you'll need guidance from me. First thing to know, Amsterdam is your home city. This mosque is your home office and I am your home contact in all things."

"Ok, that makes it easy. So all my instructions, money, orders whatever, will originate with you... here?"

"Yes." Joseph smiled. He wanted me to know that I had done nothing wrong and that he understood that I was in a learning process and not alone in this responsibility. "How much are we expected to pay Claude Arnot?"

"He told me $100,000 to be paid in American dollars today or tomorrow at the latest. Is this your understanding?"

"No. Arnot originally quoted his fee as $75,000 when the order was placed. Unfortunately, we have no choice but to pay him the amount he's asking. I will give you a briefcase with his fee when you're ready to leave. We'll call him from my office and tell him to be available today for his money payment and a new order. Is this agreeable?"

"Certainly... I don't trust him. Now what's the new order?"

"You know from your combat experience we have captured many weapons made in the US, but we don't always have parts and ammunition for them. The new order is for parts and ammunition. Arnot has an American contact in Brussels who can supply what we need."

"I see. How much will that cost?" I asked.

Joseph smiled." Arnot will ask at least a million American dollars for this order."

"Should I try to negotiate the price?" I asked.

"You could, but I doubt if it would be negotiable. He gives us a number and that's final. 'Take it or leave it,' he always tells us. This is why you are here. We don't want to do business with him any longer. By the way, He is charging us half a million to train you. Did you know that? Did he tell you?"

"We don't talk much... Oh, and just so you know, I'm having dinner tonight with our Amsterdam supplier. Is that alright?"

"Certainly. Learn as much as you can and as quickly as you can."

He then handed me the new order details which I pocketed. I'd take a cell photo later. We chatted a few more minutes and left the conference room for his office where he gave me a briefcase containing the $100,000 for Arnot. He then called Frenchy and told him I would be coming over with his fee and a new order. Arnot said he was very busy but he would see me an hour. Joseph called me a cab and invited me to return for services in the mosque. I told him I'd be back very soon and I left when the cab arrived for Arnot's office.

I was early and Frenchy made me wait. The receptionist wasn't friendly and offered no water or tea. This was not a "happy work place". So I just sat and waited for the big man to ask me in with his $100,000. After he kept me waiting for an extra fifteen minutes, I thought about getting up and leaving his office. Let him find me if he wanted his money. If it wasn't for the new order that's exactly what I would have done.

The receptionist hung up her phone and turned to me. "He's ready for you now."

I entered his office and he had his head down, reading some documents on his desk. He didn't greet me or look up, just motioned for me to take a seat. When he finally finished his reading, he snaped his fingers and pointed to my briefcase. I held back my anger and handed it over to him. He didn't open it and count the money in front of me at least.

"Let me see the new order Professor."

I said nothing and just handed him the order. He read it quickly, sighed and asked, "When do you people want this?"

Joseph told me it was needed quickly and I told Frenchy right away, who wasn't too pleased to hear that.

"I'm not a miracle worker. This order will take some time. Today is Tuesday, on Thursday you and I will take a train to Brussels to get the process started. Be here at 8 am, I'll make the arrangements. We'll be gone two days so pack a bag. Is that understood?"

"Of course, I understand and please stop asking me if I understand... we have to work together for the time being and let's try to be respectful."

Frenchy scowled and waved his hand indicating that he was finished with me. I fumed inside but just smiled, a thin lip smile I might add and left the self-important jerk to go back to reading his emails or whatever. I returned to my hotel, napped for an hour and then showered again and dressed for my dinner with Madeline. I had thought about contacting Gabe but decided to wait until tomorrow after I met with the guy at the Consulate.

Madeline arrived on time and met me in the hotel lobby. She was dressed in what you could call business formal. Me too for that matter. This was not a date as I saw it. Just business associates learning about each other in a social atmosphere.

"Do you enjoy Italian food? Or perhaps prefer something else?" she asked as we entered her car conveniently parked at the hotel curbside. The Doorman smiled as he opened her car door. I had the feeling that she was well known here.

"Oh, I'm fine so I'll leave that up to you. I never heard people rave about Dutch cuisine so I guess Italian is always a good choice."

"Italian it is then. I think you'll like this restaurant. My family owns it."

"No doubt we'll get great service then." I laughed. She did too.

A valet parked her car and we entered a somewhat ornate restaurant decorated like people might imagine an Italiano Palacio. I liked the look and feel of the place. It was crowded but not too crowded. The tables were appropriately spaced and the dinners were dressed the same way.

I imagined this was an "expensive date" location. I noticed there were many older men with younger women... cheater's hangout? I caught the sounds of English, French, Dutch and even some Spanish being spoken as we were taken to a nice secluded table. The Maître De fawned over Madeline and inquired about her father.

"He's well Franco. Travelling as usual. I'll tell him you were asking for him. Thank you."

She asked if it was alright for her to order for us and of course I agreed. She was surprised when I told her I didn't drink and said something about wine and Italian cuisine are the same. She ordered a glass for herself and left it up to the Wine Steward to make the selection. She also told our waiter that she would call when we were ready to order, but to bring a small cold antipasto to our table now.

She looked at me, smiled and asked, "So tell me Paul... how long have you been a terrorist?"

Hmm... rather getting to the point, I thought, but she was smiling when she asked the question. She wasn't making a judgment. "Ah, ever since I attended Catholic school. Oh, sorry you said terrorist... not terrorized." She laughed. As I continued. "I don't think of myself as a terrorist, just someone who is serving Allah and his people. I understand that our ways are not generally accepted... even hated. Sometimes, well I'm not so sure myself." It occurred to me that her family had no problem taking terrorist money.

"How did your organization come to work with Claud Arnot? He's not my favorite person by the way. You probably already know I am going to be his replacement at some point."

Madeline rolled her eyes at Arnot's name. "He's a little prick. If I had a choice, I'd have nothing to do with him. But business is business. He makes the expression "honor among thieves" a mockery. I think at some point he will find that he has crossed the line too many times. He can't be trusted. I tell you this because I feel you're not like him. I hope I'm correct."

I thought, *The expression is "there's no honor among thieves" but I wasn't going to correct her.*

"You're an American Paul, where in the States do you come from?"

"Brooklyn, New York... all my young life."

"Has anyone ever said you look like a young Al Pacino... only taller and better looking? I've visited Brooklyn by the way, have relatives there. Your English sounds Brooklyn. Are you Italian?"

I was a little flattered. "Yes, I've been told that before. And yes, I've never lost my Brooklyn accent either. And no, I'm Lebanese and Irish. When were you in Brooklyn?"

Our antipasti came and she ordered another glass of wine while she told me about her visit to my home town. I knew she was the daughter of a mafia kingpin but I didn't want to seem inquisitive and avoided asking her anything that would get her cautious. It was really none of my business anyway. We talked about the World, its problems, religion, politics and life's ups and downs. I was really enjoying her company and I could tell she liked mine as well. Eventually she ordered us dinner and it was exceptionally good. We sat there for about two hours before I mentioned I had an early morning appointment and she offered to take me back to my hotel. I declined and she asked the waiter to have a cab come to the front door. I offered to pay for dinner but she was insulted in a kind of mocking way... "No, no... I enjoyed and appreciated your company tonight Paul you're my family's guest and I look forward to continuing our relationship. My father will be back here in two weeks and I'd like you to meet him. Here's my private number. Let me know when you're available and we'll be sure to meet again."

We said our goodnights at the table and I left for my hotel.

CHAPTER 41
Two Masters

I arrived at the US Consulate at the appointed time but it was almost an hour later before I was finally escorted to Bowman's office. Why is it that anything you do in life that requires any sort of governmental interaction is always unpleasant?

Bowman was huge. How could a man who weighted at least 300 lbs., obviously in bad health by the way he looked and his heavy breathing, work for the government? His top shirt button was undone, his suit was wrinkled and his shoes hadn't seen shoe polish since they came out of the box he bought them in. I noticed a cigarette burn hole on his tie and the guy looked like he'd have a heart attack at any moment.

"Sit Asoph," he grunted pointing to a chair in front of his cluttered desk.

I sat and had already decided to say as little as possible. Now after seeing this big mess of a government official even more so.

"Why the fuck are you working for the Israelis?"

Now that surprised me. I decided that he had information and wasn't just probing so I'd admit my relationship with the State of Israel. The question was how much did he know?

"I have helped them from time to time but I never considered I was working for them. Am I breaking any laws?"

"Bull shit! Yes... you're not registered with the US Government as working for a foreign government... so you are breaking at least one law. How long have you worked for them and what do you do for them?"

I decided to become confrontational. "Who the hell are you Bowman? Why did you bring me in here?"

"Look asshole I ask the questions. You want me to pull your passport. I can have an FBI guy here in two minutes and you'll go back to New York on the next plane... in handcuffs and leg irons. So just answer my fucking questions."

"Go ahead. Take your best shot Bowman. I'm leaving."

I got to my feet and walked out of his office and the Consulate. I found a pay phone and contacted Gabe. I needed to meet with him. I took a cab to the Red Light District and found my "girl's" store front. The curtains were drawn and I had to wait a half hour before she opened them and beckoned me inside. She left me alone but it didn't take long for Gabe to show up. I told him about my meeting with Bowman. Gabe had heard of him before.

"He's CIA."

"Gabe how did they find out about me? What do you think they want?"

"I image it was the request that Jake made with Dutch Security asking them to not bother you in any of their internal operations. Someone there must have passed on the request to Bowman. This was bound to happen at some point. All these European agencies share information with the US. I doubt if they know anything more than you might be working with us on something. I'll update Jake later today and see what he wants us to do or perhaps he can do something on a higher level. I don't really know. But I don't think you're in danger of being arrested or deported. You read it correctly, Bowman was just probing." I told him my impression of Bowman. "How can a fat pig like him be CIA?" I wondered.

"Chuck Bowman actually is a living legend in the Agency. He's accomplished more than any another agent in helping close down terrorist activity throughout Europe. He's based in London but travels all over. I imagine he has a vast network of undercovers working for him. I've never run into him but Jake has. The only problem is that you're on his radar now and he will watch you and do a deep investigation on your background. Since the CIA is not known for sharing information, your FBI and Homeland Security will most likely be kept in the dark. In all likelihood Bowman will bring you in again as soon as he knows more about you. Be ready Professor."

"Ok Gabe. We don't have much time, so let me fill you in on what's happened the last few days."

The first thing I did was send my cell photos of the supply requests and the information I had on Madeline's company to Gabe's phone. I then recounted my meeting with Joseph and all he told me about the Al-Qaeda supply chain operation. I didn't tell him about my social meeting with Madeline. Gabe recorded our conversation on his phone for Jake. We made tentative plans to meet back here after my return from Brussels. We had to be careful meeting too often in the brothel. No doubt I was being tailed and someone might get a little suspicious if I appeared to be a little too "Horney" and showed up for sex too many times to be normal. Gabe said he'd figure something out and send a message to my hotel about a possible new meeting location. He left fifteen minutes before I did and I grabbed a cab back to the hotel. I called Joseph on the way and told him about my meeting with Bowman. He seemed a little concerned and said we needed to meet when I returned from Brussels.

I hadn't had time for my run this morning so I did an extra long one and completed my exercise regimen back in my hotel room. I did notice a woman casually watching me on the street. I had remembered her seeing her from another day and surmised she was part of my surveillance team. Who she worked for... well that was another unanswered question?

I had a good night's sleep and rose early on Thursday morning. I took a quick shower, packed some overnight stuff and stopped in the hotel restaurant for an early breakfast. Frenchy said to meet him at the train station. I guess he didn't love me anymore so no pick up in his elegant BMW this morning. The cab ride there was about fifteen minutes... I checked the train schedule board and found the track for my train to Brussels. I'm not a big train guy but "training around" is very popular in Europe. I was watching for a tail but I couldn't see anyone looking me over. Frenchy showed up just as the train pulled into the station and I went up to him.

"Hello Claud. How are you?"

"Fine... fine. Let's board and find our seats. This is a short trip and I have set up an appointment with my supply contact for 3 this afternoon. We'll be staying the night. Tomorrow we visit our transportation and warehouse sources so we'll be busy. Don't make any sightseeing plans."

"Do you plan to fill me on the train? I'd like to know more about our contacts before we meet them."

"No. That wouldn't be wise. You never know who might be listening. I'll wait until we check in at the hotel. If that's alright with you Professor?"

"You're the boss... I can wait."

Frenchy made a few calls while we were traveling. Surprisingly, he spoke English on one of them. His English was excellent. He also spoke Russian on another. From what I could surmise, the calls had to do with other business activities his company was working on and I couldn't pick up anything that he shouldn't be talking about on an open telephone line. I napped a bit and woke when we pulled into the Brussels Midi Station.

"Let's find a taxi," he said as we stepped out onto the busy boulevard.

"Take us to the Rocco Forte Hotel please," Frenchy told the driver as we entered the back seat of this extra large cab. The driver took our overnight bags and placed them in his trunk. It was a short drive to this very elegant hotel. Frenchy always paid for everything while I was with him. He told me his expenses were covered in his commission. Inflated no doubt. We checked in... separate suites, and planned to meet back in the lobby in an hour. Our rooms were adjacent and the bellman carried both of our bags. I took mine and my key while Frenchy waited for him to escort him to his room.

There wasn't' much unpacking to do... I took off my jacket and shirt, washed up, brushed my teeth, dressed again and decided to wait in the lobby a little early. Frenchy came looking for me at exactly one hour later. He exited the elevator, stopped and looked over the crowded lobby over before approaching me. I was sitting in a quiet corner reading a French newspaper but noticed him get off the elevator. He had changed into a sport shirt, no jacket. He sat across from me.

"Our contact will meet us here. I know a spot in the Hotel where no one will overhear us and even notice us. But we'll wait here until he arrives. When he comes, I'll go and meet him. You stay seated but don't follow us. I'll return for you. He doesn't know you're coming and will want to know who you are before I bring you in. Don't worry, it will be alright, all is good."

We sat there for another half hour before he came. Of course, I didn't have any idea what he looked like but Frenchy stood and walked over to a tall guy who had just come in. They talked a bit and then turned and walked away. Frenchy was gone for fifteen minutes or so and when he returned, he looked concerned. I hadn't seen him look like this... he's a cocky bastard, always sure of himself. I stood and in almost a whisper he said,

"He's nervous. He doesn't know you and he's afraid you're some undercover agent. He wants to speak with you alone before he'll talk business. Follow me."

I followed him down the hall and we turned in at the Bellman's storage closet. Frenchy opened the door and ushered me in. Closet is not a good description. It was really a mid-sized room for storing baggage and other items people had left. I imagine Frenchy paid the head bellman off to use the room. No doubt it was secure enough.

"Close the door and lock it," the tall guy ordered. I did. He was definitely an American. He looked military to me.

"Ok... now strip down to your underwear."

"I don't wear underwear," was my laughing reply.

"Better yet. Now take it all off buddy."

The guy was either a pervert or wanted to be sure I wasn't wearing a wire. I stripped and he checked my clothes. He threw them back and I began to dress.

"Ok... you're good. Now you can tell me who you are."

"I thought Claud would have already told you. What do you want to know?"

"Name, where you're from... who you represent, the usual shit. Start talking."

This guy had a commanding manner and I figured him for an American military officer. Crew cut, good physical shape and a lot of confidence that when he gave an order, he knew it would be obeyed.

"Paul Asoph, Brooklyn New York, supply agent in training for an international organization whose name I will not mention. I don't know you buddy, maybe you should strip for me now," I laughed when I said it... didn't want to piss him off. He smiled.

"Ok you pass, get your asshole friend back in here and let's get this business done. I'm in a hurry."

"Before I do that... what's your name? You can forget about telling me your rank and serial number."

He laughed, but took a heartbeat before answering. "Ray Shadow."

I left and returned with Frenchy and we got down to business.

"I need a few weeks to secure all these items. They come from different sources and will take time to assemble. I want $500,000. Delivered the usual way. I need $250,00 right away. You provide me with the drop off location and I'm done. You'll have to re-crate the product before you ship it out of Brussels. That's it. Is it a go?" Our conversation was conducted in French. Ray Shadow didn't speak it all that well.

Frenchy turned to me, "Well?"

"It's a go," I answered in English.

"Your $250k will be wired tomorrow. Contact me in the usual way with the date the product is arriving and I'll give you the delivery location. Now gentlemen, let's come out of the closet."

Only when we left the hotel, were safely in the cab, and Frenchy had instructed the driver to take us to a warehouse storage location, did he turn toward me and spoke in a whisper, "We're meeting our storage contact next and then we'll arrange for the supply transportation out of the country."

The warehouse storage guy turned out to be a woman, an old woman. Frenchy was charming and flirtatious and I could tell she loved it. He told her the type of product she would need to store, the quantity and most importantly it would need to be re-crated with new stenciling and put on pallets in bundles suitable for air cargo loading. He introduced me as his replacement and she didn't seem to care all that much. She gave him a price of $50,000 and said he needed to get her a $10,000 down payment in a few days. The rest would be due upon his inspection. She called us a cab and we left for the air cargo contact's location.

Nothing difficult here as well. The air transport guy accepted me and was really only interested in the size of the load, how it would be crated and the destination. He did a calculation and estimated $30,000 subject to weight and handling. Full payment would be made at the time his trucks picked up the load.

It had been a busy day and I began to appreciate the complexities of the supply chain. Frenchy had a good thing going and it must have taken him years to create the various middlemen contacts, and that was only in Brussels. On the way back to the hotel he told me the total cost, including his commission, would be one million dollars, just as Joseph had predicted. I had a feeling he was also getting kickbacks from his middlemen as well. There had been no negotiations with the middlemen. They gave Frenchy a price and it was a done deal. I don't know much about business but I think this is not the normal way it's conducted. I guess he hadn't read any books on "How to Negotiate A Deal."

I now had all the Brussel's middlemen details, names, locations and full details on this order. When Gabe and I met, I'm sure he'd be pleased. I could imagine Jake dangling this information in front of his American counterpart and bargaining for new jets or armored vehicles. The name of that American, Ray Shadow, would be worth almost any price to Military Intelligence as well.

The next day Frenchy and I went to his bank to complete the money transfers. When we arrived, we were treated like royalty. "Come this way sir. Would you care for coffee, sweets?" and on and on. I can't begin to image the commissions these bankers made from Frenchy's money transfer and other transactions. I suspected the whole banking system was crooked anyway. As a kid growing up in Brooklyn, we rarely went into a bank let alone have any business being there. Frenchy had money no doubt about that. He fronted Al-Qaeda for the down payments, this time amounting to $300,000 American dollars. I was a little impressed. Our work here in Brussels was done... completed and we headed for the train station. He was happy. Maybe the service he received at the bank fueled his ego. I don't know. But he actually chatted in the cab and later on in the train ride back to Amsterdam.

"Professor, tell your associates that I require $600,000 in cash in two days' time." It didn't sound like a demand, more like something the tone you'd use to remind a kid of a chore they had to do.

"Of course. I'll deliver it myself. I wonder how much $600,000 cash weights?"

Frenchy smiled at my question. "I'm sure you can could easily carry about 12 lbs. Professor."

We arrived in Amsterdam and went our separate ways. I called Joseph from the cab and told him all went well and I needed to deliver a lot of cash to Frenchy in a few days. He didn't seem concerned with the amount and told me to come in as soon as I could. He really wanted to know more about my meeting with the Embassy guy.

When I got back to my room, I changed into my jogging clothes and went for a run, I hadn't had time this morning and I needed it. I found that running calmed me and gave me time to think. I had made photos of all the documents gathered during the three transactions in Brussels together with middlemen names and contact information. I took my cell with me on the run; couldn't take a chance of leaving it in my hotel room. I had run about three miles down the semi-crowded Amsterdam streets when I noticed that a cab had slowed and was following me. I kept running, slow jogging is more like it, and when I reached the corner and waited for a light to change green, the cab pulled up next to me. I was on high alert but when I saw that Gabe was driving, I broke into a smile.

"You moonlighting Gabe? Your regular job doesn't pay enough?"

"I have a lot of girlfriends... a lot of expenses. Hop in sir."

I got in the back. "I'm a little sweaty. You're gonna have to clean the seat up after I get out."

"Look in that bag next to you Professor, there's some clean clothes I brought for you."

I stripped off my running shorts and shirt and put on the fresh clothes while we chatted a bit. I mentioned the woman I had "made" following me. "Don't worry about her Professor, actually, she's following in the car behind us, blocking any tails we might pick up. I'm gonna have to talk with her about improving her surveillance skills. Not so good I guess if a neophyte like you can spot her."

Finally, I asked him where we were going.

"To a safe place to debrief. We won't be bothered there and you'll have time to talk. Oh, and I have a guy at your hotel keeping tabs and he'll call if anyone suspicious should come looking for you."

Gabe drove up and down, back and forth... the best way to lose a tail. I got to sit back and sightsee. We eventually left the city for the suburbs. Gabe stopped at a high black iron gate, pressed the code box combination and we drove up a tree lined roadway to a stately old mansion. He parked in the garage and we entered the house through the immense but empty kitchen. The house was as still as a church on a Monday afternoon. He led me to the library room and asked me to wait while he got Jake.

"Jake?" I was both shocked and overjoyed. I hadn't seen him since Lebanon and I was doubly delighted that he was here. First because I liked the man and second, maybe he had figured a way to get me out of all this. My life had become too complicated. I wasn't afraid of dying, well maybe a little, I was afraid I was going to screw it all up. For the most part, you already know I didn't believe in religion, ergo, I was a lousy "Muslim". I surely didn't ascribe to the nonsense that Al-Qaeda and all the other radials were preaching either. I could see myself one day getting on top of the highest mosque and broadcasting... "You're all a bunch of assholes". I needed to disappear and maybe Jake would make it happen.

I waited just a few minutes before Jake entered, alone... no Gabe. He looked the same. Urbane, erudite and confident. "Hello Paul. You're looking fit. I guess all that running around in the mountains was good for you. I understand that you have been doing some great work for us all here in Amsterdam. I always knew you'd be a treasure."

My dream of Jake making me disappear vanished in a burning flash. I already knew what was coming next.

"Sit... sit. Let's chat. We will be having a guest join us in just a little bit. But I wanted to see you first so we could talk before he came into the conversation."

This sounded ominous. "A guest? Who?"

"Someone you've already met... perhaps under difficult circumstances from what he told me. But you'll be getting important news and Paul, your future life anywhere in the world will most certainly reap the benefit of his association. It's Chuck Bowman."

"That guy's a prick Jake. How did he find out about me and you?"

"I passed your name along to Dutch Counter Intelligence and they passed it along to the Americans. The CIA didn't know who you were and why you're working with us and not them. It must have annoyed them to say the least. In any case Bowman is good at what he does and respected in a field of otherwise unscrupulous characters. Myself included of course. I asked Bowman if we could speak first before he met with us and he agreed. The Americans want you to work for them. I imagine you'll be paid well and receive other benefits, by the way, there's already half a million deposited in your name in an Israeli bank. And in case you're still concerned, that problem you had with the young woman in Beirut is "gone away" never happened, forgotten... all evidence has been completely destroyed. And don't concern yourself about Bowman asking about you and Beirut, Bowman never asked... wouldn't ask... why you were working with us."

Jake sat back and waited for me to consider all he just told me.

"I want to end this spying business Jake. I'm tired, maybe a little frightened too. Years of living a lie and the thought I could be found out at any moment have beaten me up. Actually, I was going to ask you to let me go today. Now Bowman wants me to work for him. This is "fucked up" in plain English. How can I get out of this?"

"Unfortunately, my friend, I don't think you can... at least not right now. The terrorist menace is overwhelming to the West, especially America. They are only just learning to fight them. Of course, we know how, Israel has been fighting terrorists since its birth. But someone like you, already inside Al-Qaeda, is important to them. Let me bring Mr. Bowman in and you can talk to him. Ask him what he wants from you? How much more do you need to do? You'll think of the right things to ask. Wait... I'll go and get him."

Jake left and returned with Bowman. The fat man was actually smiling when he shook my hand.

"Professor, I'm sorry I was rough on you last time we met... but my work is important and I need someone like you working for me. I want you to join us..."

"Me? I junior CIA agent? I don't think you really want someone like me. I'm not a spy. I just told Jake that I'm burned up after two years of undercover in Al-Qaeda. I'd like to get my life back if I could."

"I understand... I've seen agents like you... too much pressure, pressure that starts when you get up and stays with you all day. It's an almost impossible job. But I deal in impossibilities. You are established, accepted, someone they already trust. You already operate on a "management" level. You see things that could be vital to us. Look, I understand you want out. Just stay here in Europe a little longer and I'll get you back to Brooklyn... ok?"

"And if I don't agree?"

"Professor I really don't want to go there."

"No, go there Mr. Bowman... I have to know. I need to make my mind up. Stay or forget it. So tell me... what will happen if I refuse?"

Bowman thought a second before answering... he had a hard look and his eyes grew cold. "I will personally send you back to New York in chains. You'll be sentenced to life imprisonment in a high security Federal prison for aiding and abetting a fanatical enemy of the United States. Your grandparents and your father will be deported back to Lebanon." His tone softened. "But this doesn't have to happen. Work for us... keep doing what you're doing now. Get us the information we need and you'll be released in time and move on with some money in your pocket, a good passport and airplane ticket to where ever you want to go."

It really wasn't much of a choice so I gave in and agreed with one condition.

"Ok, fine, I'll stay and work for you. But I want Gabe and his team at my back while I'm in Europe. I trust them and Gabe especially. He knows what I need and I can always count on him."

"That's alright with me but it's Jakes call not mine. If he agrees, I want all to accept that I'm always in charge. I give the orders, just me... no debriefing without me present. If that's ok with you Jake we have a deal."

Jake answered, "I'm fine with this arrangement but I want the opportunity to hear all Paul's debriefs and if there's information Israel can use or pass on to its allies then it's a go for us too."

Reluctantly, now it seems I had a new master, the CIA.

I then debriefed about the last two days activities. Bowman couldn't hide his shock when he heard about Roy Shadow's betrayal. Apparently, he knew the guy. Shadow was a Colonel in the Quartermasters Corp. and responsible for ordering supplies for NATO. Bowman said that he had to have a ring of helpers to pull this off.

I gave them the cell phone photos for the middle men information together with the supply order details.

Bowman said it would be more than useful but he really needed to get me somewhere for a few days or even a week to do a complete debrief. I asked him what he was going to do about Shadow?

"We can't let that order get through. American soldiers will die because of it. We'll stop the shipment at its destination point so you don't get compromised. Shadow is another problem altogether."

I asked, "Are you going to kill him?"

"Yes, but first I'll find out how deep this goes and get all of the bastards and you're gonna help me."

CHAPTER 42

On my own

Gabe drove me back to my hotel but dropped me a few blocks away. On the walk over I looked hard for a tail, I couldn't uncover one, but then again, what did I know about surveillance. The streets were crowded and the weather was still warm. Lots of people out walking. I entered the hotel, my bag full of my still wet running clothes tucked under my arm and was heading for the elevator when the desk clerk called my name.

"Mr. Asoph... could I see you please?"

I walked over and he smiled and asked how my day was going while handing me three messages. I thanked him but didn't look at them until I was safely locked in my room. One was from Joseph, then Madeline, and the last from Frenchy. No messages, just that they had called.

I called Joseph first. He wanted to see me, tomorrow if possible. He already had Frenchy's money. I set it up for 10 am. Then I called Madeline. She invited me to join her and her father at their restaurant on Saturday night... he wanted to meet me. I accepted the invitation. I finished with a call to Frenchy. I arranged to meet him the next afternoon with his money. Before hanging up he told me he was going to Paris and asked if I wanted to come along and meet his French middlemen. Next week, Monday... train trip. I accepted. I was a popular guy.

The next morning, I did what I always do... run, exercise had a simple one coffee breakfast and dressed for the day. I don't read newspapers, watch news TV or concern myself with anything that I have no control over. The World does what it wants without my permission. It has no interest in me nor I, it.

I'd be meeting with Joseph at 10 and Frenchy sometime in the early afternoon. I decided to take my knife. I don't like carrying a pistol especially in Europe when the penalties are high for being caught with one. My knife would do.

I took a cab to the mosque and thought about asking the driver to wait for me. But then again, I didn't know how long I'd be with Joseph and I had no set time to meet Frenchy. I gave the cabby a nice tip and sent him on his way. Something told me I was being watched. I guessed it was one of Gabe's people so I ignored my "sixth sense".

Joseph was obviously pleased to see me back safe in Amsterdam. "Thanks be to Allah that your journey was successful and you arrived safely back."

"You were worried about me Joseph? Why? Did you think I might be in danger?"

"Claud Arnot is an evil man Paul. I never trusted him. You're to be his replacement and that will cost him millions of dollars. It seemed possible that he might kill you and give himself more time to steal our money while we looked for your replacement. Please be careful with that man."

"Of course. Now let me tell you what transpired in Brussels."

I recounted my meetings with the middlemen and the money each wanted for suppling, storing and delivering the shipment. I described the visit to Arnot's bank and the money transfers that were arranged. I finished with Arnot's invitation to accompany him to Paris on Monday to meet his French middlemen.

"Why do we tolerate this man? He's a thief and can't be trusted. I believe that once he hands this business over to us, he'll notify the authorities. We should kill him now and let me work on my own. I've already established myself here and in Brussels and only need to work France and Germany. The middlemen don't really care who they work with, they only care about the money. Oh, and I believe that he's taking money, what we call "kick-backs", from the middlemen. They can't be happy about that Joseph."

We talked at length about eliminating Arnot early. Joseph obviously was concerned about any disruptions in the European supply chain but grasped the possible outcome of Arnot's eventual betrayal and my elimination before completing the transfer.

"Paul, I trust your judgement. You bear the ultimate responsibly here so I will ask you to do what you think is the best course of action for our organization. This entire critical operation is now under your control. If you believe you can accomplish what needs to be done without Arnot's help... so be it. I will support your decision."

That's all I needed to hear. I'd do what I needed to do. But I'd take the Paris trip with Frenchy and make the contacts there first. Joseph also asked me to make contact at a particular mosque in Paris. There were brothers there planning an attack throughout the city and that plan needed objective scrutiny.

He gave me contact details for this mosque and surprisingly said, "Be careful with these brothers. I've met them and I think that they have become insane... "

Joseph called a taxi and gave me the $600,000 to bring to Frenchy. I said I'd call him when I returned from Paris and he asked me to try to join him for prayers. I promised I would.

I left his office and quickly walked to the waiting taxi. I was relieved that he supported my position on the early removal of Frenchy, but at the same time thought, *What the hell have I just done? I'm not ready to take over Europe. I barely know my way around Amsterdam.*

The cab stunk of stale cigarette smoke. I had thought there was a ban on public smoking in the Netherlands, apparently not... at least not in this taxi. I gave the driver the address of Frenchy's office building we started off. My mind was swirling with thoughts of my conversation with Joseph and the implications any decision I'd make on Frenchy, not only with Al-Qaeda but with Jake and Bowman. This was complicated. I was mentally distant and didn't react fast enough to the two men who pulled opened the taxi doors and roughly entered. One jumping in the front and the other in the back seat with me. My guy had a Sig-380 pointed at my side. The guy in the front turned and smiled.

"Good morning Professor Asoph. I believe you have a case full of dirty American money for us?"

As he spoke, my guy patted me down. He missed my knife, firmly encased in a sheath strapped to my left ankle. I had no illusions of what would happen next. I would be killed and the money in the case on floor of the taxi would go to Frenchy. Sweet plan. He'd go back to Joseph and claim I never arrived and demand another payment. I'd be dead and he'd buy more time to steal from Al-Qaeda.

I knew they wouldn't kill me in the cab, most likely someplace quiet where they could easily get rid of my body. I didn't have much time. I am a calm guy in situations like this. My mind could see how I would kill these idiots and then kill Frenchy.

"What's so funny Professor? Why are you smiling?" front seat guy asked.

I didn't answer. My plan was simple. I'd wait until the taxi made a right-hand turn and we were moved slightly to the right. I'd pull my knife with my left hand which I had practiced pulling so many times, reach across my body and push it into the throat of the guy sitting next to me. I'd then grab the driver around his neck with my left arm and stab the face of the guy up front; I'd aim for his eyes. The tricky part was reaching across my body, killing the guy next to me switching the knife to my right hand and then getting to the driver with my left arm while stabbing front seat guy with my right. It had to be beyond quick, but I knew I could do it.

It all happened just as I saw it in my mind. They were shocked. I had no trouble taking out the guy sitting next to me and actually the front seat guy made the mistake of trying to come over his seat to help this friend. He was closer. I stabbed him in his right eye. The driver was a little more difficult. He swerved the car some when the fighting began and it took me an extra second or so for me to choke him out. I wanted him alive for a bit. Somehow the cab jumped the curb on an almost empty street and I exited as it came to a slow rolling stop. The few people who saw me didn't seem to know what to do. I was focused on the driver.

"He's had a heart attack!" I yelled in English as I pulled him from the cab. His eyes opened and he looked confused. I guess I'd be confused too after what just happened. I put my knife to his throat.

"Do you want to live?" I hoped he could understand me.

"Yes."

"Do you work for Claud Arnot?"

"Yes"

"Thanks buddy, just wanted to be sure," I said as I rammed my knife up to the hilt under his chin. His eyes rolled back and he was gone. I stood, walked to the cab and retrieved the money case and just walked away. Nobody approached either me or the bleeding body on the sidewalk by the cab. I wasn't even breathing hard when I reached to corner of the block. A car pulled up driven by the woman Gabe said needed more training. She reached over and opened the passenger door for me. I got in.

"So, tell me, how's your day going?" I asked her. She dropped me off at Arnot's office building.

Frenchy's receptionist announced me. I could tell there was a pause on the other end of the line. I guess he wasn't expecting me. "Mr. Arnot said you could go right in sir."

"Thank you. Oh... you might want to hold his calls for a bit. We're going to be busy."

He was seated behind his desk. A sickening smile was plastered on his pasty face. He stood and came toward me, his hand outstretched. "Hello my friend, I see you have my money. Good, good."

I handed him the bag and sat. He returned to his desk and I thought he was going to count his money. He didn't.

"See, I told you it wouldn't be too heavy for you. You had no problem?"

"Nothing I couldn't handle. I want the information for all your middlemen... now if you please." I wasn't asking... I was demanding and he knew it.

"That's not possible Paul. I don't keep such confidential information in my office. Come in tomorrow and I'll have it for you."

I thought, *That might be true.*

"Alright. But I'll need something else then before I leave. And I know you have it here."

"Certainly, if I can provide it. What is it you need?"

"Your thumbs. That will do for now." I pulled my knife and stood. "Don't try to pull a gun from that desk or you're dead right now. Put both your hands flat on the desk. Spread your fingers. It will make the cutting easier for me."

"Please Paul, Professor... can't we talk? What have I done to you? I've helped you... cooperated. Haven't I cooperated?"

"Yes, you're been a real peach as my dear old mother use to say. Are you sure you don't have the middlemen info here? It would save us both a lot of trouble. Maybe you could take a look. Perhaps you forgot you had it here. I can wait."

"Yes... I forgot; I have a copy in my safe. Can I get it for you?"

I stood him up, walked him to his wall safe and he retrieved what I wanted.

"Sit back down," I ordered.

"You have what you asked for. Could you leave now."

I switched to English. "Naw we have a few telephone calls to make. I want you to call your middlemen in France and Germany and introduce me. And call Roy Shadow too. Tell them I'll be by to see them, very soon, that I'll be handling all our business from now on... what do you think Claud, can you handle that right now? When we're finished calling, I'll leave you to get back to work. Ok?"

Frenchy answered me in English. "I'll try, but they all might not be available."

"Put your phone on speaker so I can hear what's said. Don't screw up... I might get angry if I hear something that doesn't sound right. Ok?" I stood next to him while he placed the calls. There were no problems. A few asked questions... what did I look like, how would they know me? I told all of them I'd bring a dozen red roses to our first meeting. That actually got a laugh from them. The calls were done in less than 45 minutes. Frenchy was sweating like a pig at the end of it. I was satisfied that I wouldn't have any problems in France and Germany now.

"Are you satisfied now Paul. Can you leave? I've done as you asked. You promised that you'd leave after I made the calls." He was back to French now.

"Aw, you know what Claud, I lied. There's still something I need to do before I leave." I stuck to English. I had decided that killing him here in his office would create too many problems. His killing would wait for the proper time and place. But I was still "pissed off" that he tried to have me killed a few hours ago. I couldn't let him think he got away with that. I slashed his face, leaving a long red blood line from his jaw to his ear. He screamed. I hit him and knocked him out. *What a cry-baby*, I thought. *Now I'll have to wait till he regains consciousness*, which thankfully came in just a few minutes. He began whimpering when he realized I still stood above him, my knife dripping his blood.

"No more. For God's sakes, no more. Please, please."

"I'm leaving but I want you promise that you'll forget everything about my organization and what work you've done for it. This is very important to me. I will finish you if you forget what I just said."

"I promise, I won't."

"You won't what Claud... what will you forget?"

"That I ever did any work for Al-Qaeda and I'll forget you and everyone you work with. I promise. I'll forget."

"I know you will. Thanks for all your help buddy. Good luck in your life. I hope I never have to meet you again." And with that, I picked up the money bag, the documents and left. I'd finish him off soon.

Five minutes after Paul left, Frenchy called Roy Shadow. He was bleeding heavily but needed to make this call first.

"You bastard... the morons you sent me to take care of Asoph failed. They're probably dead. He was just here and attacked me and took my money. What are you going to do now?"

"I guess I'll kill him myself," Shadow answered.

I thought about what I did to Frenchy in the cab. *I should have killed him.*

An hour later I was safely tucked in my room. I looked at the money bag. I didn't want the money. Money was not important to me and never a temptation, but this money was blood money and I had no intention giving it back to Al-Qaeda. I'd contact Gabe. I wanted to thank him for sending his agent, it saved me cab fare; too bad she didn't arrive soon enough to help me take out those three killers. I then began to put together a plan for eliminating Frenchy. I knew he'd be quiet for the short term but eventually he'd rat me out. I'd ask Gabe to track him for a couple of days and we'd figure out the best time and place to kill him. Meantime I'd work out the details for my meeting with the French and German middlemen. I called Joseph and reported all went well and that Frenchy was still alive. He seemed relieved.

The next day I met Gabe at the "hooker's haven" in the Red Light District. He began by thanking me for keeping him on the team. He told me that Jake was pleased with the outcome of our meeting with Bowman. I handed the money bag to Gabe and filled him in on what had happened and how I came by it. I told him I will never take blood money from anyone and he and Jake would decide what should be done with it. I made copies of the middlemen info and gave him that as well. I assumed that too would wind up with Bowman, I had no intention of doing another "debrief" anytime soon with him. I asked Gabe to help track Frenchy and with my plan to kill him. He agreed that was necessary and would take care of... including the killing as well. "Consider that task off your plate Professor. This is something we're very good at."

"You're going to have to make it happen in the next few days. That punk will be signing his guts out within a week if you don't."

Gabe grew pensive. "You're changing Professor. You're not the same man I knew so long ago in Beirut."

"How so? You think I've changed Gabe?"

He thought for a second or two before answering. "Yes, I think you just don't care about anything anymore. You were always retrospective and reserved but now you seem angry. I know how difficult your life has become. It can't be anything but a nightmare at times. But this will end and you can go back to Brooklyn or wherever you decide to call your home."

"Gabe I can't ever go back to the States. I've burned my bridges there a long time ago. I was before and have become a professional killer or perhaps better stated, a murderer. I can't control it, actually I could never control my need to kill... you're my only friend and I feel comfortable with you. I want to tell you about me... I killed even before Beirut. Back in the States. Some were innocent... they didn't deserve to die but I can't change that. I'm afraid of living in any civilized society. I suppose that's why I can stand living with Al-Qaeda murders, they're like me. I know it will end with my death. I've come to accept that is the only way it can end for me." I was drained after making my spontaneous confession but in some strange way I felt better for it.

Gabe just put his arm around my shoulders and we spoke no more.

CHAPTER 43
Friends and neighbors

I spent the next few days decompressing. I read, visited a few museums and worked out in a real gym, something I hadn't done in a long time. I felt better; not necessarily better about what my life had become but better mentally, physically. I needed this little break. It was Saturday and I was meeting Madeline and her father for dinner. I liked Madeline... not in a boy-girl way, but I enjoyed her intellect and her mental strength. She was the daughter of mafia royalty. Being Rocco's "daughter" got her in, being strong kept her in.

I arrived at the restaurant a few minutes early, introduced myself to the maître de and was escorted to a private dining room. Madeline and her father were already seated and waiting. He was in his 60's, thick snow-white hair, tanned Roman face and looking at me through the lightest blue eyes I had ever seen. When he shook my hand, I could feel his physical strength. He smiled and in a pleasant voice said, "I've heard a lot about you Paul. I understand that you taught university in Beirut. How are you finding life here in Amsterdam? And thank you for joining us this evening. Please call me Rocco."

I thought, *He must have done some deep Paul Asoph research*. I had never mentioned my Beirut teaching to anyone in Amsterdam, not even to Frenchy.

I sat and he began to pour me some wine but Madeline held his hand, "He doesn't drink Papa."

"Really, well I hope he brought his appetite then. Gino, some sparkling water for our guest please."

The waiter filled all our water glasses and removed my two wine glasses from the table.

"Paul, tonight we eat as the Italians eat. Many courses... much conversation. Two or three hours sitting at the table... restroom breaks when necessary." And he laughed. I liked him.

We spoke about many things, but not our work. Rocco grew up in Sicily, lived in Salerno much of his life and enjoyed fishing. I described my boating experiences in Beirut and we had something in common from the start. Madeline contributed to the conversation but tended to defer to her father on most topics. We ate, laughed and were genuinely enjoying each other's company.

"Madeline mentioned that you had relatives living in Brooklyn."

"Yes, a cousin and his family. I understand you come from Brooklyn. Whereabouts Paul?"

"I grew up in Bay Ridge. Do you know it?"

He began to chuckle. "Of course, I know it. That's where my cousin lives. His name is Joe Gambadela... good friends with others who came from my little town in Sicily. The Lepore family comes to mind. Now don't tell me you know them."

I was shocked beyond belief. "If it's the same Lepore's... they were my next-door neighbor growing up. Franky Lepore... two kids, Marie and Little Frankie. He's a tall guy, moustache, good singer. Mrs. Lepore and my mother are best friends."

Rocco starred at me. I imagine he was thinking I was playing a joke on him.

"No really Rocco, the Lepore's were my friends... neighbors... we went to school with their kids, church, played games on the street. I'm not joking. I really know them."

Rocco got serious and said in a soft voice, "Then tell me what terrible thing happened to little Marie?"

"She was raped by a priest, Father Sullivan and I killed him."

He just sat there looking at me. "You're not lying, are you? You really killed the priest."

"Yes, I murdered him in his church. I cut his throat and was glad I did it. It was one of the reasons I left America."

"Then Paul, I'm forever in your debt. My cousin Joe told me about it... asked if there anything our "friends" in Brooklyn could do to this pig priest. You got to him before we did. Now my new friend Paul, should ever need my help I'll always help." He stood, came to where I was sitting and kissed me. There were tears in his eyes. Honestly my revelation pretty much put an end to our dinner talk. I asked him to mention that we had met when he spoke with his cousin and perhaps do me a favor.

"Please ask Joe to get word to my mother, tell my her that I'm fine and love her." I explained that it was better if my family didn't know where I was. Rocco understood.

The next day, Sunday, I made my own train reservations for France. Frenchy had made train reservations for Monday but I decided it would be better to make my own. As far as I knew he was still alive and if he knew where and when I'd be, he might just try to kill me again, especially since I took his $600,000. I'd leave Monday night, get to Paris late and spend Tuesday visiting the mosque Joseph wanted me to go to. I'd call ahead and make sure the people I needed to see were going to be available. I would contact the middlemen from my Paris hotel and see if we could meet on Wednesday. I imagined that Frenchy would no longer be among the living by then. The plan was a little "iffy" since it depended on availabilities. *Oh well, I'll get to see a little of Paris anyway*, I thought.

Sunday passed quickly; my exercise at the gym, a little reading, and a call to Madeline to thank her and her father for their hospitality the night before.

"Hello Paul, I'm so glad you called. Please wait... my Father wanted to speak with you. Please hold."

Rocco came on. "Ciao Paulo, I wanted you to know that I spoke with my cousin and he will pass on your message to your mama. He is grateful for what you have done for his friend Franco and his family. And I am grateful and in your debt. I would like to invite you to my home is Sicily when it is convenient for you. This is an open invitation my friend. Please plan to visit us. Call Madeline when you can. I would enjoy seeing and talking with you again." Rocco put Madeline back on the phone.

"I hope you can find some time to visit us Paul. I think you'd enjoy seeing my beautiful Island. Ciao for now."

I thought I'd like to visit Sicily and would try to find time. Maybe just a week away, including travel time would work. I didn't know whether Al-Qaeda gave its loyal employees vacation time but I operated on my own schedule anyway, so dropping out for a week was possible. Meeting Rocco and learning of his connection to my life growing up in Bay Ridge was in some strange way comforting.

Monday was a jumble. I packed for my trip, ate a little and met with Joseph to discuss my progress. I hadn't told him about the attempt on my life or that Frenchy didn't get his $600,000. I wonder what he'd say if he knew the money was now safely in the hands of the State of Israel.

"Professor, the brothers and sisters you will meet with in Paris are part of a very active unit. I am told that they are planning actions that will electrify the World and make them fear us. Please make sure that all they plan to do is in accord with our beliefs."

"What exactly do you want me to do when I meet with them. Am I authorized to approve their plans?"

"No... they might not even share the details with you which might be better anyway. You're there only to discuss the overall plan, make sure it fits our International goal and that they have a plan that makes sense. Our cause is being perverted by the Western Press. We are viewed as crazies, fanatics. They never credit our love for Allah and our desire to bring the World to Him."

I could already tell this meeting with the Paris cell was going to be a disaster. "Alright Joseph, I'll make sure they understand our Global objectives. Do you have any money for them? I'm sure they will be looking for some financial support."

We discussed my visit to Paris in greater detail and before I left Joseph gave me a large packet of Euros.

When I arrived at the Amsterdam train station, I made a call from a pay phone to my Mossad control. I needed to speak with my handler and when she came on, I reported where I was going, what I'd be doing and where I'd be staying in Paris. The call lasted about three minutes... I made sure most of it was cryptic and followed the protocols I had been trained in. I could never be certain someone, somewhere was listening in. She told me that I should use room service tomorrow night.

When I arrived in Paris, I took a taxi directly to my hotel. The city glowed beautifully from my cab window and I looked forward to seeing it in the morning.

"Are you from Marseilles?" my taxi driver asked.

"No... do I sound like I'm from Marseilles?"

He laughed. "Excuse me sir but your French makes you sound like a gangster from Marseilles."

We both laughed. I wasn't insulted, actually I was pleased to hear I sounded French.

My hotel was pleasant and centrally located in the heart of the city. I had a very nice room, a suite actually and after unpacking I called my contact at the mosque to let them know I had arrived and was ready to meet my "friends". I was given the name and location of a Middle Eastern restaurant and asked to be there at 6 pm tomorrow. The next day would be a busy one. I had Wednesday meetings planned with my middle men, including a banker that Joseph had arranged for me to meet and most importantly, the Al-Qaeda brothers at 6. I finished a quick workout, showered and went to bed. My last thought before sleep was, *Is Frenchy dead yet?*

Tuesday went well enough, no problems with the French middlemen I had rescheduled two of my Wednesday meetings without a problem. When I met with the supply and warehouse middlemen, they all more or less told me that they didn't particularly care for Frenchy and that they didn't trust him. They enjoyed the bouquet of roses I brought along with me too. The banker on the other hand was a little weasel. It was a quick meeting. I felt uncomfortable speaking with him. He obviously hated doing business with us and set down a long list of "rules" for future transactions at his bank. Joseph told me Al-Qaeda, under another name of course, had deposited two million dollars with this bank. I signed papers allowing me to control the account. The bankers name was Paul Ambrose and he and his bank would be prominent on my report to Bowman.

I was a little tired when I reached the restaurant about fifteen minutes early. It looked fashionable from the outside and inside was tastefully decorated. I was a little surprised. Somehow, I thought it would be a hole in the wall joint since my "brother jihadists" were its owners. Go figure. I gave my name to the young lady at the door and she said I was expected. She led me to a table in the back away from most of the dinners. There was already a mid-size crowd... they did a good business by the looks of it, especially since it was a Tuesday and most Europeans don't dine until 8 or later.

I was brought some Syrian bread and a bottle of sparkling water while I waited for someone to join me. I read the menu. Looked good, dishes from all over Middle eastern countries were represented. I could understand why this was a popular restaurant.

In about five minutes I was joined by a large overweight man, dressed in kitchen whites and looking Arab... maybe Egyptian. He had a pleasant face, big moustache and wide grin. The kind of face and demeanor most people would immediately take a like to. He sat down, breathed a sigh of weariness, and gave me a huge, toothy smile.

"As-salamu alaykum my brother and welcome to my humble establishment." He spoke in an Arabic that sounded Syrian to me.

"My name here in France is Oscar and my brother is now called Lucas. We are its proud owners. I know who you are my brother and your renown precedes you." I held a finger to my lips and looked around to be sure that no one was listening. I thought, *Oscar feels very safe here*. I didn't. He understood my gesture and seemed chagrined. He then asked me normal questions like how was my trip, was this my first time in Paris, what did I want to eat tonight?

I responded by being as friendly as Oscar. I complimented his restaurant and its menu and asked him to order for me... but keep it light. I then suggested that we meet somewhere more private to talk and he apologized that was not possible tonight. We set up a meeting for Wednesday, early afternoon. He would have someone come and pick me up outside my hotel around 1pm if that was alright. I only had a morning middleman meeting and told him that 1pm would work, I'd be outside the hotel waiting. My meal came and Oscar left me to enjoy it. I left a large tip for my server, tips in Europe generally are small if even given at all.

Back in my hotel room I called room service and ordered coffee and some munchies. I had some old pot which I smoked out on the balcony before I ordered. Fifteen minutes later my order arrived delivered by Gabe of course. He smelled the pot and laughed.

"Bad habits from Beirut Professor?"

"Gabe this is my only bad habit if you don't count killing people. How's Frenchy?"

"Ah, suffering in Hell I imagine. Or maybe he made peace with his God and is playing a French horn somewhere in Heaven's suburbs."

"How did you take him out?"

"Easy, we called him and told him his doctor wanted a nurse from his office to examine his 22 stitches and would be at his apartment in a little bit. He baulked but finally agreed. My "nurse" arrived and told him he needed a shot of antibiotics. Two minutes after she gave him the shot his heart stopped. Frenchy is gone, gone, gone. Do you think you'll have any problems because he's dead?"

"I don't think so. I met with most of his contacts and they didn't seem to care whether they dealt with me or him. So, I think I'm ok. If any of them should ask me about him I'll just tell them he had a bad heart. That should satisfy them. Now let me give you an update."

I reported on my meetings with the French middlemen, and my quick meeting with Oscar, the leader of the Paris Al-Qaeda cell and the follow up meeting planned for tomorrow.

"Professor that could be dangerous for you. You don't know them and they don't know you. There could be a problem. I'll have you watched. Is that alright?"

"Ok... but Oscar, the guy I met, seemed to know my reputation and was friendly. But we need to know as much as possible about these guys... so have your watcher note license plates, where they take me and anything that might be interesting to Bowman. You still report to Bowman now, right?"

Gabe hesitated. "Well... he gets the reports that I give to Jake, so I guess you could say I report to him indirectly. Professor, I suspect he is watching you here as well as we are. But I don't know that for sure. Do you need a weapon?"

Gabe held out a new .45 and handed it to me. I wasn't sure I would need it but took it anyway. I checked the chamber and removed the clip; it was ready to go. I had my knife and that always seemed to be enough for me. I'd go armed tomorrow.

CHAPTER 44
A little surprise.

Roy Shadow actually liked the new plan for him to personally take out Asoph. He was a full colonel in the Quartermaster Corps, but had seen combat Afghanistan. He hated these motherfucker jihadists and enjoyed killing them. He decided to use his sniper rifle. Arnot had told him where Asoph would be staying in Paris but Shadow decided he'd use one of his contacts to watch the train station just in case Asoph changed his original itinerary. And it paid off. Asoph arrived later than scheduled and his guy followed him to a hotel other than the one Arnot had told him. *Smart of Asoph*, Shadow thought. It didn't matter. Asoph knew Paris well and this asshole wouldn't get away.

I had my meeting with the transportation middleman and spent another 30 euros on a bouquet of roses. Like the other two I met with yesterday, this guy actually seemed glad that Frenchy was out of the picture. I got back to my hotel early and had time for a quick lunch and to pick up my knife and .45 for my meeting with Oscar and his brother. The .45 is a big bulky weapon and I had a little difficulty getting it situated so it wouldn't be too obvious. But it felt good having it and I'm glad Gabe gave it to me. I stood outside the hotel and searched for my watcher. Whoever Gabe sent to track me was good. I couldn't find them and I really looked carefully. I thought, *Maybe they aren't there.*

An expensive and new MB sedan pulled up exactly at 1. It was driven by a young good-looking woman, fashionably dressed. She was the receptionist from the restaurant.

"Get in please," she said to me in Arabic through the rolled down passenger side window.

I got into the car and decided to speak English first. "Thank you for picking me up."

She looked at me like I was a little crazy. "Of course I picked you up. What did you think?" I'm sure she was thinking.

"Yes, of course my brother. I am honored to take you to our headquarters," she answered in perfect English.

We quickly pulled away and drove off in the direction of the river.

Ray Shadow followed, but not too closely. He constantly checked his mirrors to make sure he was the only one following Asoph. His sniper rifle lay on the back seat... fully loaded and ready for use.

We didn't speak during the drive. She drove very well in the crazy Parisian traffic. She headed for the warehouse district and we stopped about 20 minutes later in front of a one-story building. It looked like every other building on this deserted block. This lady did not practice "spy-craft"... no zigging and zagging though the crowed Paris streets.

"We're here. Please go through that door while I park the car out of sight. They're waiting for you inside," she instructed me.

I felt a little uneasy going into the building alone for some reason. Maybe not uneasy exactly, but very cautious. I opened the door and was glad to see that the space was well lite. It was a large warehouse; mostly empty space and I immediately saw the six men standing by a long table... some were smoking and talking but all conversation stopped and they turned in my direction when I opened the door and entered.

My first impression was that five of them were Middle-Eastern and the tallest one was an Anglo. I saw automatic rifles laid out on the table and at least two of them had holstered side weapons. There were military type crates stacked in plain sight and I imagined they contained munitions or maybe more weapons.

These guys are ready for a war, I thought.

"Hello my brother. Please come and join us," called Oscar. "These are my trusted comrades and this is my brother Lucas. We've been waiting for you." He came to me and kissed my checks in the Arab fashion. Taking me by the arm he walked me to the table. "My brothers... Allah has sent us the famous fighter Snake. Our fearless brother who humiliated the Americans during a prisoner exchange in Afghanistan."

Roy Shadow found a place to park. It was mostly out of sight, semi-hidden by a large building. He saw Asoph enter the warehouse before he had parked. The streets in this district were deserted. He left his car and looked for a good sniper position. He immediately found what he was looking for. It was an abandoned water tower.

He returned to his car, cased his rifle and walked back to the water tower. It rose about ten stories in height with a staircase leading to a platform that he would use as his shooting position.

Oscar introduced me to each of his men. The Anglo was from Belgium and didn't speak Arabic. I believe the European jihadist were more fanatical then the ones I had met in the Middle-Eastern countries and these guys eyes burned with a fervent passion as Oscar laid out their plan for attack. The receptionist had returned and she was introduced as Oscar's brother Oliver's daughter. They all had phony names anyway and I quickly forgot them after we were introduced.

"Snake our plan is simple. Our goal is to strike fear in the hearts of these European infidels."

Oscar went on and on with the propaganda bull for ten minutes. He evidently had watched too many Al-Qaeda YouTube videos. I nodded agreement with the rest and gave the appropriate Allah Akbar when they shouted approval. It still amazed me that a beautiful religion like Muslimism had become so perverted in the hearts and minds of these fanatics.

"Our targets include two separate but simultaneous attacks. The Jews in Paris will be punished for their blasphemy. There is a Jew movie theater that plays a film that dishonors the Prophet. We have warned them to end showing it but they have ignored us... now they will die along with all the infidels in attendance. The second attack will be against a Jew restaurant. We will not kill all inside but many will die the rest held hostage. When the police and television people arrive, we will blow up the restaurant and kill them all and martyr our brothers and our sister who gave their lives for Allah's glory."

He then described the plan logistics which honestly was simple. He would lead three men into the movie theater attack and his brother Oliver, his daughter and the Belgium would attack the restaurant. They would use automatic rifles and hand grenades at the theater and the same type weapons, plus C-2, would be used at the restaurant. They would time their attacks to coincide with the largest number of patrons regularly in place at both locations. None of them expected to survive. But if they should, there was a plan to move them to a safe location in Belgium.

They showed me the target building layout plans. They had photos in great detail of interiors, the surrounding streets and pictures of the two Jewish theater owners who were almost always in attendance at the showing of "The Life of the Prophet". There were area street maps, marked with police, fire and hospital locations. The described how other members of their cell would ensure traffic jams wherever possible to impeded response times.

Our "official" meeting ended with a prayer. I had really nothing to add to their plan, I had wished them success and spouted gibberish about how by their great sacrifice the World would now recognize the strength of our beliefs and now know that they were not safe from Allah's vengeance of their sinful actions against innocent Muslims. I took Joseph's money from my pocket and handed the envelope to Oscar.

"My brother... please accept this small token of our love and respect for you and these noble brothers and our sister. Your great sacrifice will be eternally rewarded. Perhaps this small gift from our leaders may help your beloved families though the impossible times facing them after your heroic action against our enemies."

Actually, I had thought to keep the money. These guys would be dead anyway and I'd give it to Gabe. But there was a chance that Joseph might discover that Oscar and his nut group didn't get his gift. I didn't want to take that chance so I handed Oscar the envelope.

There were tears in Oscar's eyes as he opened the envelope stuffed with Euros.

"Thank you Snake for this generous gift. I will see that it is distributed among the families of all here. Allah Akbar. Miriam, please bring the car to the front. Drive our brother Snake back to his hotel."

I needed to alert Gabe immediately. They didn't mention an attack time just that they would be doing it in the next few days. I wondered if my cover would be blown when they were captured. Oh well, I knew it would end sometime but this attack was not going to happen. I would see it stopped and be happy to go live in Israel or someplace warm. I gave each of my new brothers a farewell kiss thinking, "You bastards will rot in Hell." Hopefully soon.

I walked out the door to the waiting car and my head exploded in a blinding white light.

Roy Shadow watched the door open and the girl exit. He was ready. He would take a head shot. He was about 600 yards from his target. An easy shot. The gusting wind was his only concern. There was Asoph coming out, centered in his sights. Squeeze the trigger. "Got him!" blood and brains flying. Shadow quickly cased his weapon and climbed down the iron water tower stairs. He drove away smiling. He'd call Arnot later, but first he'd buy himself a victory scotch.

The bullet trajectory was almost perfect. A strong wind gust pushed it two inches off center target and saved Paul Asoph's life.

CHAPTER 45

Lost in La La Land

"Why is my Grandfather calling me? His mouth is moving but I can't hear what he's saying. My sister is running. My Father is yelling. I can't hear them. Am I in trouble? My head hurts. I can't move. Why can't I move?"

"He's waking. Here Snake. Wet your lips. You'll be fine. Praise Allah."

I drifted in and out of whatever new nightmare my brain conjured up. I remember waking and someone giving me water. How long this went on I didn't know. I felt pain... real head pain every time I became conscience. I welcomed oblivion and the darkness when it returned.

My eyes opened. I stared at a man... a doctor... white coat. He was smiling at me. I didn't feel like smiling back at him. I tried to speak but nothing came out. "Don't try to speak sir. Take your time, here, a little water. Ah, that's good, now rest."

I fell back into La La Land. It was dark in the room when I woke again. I could tell I was in a hospital. I was hurt, probably hurt bad by the intense pain in my head. I had trouble moving my hand but I was finally able to touch the heavy bandages that wrapped my aching head. *What happened to me?* I thought. I remembered the warehouse meeting... I remembered leaving the building and then nothing. *I think I was shot! Shot in my head. But I'm still alive. That's strange. Who shot me?* I thought and then drifted off.

My eyes opened part way. It hurt to open them. There was someone sitting next to me. I think he was a doctor.

I spoke in French. "Hello Doctor. Where am I?"

"Good, good... you can speak. I was worried. You're in my hospital my friend. You've been shot... in your head. I thought we had lost you. Can you move your arms and legs for me please?"

I made my limbs move... not much but I could move them.

"Perfect. Do you remember your name?"

"Paul Asoph."

"Good... tell me what you remember about your injury. But don't strain yourself."

I told him all I could remember. I was thirsty and he gave me some water. I noticed that I was connected to an IV and my butt hurt. My eyes were fully opened by now.

"I thought I was shot in my head but my butt hurts. Why is that Doctor?"

He laughed. "I did a skin graft to cover your head wound. So now you're a true 'butt-head' Mr. Asoph."

That struck me funny too and I laughed with him. "How bad am I?"

"Hmm... well you were much worse when you came in. You had lost a significant amount of blood and a small piece of your skull. I added a silver plate to cover your missing bone and stopped the bleeding. Your brain functions are alright. So with rest, you'll be fine. That's enough for now. You need to sleep. I'll be back."

When I woke again Joseph was sitting there with me. "How are you feeling Professor?"

"I'm good. A little out of it but good. I met with the cell. Did they complete their attack?"

"Praise Allah... they did. They sent 168 infidels to Satan and shown the World our strength and vengeance. They are now with Allah in their final glory. We owe you great thanks for your work. I have been told you are needed elsewhere. But I will explain all that when you are stronger... please rest. You will stay here and rest, gain back your strength and be ready to serve our cause. I will return tomorrow and tell you what you have been selected for. Rest now."

"Joseph... who shot me?"

"I don't know yet but I'm looking in to it."

He left me there feeling like I was a complete loser now knowing that I had failed. I knew that getting shot prevented me from sounding the alarm but I felt guilt none the less. I realized I was changing. Before nothing really mattered to me. I didn't care who was hurt, killed or who won this "War on Terror". It was all the same to me, but now I was mad. Mad at the bastard who shot me whoever that was. Mad at the Boss who put me in the hospital, mad at Jake, mad at Bowman who both used me. At this moment, lying in this bed I hated them all and I would get revenge for what they had done to me.

CHAPTER 46
Vengeance

The nurse tucking my pillow looked familiar. She smiled. "Hello Professor, I'm a friend of Gabriel. How are you feeling?"

I recognized the Mossad agent who had given me the ride after I killed the three guys Frenchy sent to kill me.

"Hello nurse... did you give Frenchy his shot? I hope you're not here to give me one too, are you?" I smiled and she smiled back.

"No... never you. Sorry, I can't discuss my previous assignment but I know how to give injections if that's what you're asking. I don't have long to stay with you but Gabe wanted to find out how you were, so he sent me. How are you feeling?"

"I'm not great but feeling better. How did you find me and how did you get in here?"

"We followed Oscar's son who went to your hotel and removed your clothes and papers. He brought them here. I came in through the front door, no one stopped me. I told them I was a private duty nurse assigned to you and they let me come in. They may check so I can't stay long. Do you have anything to report to Gabe?"

I quickly told her all I could remember since I last met with Gabe. It wasn't much. "I'm sorry that I couldn't pass on the theater and restaurant attack information. How is it being handled?"

"Not well... every European Counter Intelligence Agency and the CIA are trying to put the pieces together. Your information may help...

unfortunately late but still useful. I'll see that Gabe gets it as soon as I leave here. Do you know how long they plan to keep you here?"

"Weeks, months.... I don't know yet. Do you know who shot me?"

She hesitated. "Yes, it was the American colonel... Ray Shadow. I saw him as he drove away after he had shot you. I was your follower that afternoon but lost you... I had a small car accident and was delayed. It was only luck that I reached you... unfortunately it was after you had been shot. They took you away in a van... to here, I guess. You were being helped and there was nothing I could do so I followed Shadow. We traced his rental car and I believe Bowman took action, but I don't know that for certain."

I thought about that. It made sense... so Frenchy got his vengeance from the grave and Shadow probably is out of the picture by now. I hoped he wasn't. I wanted to see him again.

"Where am I exactly? I know it's a hospital. Am I still in France?"

"Yes... you're still in France... in a private hospital run by friends of Al-Qaeda. I have to leave now and I'll try to get back soon. Please rest. You've been through a lot from what I read in your chart."

An hour later my doctor came in to check on me. "You're doing better sir."

"How long will I need to be here?" I asked.

"Perhaps a week more... but maybe longer. I will have you up and walking first and we'll see how that goes. Do you need anything? Books, television, telephone?"

"Sure, thanks. But I really want some "Learn Italian" language material. Can you find that for me?"

He checked my wound and left. A little later Joseph came in. We chatted a bit... small talk really and then he gave me the big "news".

"Professor our fortunes are failing. Please don't upset yourself when I tell you this... but our brave brothers and sisters fighting in Iraq are being overwhelmed in Fallujah and Ramadi by the heretic Shia army. Perhaps even as we speak, they have may have been defeated. Many of us are now joining a new movement whose goal is to quickly restore the Califate. The West calls us Islamic State or sometimes ISIS. When you are ready there is an important place for you waiting. Many of our leaders know of your work and loyalty and have requested you join them in this new army of Allah. We need foreign recruits... especially from here in Europe and perhaps even America as well. You have proven yourself time and again and they would hope that you would continue to work for the new cause and bring more soldiers to Allah."

I told Joseph that I wanted to think about it and get my health back before making a decision. I would have told him to go fuck himself, take the two million that I controlled in the Paris bank and head out into the great unknown. But something nagged at me, more like tore me up. Hate. It was "Beyond Hate". I hated these guys, I hated everyone who screwed up my otherwise screwed up life even more. Any kind of passion about anything was new to me and somehow, I liked it. I welcomed hate, the fire burning bright and hot in my belly. All I wanted to do was get revenge. On Al-Qaeda, the CIA, Mossad... and maybe these "new jihadist fanatics"... ISIS or whatever the hell they called it. I needed to think and lying in this bed with half a head would give me all the time I needed.

A few days later my Mossad nurse arrived smiling and chipper. "How are you doing today Professor? Feeling any better?"

I began my campaign to unsettle the Mossad and CIA... misinformation.

I smiled at her and tried to look as pensive as I could with a head wrapped in bandages. "I was thinking and remembered a few things."

She got serious. "Oh... what did you remember Professor?"

"It's a cloudy memory but I recall the asshole Oscar guy talking about some cell in Belgium planning a WMD attack on Tel Aviv. He said that their original plan was delayed because the CIA got wind of something coming. Oscar said, "but the Jews will still be punished."

"When did he tell you this? In the warehouse?"

"Yes, in the warehouse. He was giving us a Rah-Rah speech and it came out then. Did your people know about it? Did Bowman pass on the intel?"

She was obviously shaken. I knew she'd report back to Gabe and there would be more questions coming for me. But I had begun to sow seeds of doubt between the two "cooperating" allied agencies. I knew I couldn't take either of them down. I couldn't kill anyone. So the next best thing was getting them at each other's throats and chase their tails. My plan was to feed everyone I hated false information. I knew I was in a position to be believed and I'd take advantage of it.

Over the next two weeks I walked, talked and watched TV and learned to speak bad Italian. My head stopped hurting but the wound was itchy. I was even able to handle some limited exercise. The doctor removed the heavy bandage wrap and left me with just the long line of an ugly blood red scar.

When Joseph returned, I told him I would join this new Jihad. He was pleased and we would meet back in Amsterdam to discuss it more detail. He said tell my doctor to call him when I was ready to leave and he'd have a car pick me up and take me back to Amsterdam.

It was a week later that I was ready to get out of the hospital. They brought in my clothes, passports and other items from my hotel, I dressed... my clothes were a little big on me. I met with the doctor in his office.

"Your driver is waiting outside. You did well Mr. Asoph. I would suggest that you avoid any potential head problems such as fist fighting for a while." He was smiling when he said this. He reached into his desk and retrieved my knife and pistol and handed them to me across his desk.

"Do you have any documents here such as my medical records Doctor? If you do, I'd like to take them with me. I want no documentation on my treatment to remain."

"Nor do we. Here is all we have. You might want to keep it and it might be important for another physician to review should you ever have any injury problems."

I folded the file and put it into my jacket pocket. I held up my knife and reached across his desk and grabbed him by his necktie pulling his face close to my knife tip.

"I won't kill you because you saved my life. But I need to leave you so you can never identify me Doctor."

I blinded him. I was not going to leave this man able to ever treat another wounded jihadist.

I left to his loud screams that brought staff running to his office. My ride was waiting outside and I climbed into the plush front seat. It was the "gone to Allah" Oliver's daughter new MB he was driving. I was going to have a comfortable ride back to Amsterdam. I slept most of the way.

I had the driver let me out in midtown and hailed a taxi. I didn't want anyone to know where I was staying. I found a discrete, nontouristy hotel off the beaten path and checked in. I had cash... not a lot but enough. I'd get more later when I met with Joseph. I left the hotel and found a place to buy a throw-away cell phone. I activated it and called Madeline. She seemed happy to hear my voice.

"Now where have you been hiding? Are you available anytime soon for another meal with my Father and I? We both enjoyed your company... and I'd like to see you again Paul."

"Of course." I was available and asked if tonight was too soon. It wasn't and I'd meet them at their restaurant at 8.

I found a pay phone and checked in with Mossad. I told them I was back in Amsterdam and asked for a meeting with Gabe. They gave me a secure telephone number and told me to call in two hours. Gabe would be waiting.

"Hello Gabe."

"Where are you Professor? I was worried. The nurse went to the hospital and you were gone. It seems you created quite a bit of chaos... was all that really necessary?"

"I'd say what I did was prudent, therefore necessary. When and where can we meet Gabe? But it would have to be the day after tomorrow. I'm seeing Joseph tomorrow and I don't know what might happen to my available time the rest of the day. And oh... I have big news for you."

We set up a time and place... not the Red Light District but close. A "hooker" would approach me at a particular street corner and I'd appear to go to a hotel with her where Gabe would be waiting.

Gabe asked me where I was staying but I wouldn't give my hotel name and I could tell he was a bit concerned.

"Professor you might need watching. That Ray Shadow guy slipped Bowman and could be here in Amsterdam. Please let me put a watcher on you. It would make us all feel better."

I refused again but told him we'd talk about when we met. I didn't want anyone tailing me and discovering that I was meeting with Madeline and Rocco. I had a plan and they would be part of it if they were willing. Gabe wasn't happy but we left it at that and hung up.

I bought some jogging clothes and shoes on the way back to the hotel. I had been sitting on my ass way too long and I needed to run.

I took a taxi to the restaurant and was immediately taken to Rocco's private dining room. Madeline looked great. She's not the fashion model type, more like a Playboy Centerfold, but she knew how to dress. They both stood and seemed genuinely happy to see me. I greeted them in bad Italian and they seemed amused. They asked about my obvious head wound and but not how I got it. Rocco ordered for us, noting I was "skinny" and needed some good Sicilian food. Now and then I try out my Italian and they corrected me but said my pronunciation wasn't all that bad. When they spoke their "fast" Italian I only got words here and there but this is how I always learned a new language.

After an hour of eating and casual conversation Rocco got serious.

"Tell me truthfully Paul, why are you a fucking terrorist?"

"I'm not. I was a once a teacher who did something very wrong and got blackmailed into joining these assholes. I'm what you might call a "counter-spy" who hates the people I'm forced to spy on. I've been at this for a few years and have never hurt any innocent Westerners... I've killed jihadists, freaks and other lowlifes along the way. But I'm not a terrorist."

He seemed to accept what I had said and asked no more questions.

"Rocco, I have a favor to ask of you."

"Perhaps... what is it?"

"I need a new identity. Passport, papers whatever. I want to break out of the box I'm in and go live the rest of my life without looking over my shoulder waiting for a bullet. Can you help me?"

"What do you want to become... French, Spanish, Syrian... but not Italian, not yet anyway. You don't speak Italian well enough."

He and Madeline laughed at his little joke.

I had given this some thought. "French-Moroccan... I speak good French and Arabic and look a little Arabic... nobody knows too much about Morocco anyway so I could pass easily."

Rocco quickly answered. "Consider it done. I will need to have passport pictures and some family information to create your documentation story. We'll pick some out of the way place in Morocco for your family origin and you can do your own research. How does that sound?"

"It sounds perfect. Could you make me a sailor too? I know a little about boats."

We would meet at Rocco's office the next morning for my passport pictures and to begin developing my new identity documentation. I asked him to have his lawyer around; there was something else I planned to do and it would require some legal work. He seemed intrigued but asked no questions.

Early the next morning I ran. Not as long a run as usual, but it was a long-awaited start and jogging again felt good. When I reached Rocco's office the photographer was waiting. Madeline applied some makeup to cover my scar and I posed for the photos open shirted. I wanted to have that "sailor look". My beard was neatly trimmed and my pictures came out looking good.

I sat with Madeline and we created a cover story for my new Moroccan life. She would have "family photos" made for me to carry... two sisters and a mother and father. We picked my "home" location in a small village somewhere in the mountains and I'd do my research. She said she'd find other personal items for me to carry in the event someone challenged my origin. All would be ready in about a week.

"Rocco, I want you to control some money for me."

"What do you mean Paul? Control money... I don't understand."

"I have two million under my control at a bank in Paris. I want you or Madeline to have power of attorney to move the money, pay my expenses... whatever comes up while I'm away. Do you think your lawyer could prepare the necessary papers?"

I trusted him and he agreed. The lawyer took my bank details and prepared the necessary paperwork for signature. Both Rocco and Madeline singed and I felt much better when I left them.

I reached the mosque and entered Joseph's office building. He was waiting for me in the otter office and we walked back to the secure meeting room.

"Tea?"

"Yes, thank you."

"How are you now?"

"Almost my old self."

"Why did you blind the doctor?"

That was from out of nowhere but I was prepared.

"I didn't trust him Joseph. He asked me too many questions. I could have killed him but he got my message should he ever think about talking to anyone. Perhaps I should have gotten your permission... I apologize if I did something wrong."

Joseph sighed. "What's done is done. I have much to tell you."

I sipped my tea as he spoke.

"Claud Arnot is dead... it appears he had a bad heart. Perhaps your attack on him caused it but no matter; he would be gone from us in any case. Now concerning who attempted to kill you... we believe it was the CIA seeking vengeance for your humiliation of the American Army in Afghanistan."

"That makes sense but it means I'm now known and perhaps useless here in Europe."

"Possibly... possibly not. It remains to be seen. There was some discussion that the attacker worked for Arnot. He wanted to continue working in our efforts and saw you as someone he needed to remove. He earned considerable money from us you know... motivation enough for him to kill you."

I never told Joseph about the three guys that attacked me, now was a good time. I gave him all the details and told him I suspected Arnot as the source of the attack. These guys weren't just street thugs but paid by Arnot to kill me. I told him that was the main reason I cut Arnot the last time I met with him. Joseph bought it. He was now completely convinced that Frenchy was behind the shooter who hit me.

"That makes perfect sense Professor. If it had been the CIA our brothers would have been attacked or at least arrested at the warehouse. So there's no need to worry that you're compromised here in Europe."

"Joseph, I want to do more for our cause. If joining our new brothers fighting under the Islamic State flag will allow me that privilege then you know I will. But why is their goal of creating a Caliphate different from our goal of removing the Crusaders and Zionists from our lands?"

"Their objectives are basically the same as ours. We are now attempting to unite our forces but they will not accept our leader as Calif... perhaps in time they will. They know of your good work and loyalty and wish you to continue recruiting jihadists here in Europe. But first they've asked that you leave for Syria and meet with their leaders in Raqqa for more instructions and learn more about their goals. There may be occasions where you will fight side by side with them before you return here. Is that acceptable? "

"Of course. But I am not familiar with all the active cells here in Europe. Could you provide detailed information on each country's current organization and perhaps the names of their leaders. That will make my future work much more productive. When I return, I could visit each of the cells and gain knowledge and support in my recruitment efforts."

"I wish that I could. But many of them are unknown to me. We never had organized rosters and most of the cell leaders are reluctant to provide such sensitive member information. I could give you the names of many cell leaders and in some instances, tell you how you could make contact with others.

Perhaps when you meet with them, they will be able to help you further."

Joseph gave me pen and paper and then asked me to prepare a cell leader list... he had no written document and all he recounted was strictly from memory. I copied down all he told me. It was a start and I was glad to have even this minimal information. He then gave me the names of each of the ISIS leaders and the ones I needed to meet in Raqqa. He said he would try to find more information for me when we next met.

"Thank you, Joseph, this will be a help and real aide in my future recruitment work. Oh, I was wondering about the Belgium in Oscar's cell. He seemed somewhat out of place. Who was he? Did you know him?"

"I didn't know him but he was recruited as their explosives expert from a cell in Belgium. His name was George Krauss and the leader of his cell is Carl Kruger. I'm sure they will help you when you call on them. It's a very active cell, experts with explosives, and has long standing ties with our French brothers and many links with other cells too. I have some contact telephone numbers for you. I'm glad you mentioned that."

We continued discussing my future recruitment efforts and Joseph added more detailed information about the ISIS leaders I would be meeting in Syria. The information he supplied was a treasure trove. I'd use it to destroy the Al-Qaeda organization here in Europe and help delay ISIS recruitment and advancement in Iraq and Syria. I took a cell phone photo of the page I had written and then destroyed it.

I told him I would be leaving for Istanbul in about a week. This is where he would have someone move me onto Raqqa and the ISIS

Caliphate capitol in Syria. It would be a long and dangerous journey and honestly, I wasn't looking forward to it at all.

Since this was to be my last face to face meeting with Joseph so I requested and received $10,000 expense funds before I left. I thanked him and we prayed together for success in my new mission.

The next day I waited at the appointed street corner for my "hooker" pickup to arrive. Surprisingly she was my nurse friend from France, seductively dressed to look the part. I'm not a guy easily aroused by sexy women but if I didn't already know why she was there I may have acted on my jumping hormones. We had a pretend negotiation in English and she took me by the hand and walked me to a seedy hotel a block distant where Gabe waited.

"Gabe it's good to see you. Oh, and I like your agent... she almost convinced me we were actually coming here for sex."

"She only likes girls so you're out of luck this time. That scar looks nasty Professor. Are you ok?"

"I'm fine. Actually, I think the scar will make me look more interesting when it heals. What do you think? Can I get work in the movies?"

"Maybe selling tickets."

There was no rushed meeting today. We both knew we might not meet in a longtime or maybe never so we reminisced, about Beirut and our adventures over the years. Gabe was really the only person in my life that I genuinely thought of as a real friend. He made tea and had some pot for me to smoke. Eventually we got down to business. I returned the .45 pistol he had given me. I'd never get it through airport security where I was going.

"Jake was concerned about your report of a possible WMD attack on Tel Aviv. Do you remember anything else Professor?"

"Gabe, I told you it was only a vague recollection. Something Oscar just said in passing. Just that the CIA prevented it from happening for the time being. I really can't remember much beyond that. Sorry."

"Jake plans to meet with Bowman and I'm sure this will come up. Now, how was your meeting with your friend Joseph? Did he give you some combat bonus money, a Purple Heart?"

I then recounted my visit and presented the information gathered during my meeting with Joseph. Gabe copied my Al-Qaeda cell phone data and seemed impressed but concerned with my decision to become a jihadist with ISIS.

"Gabe you can tell Bowman that the cell in Belgium may be planning an attack on NATO. They specialize in making bombs... also my guy Joseph is going to join them so he should be taken out by the Dutch Counter-Intelligence as soon as possible. He controls Al-Qaeda money in Europe and taking him now would be a double whammy. But wait a week or so until I leave for Istanbul. He's making all the arrangements for me to join ISIS in Raqqa, the hometown of the Caliphate in Syria."

"Alright Professor, but you probably don't understand how evil and vicious these ISIS thugs are. Al-Qaeda was bad but these guys are ten times worse. They seem to enjoy killing and will kill anyone and everyone they meet. Jake thinks they do it to make sure the World understands that nothing matters to them and they will do the most horrible things imaginable to reach their goal of creating a Caliphate. Now you're going into the heart of that inferno... you may not come out. Even if you survive, you'll never be the same. Just being part of that shit will change you forever. Do you really want to go?"

I laughed. "I'm not crazy Gabe.... No... I don't want to go to Raqqa and become part of ISIS. But I feel I have too. I want them destroyed just like Al-Qaeda and I have a mission to be a part of their destruction. I'm no hero... I'm not patriotic, I just hate these bastards. Does that make any sense?"

"I guess. But I think you're a hero Professor. God willing you survive."

"Now what's happening with Ray Shadow. Did Bowman find him yet?"

"I don't think so but I'm sure Jake will find out when he meets Bowman. Bowman's having problems holding his job by the way. We heard Washington is not happy that a big shot traitor in charge of supplying NATO went under the radar all these years. Now if Jake passes on that a European cell was planning to attack Tel Aviv and he didn't share the intelligence; I think he'll be put out to pasture."

I thought, *If Bowman goes... the CIA network in Europe will be screwed for a long time.*

"Gabe before I go, I have a favor to ask. I know your agency is holding some money... paychecks... whatever, for me. Could you get that money back to my family in Brooklyn if I don't make it?"

"Of course. But I know you'll be back. Now how do you plan to communicate from the 'Belly of the Beast' in Syria? You won't have access to a phone that's secure. Have you figured that out yet?"

"Like always Gabe, I'll play it by ear when I get there. What's the most critical information you need to know about ISIS?"

"Hmm... troop movements, planning, where are when the leadership is going someplace new. Civilian attitude... you'll know what's important when you see it."

Our meeting ended with a bit of sadness. I already knew I wasn't coming back. I had a plan to drop out completely... no more Mossad, CIA, Al-Qaeda... and going to Raqqa and ISIS would get me out. I would "die" in Syria and then use Rocco's new ID to go far far away from this life.

A day later I met with Madeline. She had called to let me know all my new ID's were ready. We met at her office. As usual, she looked great.

"Look these documents over Paul. I think you'll be surprised to see how well we did with creating your new identity. The passport is a genuine issue from Morocco. The family photos and other letters will pass any inspection and your Seaman's ID is real and done with the help of my Father's people."

I noticed that the Passport had entry stamps from a variety of different countries. I had a letter from my "Moroccan mother" and a love letter from a beautiful girl along with her picture. There was even Moroccan money in the package.

"This is a great job Madeline... I can't thank you and your father enough." She was pleased that I was pleased. "I want you to know I'll be leaving for Turkey in a few days and I might not see you for a long time. Who knows, when I get back, maybe I'll be able to take you up on the offer to visit Sicily. I'll keep practicing my Italian."

I made my flight and hotel reservations for Istanbul and called Joseph with the details. He said he'd have someone meet me at my hotel and gave me a phone number for his Turkish contact. I was to call when I got settled in. I asked him how I would get into Syria.

"Most likely by car. It will be a very long journey but it's the safest way... most European recruits take this journey and our transportation people are very capable."

When I hung up, I figured this was the last time I'd be speaking with Joseph. I felt a little depressed... I was burning all my bridges in Europe. First Gabe, then Madeline and now Joseph. I didn't really care about him and wouldn't miss him, but down deep I knew Joseph was a good guy... just screwed up in his Muslim beliefs. Maybe a few years locked up somewhere would cure him. Probably not.

CHAPTER 47

Bowman and Shadow

Bowman was "old-school" CIA, a genuine dinosaur. He grew up learning his trade during the cold war. He was part of Hollywood's romanticized "agent on agent" fighting it out on the dark streets of a divided Berlin. Bowman smiled as he reminisced his early years as an agent... *I never wore a cloak but I sure used a dagger a few times,* he thought.

He accepted that the Agency now depended more on electronics than it did on its agents on the ground. "But didn't I prove myself again with my on-ground agents? That Asoph kid brought in a treasure trove of information no satellite could match. Didn't he tell us first to look for bin-Laden in Pakistan while we were spinning our wheels playing hid and seek with the asshole in Afghanistan's caves. Didn't he give us impossible intel on Al-Qaeda? Now Asoph had passed on intel for at least 60% of the Al-Qaeda cells in Europe. So why are these bastards in Washington looking to give me the boot?"

He knew why... Colonel Ray Shadow.

He tried to adjust his bulky frame into a more comfortable position. *Not gonna happen. I gotta lose some weight,* Bowman thought. He pulled his sniper rifle up and sighted the hillside cottage for the thousandth time. The sun had been up for over an hour so Shadow would be coming out soon. He'd be ready.

Montenegro had no extradition treaty with the US. It was a NATO member and Ray Shadow had been there many times over the years. He liked it. Nice people, good beaches, beautiful countryside, high mountains and at the end of the World to most tourists. He had created a new identity years before and set up part time residence in his pretty little house on the hillside overlooking a white sandy beach. He was safe and secure in Montenegro. Bowman had little trouble tracing him.

Shadow put the morning coffee on to boil, opened the cottage door, did some warm up exercises and started his morning run.

What the hell is that doing there? he thought, noticing the gaily wrapped small box lying at the end of his walkway.

He stopped, picked it up, and opened it. Inside was a single piece of paper. "Fuck you Shadow!" it said. The high caliber rifle bullet struck him square between his eyes and he was dead even before the message registered in his brain.

CHAPTER 48
The beginning of the end

My mind kept playing an old song, popular long before my time. Something like "I wanna go back to old Constantinople... you can't go back... dah dah de dah... why did they change the name... it's was the idea of the Turks." Crazy. I was landing in Istanbul Turkey.

I was at flying at least five thousand feet above Istanbul, this beautiful and historic city, and I was thinking about a dopey song probably written 100 years ago. My thoughts went back to my high school teachers talking about the ancient Greeks... the Hellespont, Sea of Marmora, Dardanelles... ancient battles. The Byzantine Empire... fall of Constantinople to the Turks. La da de la de dah. I imagine letting my mind wander, thinking about nothing was better than thinking about the fate that may await me with ISIS.

We landed and I whisked through Customs using my Lebanese passport. I mostly used it in lieu of my American because I didn't want to leave any trail for the CIA, State Department... FBI or whomever might be interested in tracking me. It probably didn't matter anyway. Bowman told me that he would make sure my name didn't appear on any "watch list" but I thought the opposite.

I taxied to my hotel, checked in... changed into my running outfit and took off. The streets were crowded and semi-exotic. I enjoyed the colors, smells and hearing a foreign language I didn't understand. This was a vibrant city and I immediately liked it. Once again, I got some strange looks from people who were not use to seeing "runners" on their streets. I stopped at a currency exchange and converted some of my Euros. I found a pay phone that was working and checked in with my Mossad handlers. This might be the last time I could... we'd have to wait and see.

When I returned to the hotel there was a telephone message waiting. It was from my Al-Qaeda contact; the guy Joseph had arranged to call me. I showered first and then returned the call. A woman answered in Lebanese Arabic.

"Greetings sir. Welcome to Istanbul. I hope you had a pleasant flight," she said.

"Why yes I did thank you. I am happy to be in your beautiful city and looking forward to meeting you and your colleagues. Do you have a travel plan for me?"

"Yes, of course. If it suits your schedule, my associate is ready to help you begin your tour as early as tomorrow morning. Would that be convenient for you sir?"

I noticed that she kept our conversation somewhat cryptic. If anyone was listening... it might sound like she was a travel agent speaking with a tourist.

"I think that would be excellent. Perhaps I could meet them in my hotel lobby around 10 tomorrow morning?"

"Yes, that would work. My associate will be in your lobby at 10 am. He will wait for you at the reception desk. He is a young man and his name is Tarad. One of our very best drivers. He will give you a wonderful tour of our city. If there's nothing else then, please enjoy your stay."

I was set... for what I didn't know. I'd find out in the morning. For now, I'd get a good night's sleep and hope for the best.

Tarad was young... probably about twenty years old, tall and good looking. I took him for a Syrian. He recognized me immediately and stood quietly as I checked out of my room. He grabbed my bag and we left. He drove an old MB in good condition and I sat up front with him.

"Allah Akbar Snake... please relax, we have a long drive ahead... but it won't be unpleasant. The roads here are very good and the traffic will not be a problem. We will stop for fuel and food along the way. There is a weapon in the glove box if you want it."

I opened the glove box and removed a Glock 23... it's a .40 automatic which I had used before in my training. I think I liked it better than my old favorite, the .45 Colt. It was lighter and smaller. I checked the magazine and chambered a round. I shoved it into my belt and wondered if we had to cross any check point where they might search me and the car. I asked Tarad about that and he said not to worry, we'd be fine if we were stopped anywhere along the way. He said that we were going through some dangerous country and we needed to be armed. No one would question why we had weapons. That was good enough for me.

"So Tarad, do you transport many foreign jihadists?"

"Oh yes... they come from all over the world, but I usually drive as part of a convoy. We always wait until we have ten or more to transport and take two or three vehicles." He laughed. "Not a MB like today... just pickup trucks. But you are, as the Americans say, a VIP. So, my brother Snake, you get special transportation."

That made me laugh, a VIP... "Do you see many Americans Tarad?"

"Some, but mostly I drive Russians, Chinese, and Saudis... our brothers come from many places. Having proclaimed the Caliphate has set our cause on fire. Every jihadist in the World wants to be part of the last battle and be in the Caliphate when it happens."

I had listened to this BS so many times before so I just shut up for the next hour. I really had no idea where we going and it didn't really matter at all to me. "It is what it is." As my old Brooklyn mother would say. I wondered what she and grandpa are doing right now?' Did they miss me?

We stopped for gas a few times and something to eat. It still amazed me how many countries now had Kentucky Fried Chicken and MacDonald's franchises. The food they served was pretty much like back home. But sometimes the side dishes were different... rice being one of them. We talked some... mostly he still spouted the jihadist BS but I learned he was from Syria and had lost everything including his family to the incessant civilian bombings. He didn't know if they were killed by the Russian, American or Syrian air force. The guy hated all of them.

"How long until we reach Raqqa?"

"Sorry but I will not be driving you all the way Snake. I was instructed to take you to a location on the Turkish-Syrian border where a brother waits who will take you on to Raqqa. The transfer point is about an hour or two down this road. I can never drive all the way in anymore... the bombings and enemy ground forces have taken much of our territory and also control the roads. I would not know the best way into Raqqa since it changes all the time."

I thought, *The Islamic State is on its death bed and I'm visiting the grave site.*

In time, Tarad left the main highway and took a dirt road that seemed to go on and on. Past deserted farms, bombed houses and just desolate space, empty of life. The fight had obviously come to this part of Turkey too. Maybe the Turks were ridding the land of Kurds, maybe young inexperience bomber pilots emptied their plane's ordinance here rather than taking their deadly cargo back to where they took off. It didn't matter. This was war and no one was ever really safe.

We finally stopped at a bombed-out hamlet. All the houses and shops were empty, many in varying stages of decay. This had been a little way station village for a farming community now abandoned. We ate the rest of our KFC chicken and Tarad fell asleep in the shelter of one of the wrecks of a shop of some sort. I walked around and took in the destruction. It was dark when we heard the sound of an approaching car engine.

The Humvee rolled in without headlights on. It stopped and the driver shut off the engine. I could hear the tick tick of the engine cooling. The driver just sat and waited. Tarad and I drew our weapons and slowly approached. Tarad whispered, "It's our brother... he's just waiting for me to call with the password... Death to all Apostates," he shouted.

The driver's door opened and a gaunt figure stepped out. He was dressed all in black and I couldn't see his face, but he saw mine.

"Snake... Snake my brother. Say hello to your old comrade... The Wolf."

CHAPTER 49
Raqqa

Considering what I expected... seeing Wolf again was a very pleasant surprise. I didn't consider him to be a friend but he was close. I knew him... kinda liked him, maybe pitied was more how I felt about him. We had trained together at the palace in Pakistan and then I ran into him again in Afghanistan. He had been seriously wounded by then and I could tell he was used up as far as any fighting went. I was surprised he was still among the living after all this time.

"Hello Wolf my brother and comrade... I'm glad to see you again. Have you come to take me to Raqqa?" We spoke in English. That seemed strange in a way... aside from speaking with Gabe, I hadn't used English all that much for a long while. "Are you hungry? We have some fried chicken."

Tarad stood listening... English was not something he understood so I explained my former relationship with the Wolf in Arabic. He smiled, glad that he was turning me over to someone I knew and trusted.

"Give the Wolf something to eat Tarad. I'm sure he's hungry."

Tarad had built a small camp fire and we all sat while the Wolf ate. Tarad wanted to know how the battle was going in Raqqa but since the Wolf only spoke rudimentary Arabic, so I acted as the go between interpreter.

"Not well my brothers... daily bombing attacks all day long and the Syrian and Kurd armies come closer each day. Many of our brothers have fallen," the Wolf sadly recounted.

I thought, *Why in the hell am I going to Raqqa? The city would fall and I'd really be killed in the fighting. I have to think about continuing.*

We slept for a few hours and then got ready to leave. I bid farewell to Tarad and thanked him for his help in getting me here. He seemed like a good kid, maybe he'd survive. He had a full five-gallon gas can in his trunk which he gave it to Wolf who then topped off his Humvee before we left. We had to make Raqqa on whatever gas he had. He said that it would be close. There were no friendly stops anywhere along the way.

"What's going on with you since I saw you in Afghanistan Wolf?"

He thought a bit before answering me. "I've seen too much Snake. I'm close to going crazy. I'm done, I want to go home. Sorry, I shouldn't have said that... I could get killed for saying that."

"Why? What have you seen? Were you wounded again?"

"No, not wounded, but I guess you could say my soul has been destroyed. These Islamic State leaders are crazy. Can I talk to you Snake? You wouldn't turn me in... would you?"

"Wolf, are you on drugs?" I asked him this in a serious way. Wolf looked like he was on something... he was a physical mess. Gaunt, sunken eyes... 100-yard stare. This guy was at his wits end. But could I really trust him?

"I'd never talk about anything you said to me Wolf.... What are you using... heroin, crack meth... what?"

"Anything I can get... most of us are using something. If you're caught, they execute you."

"Do you have anything with you?" I wanted to be sure he was serious and not just setting me up for something.

"Yes, I do... do you want some?"

"No... just pull over and show me what you have. I want to see it before we talk some more. Ok?"

Wolf pulled over and showed me his drugs. "I understand why you asked me that Snake. Nobody here trusts anyone."

"Thanks for understanding Wolf... I didn't want to offend you, if I did... I'm sorry. I just had to be certain of what you said. Now tell me about the leaders you mentioned."

"They are mostly displaced Iraqi Baathist officers from Saddam Hussein's old army. Bakr al Baghdadi, our new Caliph, made them leaders in all the Caliphate Provinces. Some he made Princes. These guys like to kill people. I've seen them take ordinary people off the street and have them executed in front of their families for no reason. They captured the few Christians left in the Caliphate and crucified them. You can get beaten or worse for just looking strange and any Shia they find are killed on the spot for being Apostates. I'm not a coward. I came to fight for Islam. I didn't come here for this. It's wrong and I have to find a way to leave. Can you help me Snake?"

I had heard much of this before. "What do you want me to do Wolf? How do you think I can help you? I'm caught in the same web... I really don't want to be here myself. Perhaps we can work together and come up with a way to leave. Do we have to go to Raqqa now? Maybe we can turn around and go back to Istanbul."

"We don't have enough fuel and I don't have any passport and other documents. I could hoard fuel back in Raqqa and we could make our escape then. I think I could be ready in about a week. What do you think?"

I thought about it for a few moments. "Ok... we go as soon as you've stashed enough fuel to get us over the Syrian border. I have money so that won't be a problem. Now promise me you'll stay of the drugs until we get out of Raqqa."

I could tell Wolf was instantly relieved. But then he dropped the bombshell.

"Snake I need to warn you. The Boss is in Raqqa."

"Really... when did you see him?"

"All the time. He's in charge of routing out Shia and leads a detachment of fanatics just like him. He rides around and takes any women he finds off the streets and he and his animals' rape and kill them. No one cares, he does what he wants. The leaders praise him... they say he's doing Allah's work. If he sees you Snake, he will kill you. Remember, we leave in a week... just be careful. He knows you're alive and coming to Raqqa. He'll be looking for you."

"Well now Wolf, I'll be looking for him. I owe him something... do you know where he is? I'd like to pay him a visit. Say hello, talk about old times." I could feel a new energy flooding over me... like the times I killed without reason. A minute before I was depressed about the way things were going. Now I felt alive, a tingling in my gut. I had a mission. I'd find and kill that pig before I left Raqqa.

"I know where to find him," Wolf answered.

Raqqa was on fire and vomiting black smoke into the clear blue sky filled with aircraft, each strafing and bombing at will. The city was in its death throes. I began to think... "Raqqa won't last a week... if we were leaving, it would have to sooner."

"Wolf I think we'll have to leave as soon as we can. Raqqa is ready to fall. Can you get extra fuel today and we can leave sooner?"

"I know it looks bad be we'll be fine if we don't get crushed in some falling building. The Syrian and Kurd troops are 50 miles away. They're cowards. They know that there will be house to house fighting if they enter the city and they want the fighter bombers to soften us up first. We'll be fine for the next few days."

"What are you orders concerning me? Who am I to see?"

Wolf smiled... "We just drove by headquarters... that big building that was bombed and burning. That's where I was ordered to leave you. So, I don't know what I'm supposed to do with you now."

"Ok... then take me to where the Boss lives. Can we make it there?"

"I don't know but I can try. We may have to leave the Humvee and walk a bit. Depends on what streets are open for traffic. Are you alright with that?"

We drove down the bombed-out streets making detour after detour. Eventually Wolf was able to get us within a block of the Boss' shelter. He parked within the overhanging debris of a destroyed business and we walked through the empty streets. It was growing dark and suddenly very quiet. The planes had left for now. I had my Glock handy and Wolf carried an AK.

"There it is. They all live in the cellar of that building. They park their trucks over there. I don't think anyone is there... what do you want to do?"

"I want to go in and wait for him."

Wolf smiled. "You are a crazy fucker Snake. What do we do when they come back?"

"I say hello and then I kill him."

We entered the darken bombed out building and found our way to a door leading to cellar stairs. There was a faint light coming from below along with the sounds of women crying. We followed it down and entered what was a dormitory of sorts... bunk beds, tables... some

AKs stacked against the wall and assorted dirty men's clothes strewn about. It stunk of sweat, blood and excrement. There were three naked young women chained to the far wall. Their bodies showed signs of beatings and they were terrified when they saw us enter this hell hole.

I spoke to them in Arabic. "Be not afraid children. We mean you no harm. We will help you escape from here shortly." This seemed to calm them. Wolf found some of their clothes in a pile and gave them to dress as best they could. We also found a box loaded with C2 and detonators. I was in a rage. If I never wanted to kill the Boss before, I did now. Long ago memories of my young neighbor, Mary Lepore, and her rape by that devil priest flooded back.

"When they return you and I will kill all his men... but don't shoot him. I have a plan for him and I don't want him dead just yet. See if you can find a key to unlock the women's chains. I want to get them out of here."

Wolf found the chain lock key... in plain sight on the messy table. He set them free, they finished dressing and hurriedly left us to a chorus of "Thank you'... May Allah bless you," Now we waited. I picked up an AK, made sure it was fully loaded and ready to go.

"Wolf let's get over there... in the shadows... how many men does he usually have with him?"

"I've only seen three others when he comes out on the streets. There may be more... but there's only four bunks here... so four altogether I guess."

"Good... should be easy then... are you going to be alright Wolf. I mean... can you still kill?"

"I can kill this scum. It might even make me feel better," he laughed at that and so did I.

When they returned, they made a lot of noise. We heard them come through the front door and start down the stairs. Only one guy made it down while the others were still upstairs loudly talking. The guy coming down held a sobbing woman by her hair. I knew what to do... I pulled my knife and rushed him before he realized what was happening. I held his mouth shut and buried my knife all the way into his throat. His blood gushed all over me as I lowered his dead body to the floor. The woman screamed and I could hear the upstairs guys laughing "Abdul must have already started." Wolf grabbed the woman and moved her away.

The three started down the stairs and I didn't wait to shoot. I didn't care at that point if I took Boss down. My blood was up and I wanted to kill. My steam of AK rounds ripped through them and they all fell on the stairs. I rushed up looking for the Boss. He was the last to come down and was only hit in his leg and shoulder. I hadn't killed him... yet. The other two were dead. A full clip from an AK will do that to you every time. I kicked each of them hard just to be sure. I pushed the bodies out of my way and dragged the Boss by his hair down the stairs into the cellar.

The Boss was conscience and moaning. I slapped his face and his bloodshot eyes opened and he saw me again for the first time in years. "Hello Fool... do you remember me? It's your old recruit... Snake. I hope you're happy to see me again. I know I'm overjoyed to see you my old instructor."

I turned to the shaken woman and told her to leave. She wasted no time getting away, gingerly stepping over the corpses on the stairway.

"Wolf let's chain him up to the wall." We roughly pulled him over to the place on the wall where the young girls had been held captive and fastened the heavy chains to his hands and feet. He was fully conscience now and recognized the Wolf and I.

"Fuck you fools... you will both be beheaded when I report this... I am a servant of Allah. I have performed His sacred duties and you have attacked Allah when you attacked me." His wounds were not fatal and he knew it. I thought, *He's not going to plead for his life like I wanted.*

"I think you'll be able to give your complaint to Allah in person Boss. Tell him I said hello when you see Him. Oh, and I don't think you'll get those 72 virgins... we're not going to make you a martyr. You've already had your quota of virgins in this cellar you pig bastard."

He began to yell for help... maybe he thought someone would hear. I punched him hard in the face. Blood poured from his broken nose. He spat at me and missed. I walked to the table and opened the box of C2 explosives. All recruits at my training camp in Afghanistan had been taught to handle C2.

That was training everyone paid close attention to as I remember. The plastique had timed detonators which I remembered how to set.

"Wolf, do me a favor and get those three dead piglets and put them close to their momma. I want them all to hold hands when they fly to Paradise."

I set the timer for ten minutes and put the box of explosives where Boss could see the minutes clock down. When Wolf had arranged the others around Boss, I started the timer.

"We have to leave you now Boss. Don't forget to write and tell us how your trip went. Come on Wolf... let's leave these soon to be flying pigs."

As we started up the stairs, he began cursing us in his native language which I didn't understand. He was still screaming as we opened the door onto the empty street. The air-raid sirens suddenly started wailing as Wolf and I ran to the Humvee.

"Well... that's luck. Boss and his friends will go up when the bombs begin to hit. If anyone cares, I think that they'll believe a bomb hit his building."

We found a basement to wait out the bombing. Wolf was excited. "I didn't get to kill any of the pigs Snake... you should have given me a chance." He was laughing as he said it. I think he was happy he didn't have to use his AK.

"Sorry about that buddy. Now where the hell do we go now? Who do I report to?"

The bombing ended and we got back into the Humvee. "I'll drive around, maybe we can find someone who knows what's happening. If not, I'll take you back to the hole I am living in."

We drove up and down streets cluttered with debris. After a bit Wolf gave up. We hadn't seen anyone and I wasn't surprised. The entire population, or what was left of it was hunkered down. Wolf was able to get us to his "hole" and he parked the Humvee in a relatively safe semi-bombed out garage. I grabbed my pack and the AK and we walked the block to Wolf's lair. We entered the building that was once a school and headed for the basement. I was tired and would crash as soon as I could. There were a few foreign jihadists in their bunks and no one even acknowledged our entry. They couldn't care less... they were alive and nothing mattered to them.

"Is there anything left to eat?" Wolf shouted.

One of the men lying on the floor raised his hand and pointed toward a portable cook stove. Wolf walked over and fixed us each a plate of cold mystery food from the large beat-up pot sitting there. I was hungry and had no problem eating whatever it was. I found an empty bunk and immediately fell asleep. I made sure my Glock was close by.

I don't know how long I slept but I felt like shit when I woke. Itchy too... there were bed bugs living in the blankets and they'd found me. There were more men here now, about fifteen, strewn around the cellar bunker, some sleeping, some talking quietly and one stirring the pot on the stove. Wolf was gone. I scratched my bites for a few minutes before getting up and stretching. My whole body ached. I think I was getting something. I felt hot and certain I had a fever. I picked up my Glock and belted it. I found a Lister bag hanging from the ceiling and I poured myself some warm water. It didn't help make me feel any better. I went back to my bunk and lay down and closed my eyes. I must have slept because Wolf was standing over me and shaking my shoulder.

"Snake, Snake... are you alright?"

"What? I'm ok... what time is it? I must have gone back to sleep."

"It's early... you want something to eat?"

"No... maybe a little water. Thanks Wolf."

I sat up. Down here in this smelly dank cellar there was no day or night... just like a dirty subway station back in Brooklyn, only worse. I drank warm water from the steel cup he handed me and thought about my killing the boss. It felt very very good thinking about that and it helped me forget my totally aching body for a second or two.

"I think I'm getting sick Wolf. You have any aspirins? Anything for body aches?"

"I'll get you what we have... we all had what you have Snake... in a few days you'll be fine. Hang on. I'll be right back."

He brought me some pills. I had no idea what they were but honestly, I didn't care. I took them and lay back down and fell asleep again.

Was I dreaming? Someone was screaming for me to wake up. "What?"

"Get up and pay attention," someone shouted.

I sat up and looked around. All the men in the room were standing at semi-attention and I somehow got myself to my feet. There was a tall guy, probably in charge, telling us to get ready.

"We have an important duty to perform today my brothers. Now, everyone outside," he shouted.

I felt a little better and followed the men up the stairs into the street. On the way out, someone handed me a black jump suit to put on and I stripped and did as I was told. I left my bug-ridden clothes outside the building and caught up with the small troop in a few minutes. Wolf returned to my side and told me to follow orders or else I'd be shot on the spot. We marched about half a mile to an open area. It had been cleared of debris and there were a hundred or more men, prisoners actually, in orange jump suits, some sitting on the ground others standings waiting dejectedly. They already knew that they were to be killed, here in the bombed-out city on this otherwise beautiful day.

There were a large group of guards... laughing and tautening the prisoners. A video camera was set up and there were the ubiquitous ISIS Black Banners flying in full array. It was obvious that they were going to video tape the execution of these captives and I realized that I would be part of it.

"Attention my foreign brothers. Today you will have the honor of dispatching this miserable group of Apostates, Crusaders and blasphemers.... I will select the chosen ten who will then choose one of these scum and parade them in front of the camera you see there. On my command they will remove their heads for all to see and know the vengeance and commitment of our foreign jihadists. No hoods concealing your faces today. Be proud of what you will do... the World will know that our cause is just and accepted by all Muslim countries and they will be proud of their faithful warrior sons who have joined us in our holy mission for the glory of Allah."

All B.S., I thought. *I hope they don't pick me. This is pure evil and murder. I don't want to be a part of this.*

Of course, I was one of the ten picked. A smiling idiot handed me a long, ugly serrated knife and we were marched to the assembled prisoners who understood what was going to happen. To their credit, some of them shouted curses at us... others wanted to die fighting and ran at the guards and were immediately gunned down. I looked at their faces, some showed resignation... I'd have to pick one of them... most had only pure hate in their eyes. I grabbed an old guy whose head was down and he went without a struggle. I was weak and glad he didn't fight me. I walked in the line of ten and we stopped at the designated sport for the camera. Our "brave leader" gave the usual speech and signaled us to begin the cutting. I did my guy quickly and hopefully without too much pain. I didn't cut off his head, just let him fall to the ground and bleed out. In a minute our fearless jihadists began killing the rest of the prisoners. I now knew why Wolf was crazy... this was evil insanity and I had become part of it. An air raid began and we all ran for cover. *Fucking cowards that we were*, I thought.

With Wolf's help, I was able to make it back to our cellar. My buggy clothes were where I had left them and Wolf picked them up for me. He gave me some more pills and I threw myself on my bunk. Let the bed bugs bite. I just didn't care anymore.

I must have gone into a coma. I only remember Wolf lifting me and placing me in the Humvee; I was totally gone. Awake... asleep... I vaguely remember driving very fast and for a long time, I think. I'd wake and someone would give me a sip of water. I know I peed myself many times.

When I finally woke... and was aware of my surroundings, I have to admit I was surprised. I was in a bed with clean sheets in an air-conditioned room. I thought Wolf had gotten me to a hospital. But it was a ship's sick bay. Wolf had left dying Raqqa with me and all the other "rats" and we were able to reach the Syrian port of Banias. There was a Container ship waiting for us foreign jihadists. It had been chartered by a Saudi Prince and was bound for Mindanao in the Philippines. It seems that ISIS wanted to start a new Caliphate in South East Asia and we would eventually arrive somewhere in the Philippines to join some active insurgency there.

The ship's doctor told me that I was still a very sick man but in time I would be fine. I had an IV stuck in my arm for weeks and not too much of an appetite. But I was clean and comfortable. Wolf visited me every day and I thanked him for all he had done for me. He told me most of the jihadists escaped into Turkey or went to Iraq and Damascus. Others wanted to join the insurgency taking place in the Philippines with the hope that a new Caliphate would be formed. Wolf just wanted to get out of Raqqa, ISIS and the Middle East and a free ride to the end of the World was his choice.

In time I felt well enough to leave my hospital bed and bunk with Wolf. He truly was a changed man. Fed up with jihad... disgusted by ISIS atrocities and ready to jump ship at the first chance. He had taken my pack and I had all my passports including the new one, so I felt I had a good chance of leaving the Philippines without too much trouble. I didn't know how I could help Wolf... he had lost his passport a year ago and he knew he'd have a real problem getting in and leaving any country without proper papers. I still had most of the money Joseph had given me and I told him we'd find a way to get him out. I enjoyed the voyage. I spent a lot of time on deck and I tried to lean as much as I could about seamanship from the friendly crew... mostly Muslim Asians. There were 112 foreign jihadists on board. We ate and slept well and the Captain was friendly. He was a Saudi and in the employ of one of the Royals. He admired foreign fighters and did all he could to make us comfortable. I had gained back some of the weight I had lost and even begun a bit of daily deck exercise.

Our ship was carrying containers to be delivered to the city of Davao in the Philippines. The trip was over 4,600 nautical miles and would take 65 days to reach our destination. Our passage papers were legitimate and the Captain told me that we'd have no problem while at sea. He was concerned with our little detour to the Sulu Sea and landing us close to the city of Marawi.

I was the jihadist "golden boy" on board this ship and everyone wanted to know the Snake. Think about it, my terrorist resume was impressive. I was a very well-educated foreign fighter, a university professor no less, who joined Al-Qaeda. I had studied with the famous and respected Mullah Abdu and had protected the most sacred Mohammad al-Amin Mosque, killing barehanded three Crusaders who were attempting to deface it. I humiliated the American military during a prisoner exchange. I had survived rigorous training in both Pakistan and Afghanistan. I had recruited jihadists in Europe. I had participated in the most successful attack in Paris. I had been seriously wounded in fighting for the cause. I had joined the Islamic State and executed an Apostate for the entire World to see.

Of course, if they knew I was also an undercover agent for both the Mossad and CIA they wouldn't have hesitated a second to kill me and throw my body overboard as shark bait. Crazy life so far.

CHAPTER 50
Marawi

The Captain announced that we would be arriving at Marawi, our final destination in two days. He told us to pack up and get our weapons ready; there might be fighting when we landed on the beach and he told us he would sail away as soon as we left the ship and off-loaded supplies for the insurgents.

I thought. "My God, this will be just like D Day."

There was a bonus for me... the Captain had a fake Philippines passport stamp showing Manila as my original entry point. I asked him to stamp my three passports. I had planned to leave the Philippines as soon as I could and I didn't want to try to explain that I showed no "arrival stamp" on my passport. Problem solved.

We were all excited about finally going ashore. It had been a long voyage. I enjoyed it. I got well, had some mental recovery time and got to know Wolf better. He had stopped using and his health and appearance showed it. I owed him big time for taking care of me and saving me at Raqqa. I hopped I could repay him for kindness.

Like most Americans I had no idea there were Filipino Muslims. But the whole end of the Mindanao was a Muslim enclave and had been for centuries. From what I read, if the Spanish hadn't arrived in the 1500s all of the Philippines would have become another Muslim country in Southeast Asia, like Malaya and Indonesia. The insurrection that was now taking place happened because the local insurgences had pledged allegiance to the Islamic State and apparently this enclave became the best location for forming a "new" Caliphate.

The leadership here was a family affair. The Maute brothers, their mother and father were running it. Actually, they had been fighting the Philippines Government for years. Their Southern section of Mindanao was almost its own country. The fighting had been heating up and it was just a question of time before the Central Government took serious action and regained control. The Filipino Army was well trained, well equipped and ready to fight. We were told the American Airforce would actively assist and provide logistical support which included gunships and drones. My small group of 112 foreign jihadists was joining the horde of foreign fighters already there or now gushing in.

The Captain couldn't dock so he dropped anchor about two miles offshore. He was worried about the Filipino and Australian gun boats that patrolled the area looking to stop foreign troublemakers like us. We took our gear and climbed into our assigned life boats cum landing craft and were dropped into a very calm sea. The boats had powerful engines and we were on the beach... fully alert in thirty minutes or so. There were plenty of supplies on board the ship for the insurgents so the boats made three round trips to offload us and the cargo. I watched as they hoisted the last life boat back onto the ship and saw the anchor chain lift. The darkened ship left almost immediately and was quickly out of sight. It got very quiet on that beach. Nobody spoke much or lite up a smoke either. Someone suggested we post a guard until our brothers arrived and Wolf and I volunteered and found our way into the thick jungle that began where the beach ended. It was hot and humid. I hate that kind of heat. We stood there in the dark, swatting mosquitoes and flies for over an hour before we heard the sound of distant truck engines.

"Wolf you hear that?"

"Yes... sounds like a truck convoy. I hope it's our brothers and not the Filipino Army."

"Let's stay hidden until we know for sure. If it's the Army, we'll try to get away and hide out somewhere." I didn't want to spend years in a Filipino prison dancing the Macarena for a YouTube video.

It was our Filipino Brothers and we greeted them with obvious relief. All helped loading the supplies onto ten box trucks.... Obviously, the supplies were more important than we were. There was still room for about 30 of us on the half dozen pickups that had come with the truck convoy. Wolf and I made it out on the last one. The convoy followed a dirt track for about five miles before we entered a paved road that led into Marawi. The Sun was rising and this little city looked pretty good to me. It shone white in the early morning sun light and there was a sweet perfume fragrance in the air.

Our convoy ended at a large warehouse near the bay. I counted 40 or 50 men and boys who were already waiting to off-load the box truck cargo and store it away. The Captain had told me it was mostly Chinese weapons, ammunition and basic field supplies. They seemed genuinely overjoyed as they worked and we received a lot of handshakes, backslaps and smiles from them. None of us offered any assistance. We just stood around and watched.

It was 7 o'clock already getting hot and the humidity was building. The Filipino's spoke Tagalog or some local dialect that I couldn't understand. I knew English was a second language in the Philippines and almost everyone had some understanding of it. I was glad of that because Tagalog or whatever they were speaking had no linguistic basis in any language I knew. I did hear the occasional Spanish word incorporated into their language during the 300-year Spanish rule. As soon as a truck was emptied, it left for the beach and our remaining foreign jihadists. The pickups had already left so it wouldn't be long before our little army was fully assembled. I think the local leadership was waiting for all of us to be in here, in one place before giving us our orders. There was hot coffee, bottled water and some food waiting for us on tree shaded tables and a few women handling its distribution. They were all dressed in keeping with the strict Sharia law of this region.

Wolf and I got in line and thanked the smiling women for their kindness. The coffee wasn't too bad. Maxwell House instant, I think. I accepted a large bowl of hot meat and vegetable odds and ends mixed in with rice. It tasted very good, but maybe because I was hungry. In a while all 112 of us were assembled. We had no real leader and we just ambled around waiting for somebody to tell us what to do.

In time a man whom I took to be one of the Maute brothers, got on a bull horn and greeted us. First there was a prayer of thanksgiving for our safe arrival. He was joined by what I took at the time was the rest of his family. He handed the bullhorn to his mother and she seemed like the real brains of the outfit. She gave a fiery speech about how the Muslims of this country had always suffered under the oppression of the Spanish, the Americans and now the Government of the Philippines. Honestly, I began to get restless standing there in the hot sun. After about 45 minutes of this BS she handed the bullhorn back to her son. He told us we would be billeted with a Muslim family and there would be regular prayers held in the central mosque each day and we were expected to attend. He reminded us that we were now under strict Sharia law and no infraction would be tolerated. He told us there were Christians living in Marawi and they were not to be harmed. This came as a surprise.

Some of his men now came among us and in English, Arabic and Chinese gave out our billeting assignments. Wolf and I were to live in separate homes and I was singled out by one of the Maute brothers. He wanted me to stay with a prominent local Muslim family and walked me over to their home. He introduced me and they greeted me in broken English. There was a mother, father and a teen age son... Aya was the kid's name.

"There is a very important assignment for you Snake, but I want you to know this family first before I give it to you," he said. His English was pretty good.

That's a little cryptic, I thought.

I must admit I enjoyed my time with this family. The son was seventeen and full of energy. He and I did a lot of motorcycling around town in in the countryside. This was a strict Muslim household and we prayed a lot. The mother's cooking was good and I put on a few more pounds. They didn't really speak much English and relied on the kid, Aya, to interrupt for them. I sensed a prevailing sadness in this home but didn't know why.

We trained for war daily. More fighters assembled and I know that were at least 3,000 jihadists now waiting to begin the battle to take over the Province. Each day we could see Government drones and helicopters circling the city. Some of them were clearly American. There was no attempt to shoot them down and our fighters were given strict orders not to engage any Government troops they might encounter during their regular patrols outside Marawi. The city was being fortified, tunnels were dug from house to house, sand bags filled and supplies were cached throughout in hidden locations. I spoke with Wolf each day and he seemed happy. He liked the family he was with and told me this was the kind of war he had committed to.

After a month or so I had settled in and almost forgotten about my "special assignment", the Maute brother had mentioned when I first arrived. One evening, after prayers, I was summed to headquarters. The Maute family along with most of the other leaders were waiting.

"How do you find your stay with us Snake? Are you learning our language?"

I laughed; I had made very little progress learning their language. "My time here with you has been good. But my progress in learning your language.... Not so good." They all laughed at that.

"When you first arrived, I told you that we had a special assignment for you. We would now wish to tell you what that is and hopefully, you'll agree to complete it for us. It's very important Snake."

I sat back and he continued. "We know of your good work in recruiting jihadists in Europe and we wish you to continue. Would you be willing to undertake that assignment again?"

I think my heart skipped a beat. This was my way out of here. "Certainly. I would gratefully serve your cause in any way I could. When do you want me to leave?"

They all smiled. "Within a few days. We have money for you to take and use in your efforts and I believe you already know where you'll be most successful in finding us willing recruits. Also, you have a network in place for getting them to us."

I lied. "Yes, I do. I am honored for your trust and I pledge that I will be successful."

We chatted some more. I filled in details explaining how I'd go about my work, all lies, and they accepted everything I told them. They would give me $250,000 American dollars for my work. That was a real bonus. Now I had to figure out how I could take Wolf along for the ride.

As the meeting was breaking up one of the leaders pulled me aside. "May I speak with you Snake on another matter that you might be able to help with?"

"Certainly, my brother. How can I help?"

'The family you reside with has suffered much. A great injustice has befallen them. Their beautiful innocent daughter was taken from them and forced to live in a life of sin and debauchery. This wrong must be righted and the evil Apostate who caused their grief must be punished. A fatwa has been issued against her and it is our hope that you might carry it out for us."

He then continued describing how this woman, who had been a Muslim, had lost her faith and brought many young girls into the brothels of Davao and Saudi Arabia. Her sins were great and she was reviled by the many families she had injured. The family with whom I resided lost a daughter but she had been able to escape and returned to Marawi. She told her parents what had happened to her and the other girls who had been lured away by this evil woman. She returned to warn the others knowing full well that her father was honor bound to take her life. In my mind she performed a truly heroic deed and I accepted the responsibly of killing this Apostate devil now living in Davao.

I left the meeting feeling both sorrow and relief. I'd be leaving... perhaps I had a chance at a new life after all. I found Wolf and told him I'd be leaving and asked if he wanted to join me. I would have money and was certain I could find him a new fake passport somewhere.

"Thank you Snake, but I'm staying here. These people have a just cause and I want to fight with them," was pretty much all he said. I didn't try to change his mind. We said our goodbyes and I left knowing I'd never see him again. I suspected he wouldn't make it alive from the impending battle.

The family had been told that I accepted the fatwa and Aya said that he would go with me. There was no room for discussion on this... he wanted vengeance and would be an important help to me in carrying out our mission. We would ride motorcycles, kill the woman, and return to a friendly family in Davao who would keep us safe. After a few days Aya would then return to Marawi and I'd move on to my mission in Europe. I'd fly to Manila and connect with a flight out of the Philippines. Where I'd go, I didn't know... maybe Sicily.

CHAPTER 51

Davao

Our ride to Davao was actually enjoyable. We were worried that there would be military road blocks outside Marawi but Aya know the back roads and got us through. I was glad he came along. We stopped a few times for food and fuel and then back on the road. Pretty country. Lots of small farms and little villages along the way. When we got close to Davao we began to run into traffic. These Filipino drivers are nuts. Weaving in and out, lots of horns... but Filipino don't generally like confrontation so they all seemed to know how far to push it. We decided to go onto the friendly family house first, to rest and plan out our attack. They were Aya's relatives... distant cousins I think... and we were shown a lot of hospitality. We stayed the night. I had my knife and Glock. I planned on using my knife on this bitch. I also had the money in a separate bag. I would need to carry it with me at all times.

I realized I actually hated this woman. There was a burning inside whenever I knew a young innocent had been raped. I'm usually not passionate, except for this. Aya found out where she lived and we took our motorcycles to her home. It was located in an affluent neighborhood and her two-story house was expensive. There was a BMW parked in front of her two-car garage. The Devil had paid her well for her sins. We drove past and parked about a block away. I took the money bag with me.

Aya forced open a door that entered into her kitchen. The house was quiet. Perhaps she wasn't there... we stopped and listened. We could hear a voice coming from upstairs. I climbed the stairs first and stopped. The voice was coming from behind one of the closed doors. It was a woman's voice. I couldn't hear another voice speaking so she was probably on her telephone. I put the money bag down and motioned for Aya to follow me into the room. I grabbed the door knob and pushed the door open. She had her back to me... she was speaking to someone whose face appeared on a large computer screen. She stood and shouted something at us, in Tagalog, Aya didn't hesitate. He grabbed her by her long black hair and punched her face. She fell to the floor. The rest is a blur. Aya was yelling something at her in his language and kicking her. I lifted her from the floor and cut her throat. It was then I notice the man on the computer screen. He was yelling but I couldn't hear him. I picked up the headset, looked directly at him and said, "Fuck You." into the microphone. I then smashed the computer screen into a thousand pieces.

We rode our motorcycles back to the friendly house and washed her blood from our hands. The fatwa had been satisfied. I remembered her eyes as I cut her. She wasn't afraid. I asked Aya what she said when we came in.

"Allah forgive my sins."

We stayed three days just to wait and see if we were known. There was no report of our killing her on the TV or in the newspapers; perhaps her body had not been found. I decided it was time for me to go and I left some money for Aya's cousins. I said goodbye to Aya and wished him and his family good luck in the coming fight. He didn't want any money but I gave him some anyway. I also gave him my knife and the Glock.

Aya's cousin drove me to a very modern hotel in Davao. I checked in using my Moroccan passport and told them I'd be paying cash for my stay. I went into the gift shop and bought a razor, a scissor and a touristy polo shirt. I wanted to blend in and my longish beard didn't help. I wanted to look like my passport photo and I now needed to figure out how I could get the bulky bundles of money through Customs. I decided that there was really no easy way. I'd have to come up with a solution.

My room was first class. I would play the tourist and get settled in Davao for a few days before I left for where ever the hell I was going. I needed to call Madeline and ask if I could visit her and her father in Sicily. But first I needed to take care of the cash. It was too bulky and I probably could hide some of it but questions would be asked. There was no law in the Philippines about carrying a lot of cash. Most Countries would allow you to bring in over $10,000 but you had to have a good reason why and I didn't want to take any chances at Customs. So, I looked for an International Bank where I could deposit most of the cash and when I needed it, I could write a check or use a debit card. The problem was finding a bank that didn't ask too many questions.

I found one. Of course, I was asked why I had so much cash. I told the manager I had inherited it and had converted it into dollars. He smiled at that but went ahead and set up an account for me. I thanked him and gave a generous tip for his service. I knew there would be no questions and my money was safe and ready to use no matter where I went.

I found a barber and had a good haircut and beard trim. I felt good. I bought new clothes and a large suitcase and carry-on bag for my flight out of the Philippines. I bought a throw away cell and I would use it until I got settled in somewhere safe. To the World, I was a Moroccan citizen now and decided I wouldn't speak English if I could avoid it.

I called Madeline from a restaurant near my hotel. There's an eight-hour time difference but she answered in Dutch on the third ring. I greeted her in my bad Italian and she immediately knew it was me calling.

"Where have you been Paul? We thought you were dead," she laughed.

"I was dead but now I've come back to haunt you. How's your father?"

"Fine, fine... he mentions you all the time. I think he really likes you Paul. When are you coming back to the Netherlands? Soon I hope."

"Actually, that's why I'm calling. Is that invitation to visit Sicily still open? I'd really like to see your country and you and your father again."

"Of course it is. When can you visit us? Oh wait, we won't be there until next week. Could you plan coming after next Friday? How long do you have? Can you stay a few weeks? My father will be so happy to see you again, I think he has something he wants to talk to you about and I can be your tourist guide."

It was settled... I'd call her back with my travel schedule. We chatted some more and I hung up relieved. I sensed something else with

Madeline... she was attracted to me and I her. I enjoyed her company, her good looks and her intelligence. I wondered how she would feel falling in love with a murderer?

I decided to use a travel agent and she made all the arrangements for my flight to Palermo Sicily. I took a chance and held off on booking a hotel, imaging that I'd be staying with Madeline and Rocco. I called Madeline with my literary... my flight time from Manila would be about fifteen hours, not too bad and there were no Italian visa requirements for Moroccan citizens. She told me she be waiting at the airport or have a driver meet me. I spent the rest of my time in Davao resting, exercising and sightseeing. I was beginning to actually feel like a tourist. My new credit card worked like a charm. I'd only be carrying $8,000 when I left the Philippines.

The flight to Manila was fine... a little overcrowded and the seats were made to fit smaller butts. I did have a problem at Customs when I went to check in for my connecting flight to Palermo. It seems that if you stay more than twenty-one days in the Philippines you have to register for an extension. I spoke only French and they had to get an interpreter who then explained the problem. I claimed ignorance of the law and they let me go after I paid a $100 fine. My flight to Palermo was great. I decided to fly first class... this was the only way to enjoy a flight and I decided that in the future, this would be my flight choice. I had no problem with Italian customs and Immigration in Palermo.

Madeline met me with her driver in the baggage retrieval area. She looked stunning, no other way to put it. I felt my heart jump when I saw her. She threw her arms around me and we kissed... a real passionate kiss that left my head spinning. I knew my life had changed for the better at that moment.

EPILOGUE

Rocco received his cousin's call and thought about it. Paul was a good guy. Someone he trusted. Smart, tough and now his daughter loved him. He was here, staying in his house in Sicily. All Rocco had to do was tell him his father had been shot and crippled and they were now threatening to kill his whole family and he knew Paul would be on the next plane to New York... and probably his death. There was a simpler way to handle this and he knew just how.

The mafia had become a shadow of its former self. In the 1980s and 90s the FBI using the RICO law had brought it to its knees. But twenty years later it still wasn't quiet dead yet. Human nature never changes so people still gambled, went to whorehouses, used loan sharks and drugs. The Dominicans and Jamaicans and Columbian controlled the drug market but there was still room for the mafia. It was a huge market. New York City was still its center and the Don's, Captains and mafia soldiers kept a very low profile. They went high-tech like everyone else and used sophisticated bug checking devices, throw away cell phones and changed the places they met all the time, and never more than three guys.

"A zoo... I fucking zoo? I have to meet him in a fucking zoo. What am I? Some kid who wants to pet the animals." Bingo was fed up with everything in his life. He should have been a butcher like his father, not some low level, make no money gangster. He saw his Captain, Billy Bones feeding the monkeys.

He should be in the fucking cage with them. They're his fucking family, he thought. He moved to the railing in front of the cage and stood next to Billy. "You wanted to see me boss?"

Bonesy never turned his head, just kept throwing peanuts to the monkeys, "I got a wet job for you kid." He called everyone "kid". "You know that old prick Irishman in the Kitchen? Gerry McGuire."

"Yeah... the pain in our ass. What about him? He needs to go back to the old country?"

"You got it kid... send him my regards. Let me know when it's done."

Billy Bones always followed orders from the Big Guy. He had met with him in the lobby of Lincoln Center earlier in the day. "Billy, our friend in Sicily needs a favor. He's got a guy working for him that the old Irishman, Gerry McGuire, is gonna hit. The Irishman already banged this friend's father pretty good, made him a cripple and now wants to hit the son. Our Sicilian friend says that a no go. Get rid of the Irishman and puff, problem solved. Use Bingo. You good with that?" said the Big Guy.

"We're good. Consider it done." Both walked away in separate directions... meeting ended.

Gerry McGuire was almost bald but continued visiting the same barbershop on 41st. The old barber, Tony was older than Gerry. But he always opened early just for him on the third Thursday of every month rain or shine. Gerry always brought his big Rottweiler Harpo along and told his bodyguard to sleep late.

"Harpo is protection enough lad. See you later."

The old Irishman was starting to doze off in the chair, the hot face towel always did that to him. He never heard the barbershop door open of the phizz of the silenced bullet that put Harpo out of the way.

"Get in the back old man... now," was all he heard, not the sound of the two quick shots from the .22 directly held to his head that put him out of the way for good.

Problem solved, Bingo thought.

The Wolf was thirsty. He was covered in dust and his face was caked with dirt and grit. He checked his AK... 10 rounds left and that was it. He lay in a bombed-out Marawi City cellar and could hear the approaching Filipino soldiers slowly making their way toward his last-ditch hideout. He had proven himself in this fight. He killed and wounded many but he accepted that now it was time for him to become a martyr. He thought of his friend, the Snake, and wondered if he was safe. He wished he could see him again. The Wolf stood, brought his weapon up... now firing and yelling Allah Akbar, ran into the street.

The lawyer showed Mrs. Asoph her son Paul's last Will and Testament. She had been named sole beneficiary of $500,000.

"He died in a boating accident off Sicily Mrs. Asoph. I imagine it was quick and painless from what I was told. He wanted you to have this money."

She was shocked. She had already received a million dollars from an unknown source with the note that it was Paul's back pay. With Jake now an invalid and the knowledge that whoever had threatened her and her family had been taken care of, she was hopeful for the future. She would pray each day for Paul's soul and have masses said each month in his name.

He'd like that, she thought.

THE END

AUTHOR'S NOTES

I hope you enjoyed reading *Beyond Hate* as much as I did writing it. The story was born when I wondered, "what would I do if I saw someone murdered while I was talking with them on the internet?"

Just in case you didn't already know, this tale is pure fiction. The events and characters in the story are not real although the locations are. If something seems like it might have been a real event or that any of my major characters are modeled after someone you may have read about, it was just coincidental. It's not a history of Islamic State terrorism.

My principal character, Paul Asoph aka "Snake," is not a good guy and I hope you didn't like him. I have to admit, while he's crazy and a serial killer, he's also interesting and complex. My original thought was to kill him off at the end of this book. I just couldn't do it. So, the Snake will return in my next book *Beyond Evil* and maybe won't make it out alive this time. We'll have to wait and see, I guess.

Lastly, I want you to understand that I respect the Muslim faith. It is a beautiful and sometimes poetic religion and almost all of its followers are genuinely good people. It's a shame that it has been perverted by the terrorists of the Islamic State.

Jim Williams
August, 2020